PRAISE FOR

FLOATING CITY

Winner of the Canada-Japan Literary Award
Finalist for the Toronto Book Awards
A *NOW* (Toronto) Top Ten Book of the Year

"*Floating City* pulls us into a narrative traversing generations, waterways, legends and history. . . . Kerri Sakamoto weaves together a life from the shores of Port Alberni, to the shacks of Tashme, to the glimmering towers of Toronto and leaves us pondering how fortunes are made."

—Canada-Japan Literary Awards jury citation

"Written in a whimsically poetic and almost magical tone, *Floating City* explores themes of hope, chasing dreams, struggle and the need to belong."

—*This Magazine*

"All that is solid melts into prose in Kerri Sakamoto's entrancing novel. . . . Frankie Hanesaka is a completely original creation, and *Floating City* a marvel."

—Cameron Bailey, Artistic Director,
Toronto International Film Festival

"Kerri Sakamoto is a magician. The way she handles language is wizardly. Her gifts for imagery dazzle. She has written a tender, sad, shimmering story about a boy named Frankie who dares to dream and aspire in an unwelcoming world. *Floating City* is as vibrant as a fairy tale, as aching and rueful as a Japanese *enka* song. I loved this novel and its deep, reflective whimsy. It floated me to a spellbinding place of broken hopes and blooming magic."

—Kyo Maclear, #1 bestselling author of *Birds Art Life*

"A boldly conceived and richly provocative tale of one man's dreams, schemes and unbridled striving for destiny. You will never look at Toronto's waterfront or skyline again without thinking of the meaning of home."

—Lynne Kutsukake, award-winning author
of *The Translation of Love*

FLOATING CITY

A NOVEL

KERRI SAKAMOTO

VINTAGE CANADA

VINTAGE CANADA EDITION, 2019

Copyright © 2018 Kerri Sakamoto

Published by Vintage Canada, a division of Penguin Random House
Canada Limited, in 2019. Originally published in hardcover by Knopf Canada,
a division of Penguin Random House Canada Limited, in 2018.
Distributed in Canada by Penguin Random House Canada Limited, Toronto.

Vintage Canada with colophon is a registered trademark.

www.penguinrandomhouse.ca

Pages 241–243 are a continuation of this copyright page.

Library and Archives Canada Cataloguing in Publication

Sakamoto, Kerri, author
Floating city / Kerri Sakamoto.

ISBN 978-0-345-80990-2
eBook ISBN 978-0-345-80991-9

I. Title.

PS8587.A318F56 2019   C813'.54   C2017-905126-1

Text and cover design: Kelly Hill
Cover images: (man with umbrella) © Marco Lamberto/
EyeEm/Getty Images; (dome) © meunierd/Shutterstock.com

Printed and bound in Canada

2 4 6 8 9 7 5 3 1

For Daniel Tisch Echevarría

The timeline of *Floating City* coincides loosely with real historical events, including the internment of Japanese Canadians in World War II and various incidents and landmarks in the development of post-war Toronto. It is not intended to follow the precise history of what was, but rather to imagine a story that might have been.

"LONGING . . . is EXPANSION and INCLUSION."

R. Buckminster Fuller
Nine Chains to the Moon

"Mr. Industry!"

Bucky held out his arm to hoist Frankie from the frigid waters of Lake Ontario. Frankie clambered onto the quay in his sodden woollen jacket. Water streamed down his neck and sloshed from his shoes.

"Out there, my dear boy!" Bucky shouted in his musty dark suit, pointing across the harbour. A line of tugboats was pulling one twenty-by-twenty-foot hollow concrete block after another, each ten feet deep with enough air inside to make it lighter than the water it displaced.

The floating blocks soon filled a quarter square mile of Toronto Harbour. Workers jumped onto the floating surfaces, hooking them with cables to hitch the blocks together.

"We will soon see, Frank," Bucky said, his eyes large, blue and blurry behind the thick glasses strapped around his closely cropped head. Frankie shivered.

When Frankie Hanesaka was a young man, it was Bucky—R. Buckminster Fuller—who told him that he must dream and dare. That everyone is born naked with no external equipment and no experience. *We are all on the frontier, on a great mystery.*

Workers in coveralls and helmets began hauling equipment off the boats. Before long, torches flamed on the horizon as welders set the joints.

Bucky had a way of casting Frankie's doubts to the wind. As a young man, Bucky had himself almost given up, he'd told Frankie. *Instead I sought to discover what, if anything, can be accomplished by a penniless, unknown individual—operating only on behalf of all humanity—in attempting to produce sustainably favourable physical and metaphysical advancement of the integrity of all human life on our planet.*

Bucky now smiled his smile of delight. He clasped his broad hands together. "Next week, the ships will haul our pre-assembled living units here and cranes will lift and drop them into place. Slope-faced, omni-surfaced, terraced!"

Each unit of uniform dimensions fronting on Lake Ontario, each tiered level sloped back from the one below to overlook a garden terrace. No sheer face or drop to tempt an ill wind or dark soul on a calm day.

Frankie gazed across the harbour. He hadn't fallen into the lake on his own. The air was still. His feet had been steady on the quay. *The Priest*, he mused. The Priest had conjured a single gust of wind to topple him. But Bucky, of robust flesh and blood, had pulled him out.

Soon enough, they'd see the doors of those apartments opening wide onto Streets in the Air. The streets would spiral up the Floating City to the very top, under nothing but sky. Home for four hundred penniless unknowns, maybe more.

PORT ALBERNI,
VANCOUVER ISLAND

CHAPTER 1

Secret World

For a moment, Frankie balanced perfectly above the water. *Ta-dah!* He looked down the inlet. Beyond was the sea.

Then down he went. Logs under his feet, now closing over his head. Blood snaked before his face in the water, light worming through then disappearing. *Fu-ranki!* his mother cried from the world above.

Water filled him to bursting. He kicked and thrashed until there was no air and no up. He was sinking like any creature taken by the sea. He closed his eyes.

Then, a tug on his arm and he was dredged up, back up between parted logs and into the light, sputtering into the air.

Namu Amida Butsu, Namu Amida Butsu, babbled Momoye, half-asleep at his side, prayer beads spilling between her fingers.

Mama. Frankie gagged and woke.

His brother, Yas, stirred beside him in the moonlight but slept on. Aki, Yas's twin, along with their sisters Julia and

Augusta, slept in another bed; their father, Taiji, lay in another across the room. The ocean swell beneath them lulled their floating house. How Frankie ached all over: his ribs, his chest, his head, his throat—even his fingers and toes.

At dawn, he watched through the window as Yas and their father stepped onto the logs tethered outside their house. Without a word, they rolled the timbers beneath their feet, poles held easily across their chests, and glided effortlessly away, like Frankie never could. How did it feel, Frankie had to wonder: that sureness; Taiji's shadow always at his back, strong and tall? When they reached the dense cluster of logs in the middle of the inlet, they poked and pushed with their poles while hopping from one trunk to another, urging the swarm toward the sawmill for skinning and slicing.

Frankie could only lie back in his bed, every finger bandaged, his ribs bound, his breath wheezing through bruised passages. Frankie had nearly been a goner. But no, not Yas. He'd roar when he rolled the biggest log faster than anyone. *I rode the Colossus!* The girls scrambled after him, crying *nooo!* Others might go down like deadheads, like squashed jellyfish, but Yas would laugh, drunk from the sea.

If only Yas would go down just once. Frankie couldn't help wish it. *Just once.*

Momoye sat beside him. She'd been brewing sake and he smelled the burnt sweetness amid the ocean salt. If only she would hold him like she did when he was little, if only to lift him from here to there. She raised a bottle to the window to let the early morning sunlight glance through. *You see, Fu-ranki?* She tipped the bottle back and forth. Green, blue and white light swilled within.

This is how we came across the ocean. In giant ships riding giant waves. Before you were born.

When he opened his eyes next, the house was dark. He felt his mother there, smelled her there, as if the two of them were below decks of the giant ship on its long journey instead of drifting in their floating house.

Momoye leaned in with her hot breath, words pouring like lava in his ear. *One night, a man fell into the Sea of Japan. Down into the deep, dark water.*

Frankie's aches flared and burned with cold anew. "Then what?" he asked, though of course he knew the story. *Shush.* His mother's eyes widened, her thick brows arching in the faint moonlight; she hunched her shoulders and drew up her arms.

The Priest swept down into the water, his robes like wings.

She sighed, shoulders drooping, eyes narrowing. It always exhausted her telling this part, as if she'd rescued the man herself. Frankie shivered and tingled. "And then?"

The Priest crossed to the other side and brought him back.

She stared so hard at Frankie that he had to look away. *Did you?*

"What, Mama?"

Did you cross to the other side?

On his way out, Taiji gazed down at Frankie with a pitying shake of his head. One by one, Yas and the girls passed by his bed and did the same. Only Aki lingered to give him a gentle squeeze and kind eye.

"Bye, Frankie!" they called from outside, voices fading as they rowed to shore for school.

His mother settled in beside him, ready to tell another story. The one about the rich widow and her son and daughter. The widow had heard of the Priest and the miracles he'd performed, of walking on fire, purging dark spirits, bringing a dead man back to life. She wanted a miracle of her own.

The widow wanted her son brought back—not to life because he wasn't dead—but home to Japan from the New World where he'd ventured.

Take my daughter to the New World and find my son, the widow told the Priest. When they all three returned, she would build a shrine where followers could flock to see the Priest perform his miracles. The daughter, who was only a girl, begged her mother not to make her marry the aged and gnarled man.

Momoye held up the bottle with its swill of white cloud, sea green and sky blue inside.

"They never found the son?" Frankie drawled, though he knew. He was weak with fever again.

His mother leaned in to pat his forehead with a cool cloth, then disappeared.

She returned hours later, wobbling over him. The stink of sake leaking out as she murmured. *The embers were red. Red!* Yet the Priest walked slowly across them.

His feet turned black on the bottom but stayed smooth as a child's. Momoye reached under the blanket to squeeze Frankie's battered foot. *He sprinkled salt to cool the coals, but the followers screeched and jumped off!*

Now she tugged at Frankie's pyjamas to check his behind: that bruise-like splotch at the top of his buttocks. They all had one from the moment they came out of their mother's body. Like a well of special paint; some peoples had it, not just their own. The Chinese, and the Indians on the nearby reserve, had it too.

Yas's and Aki's spots had faded and disappeared by the age of four. Julia's and Augusta's too. But Frankie's had only darkened.

She helped him up to pee into his bucket. When he was done and settled back, she drew something from her dress pocket. It was a photograph, cracked and grey, creased in four as if to be thrown away. *Bad-luck number four*, she'd often warned him. A girl in a kimono stood pigeon-toed on a dock by the hull of a great ship. Beside her was a man in white robes—robes that could turn to wings. His face blurred.

Frankie stared at the photograph, at the girl: the eyes, the brows; the purse of her lips. Puffy hands dangling at her sides.

Momoye pressed a calloused finger under the man's chin.

"The Priest?" Frankie blurted. The face dissolved to dust the longer Frankie looked. "You knew him?"

Momoye fell silent and wrapped her arms around herself. She searched Frankie's face and eyes—for what? As if he might know the why of it all, which frightened him. Frankie understood that the girl, not so much older then than he was now, was his mother. Married off by her own mother. Sent away. How unwanted she must have felt! Her brother the favoured one. Just like Taiji preferred Yas.

Frankie struggled to sit up, close to his mother. He began to cough; gently she pushed him down, brought him water and then drew away. The photograph slipped back into her pocket. *Sleep, sleep,* she urged.

He dreamed of the powerful ship that could sail from one side of the world to the other. Waves like clouds below his mother and the Priest, and clouds like waves above them: white and billowing like the robes the Priest wore in the photograph. He heard the voice of the Priest as if it were his own, chanting the same blessing Momoye had chanted for Frankie; someone tugged at his arms, whether down to deeper waters or up to the surface he couldn't tell.

If only these quiet days could go on. Momoye flapped her arms to make her boy laugh. *Caw! Caw!* It was the Crazy

Birdman, one of the Priest's followers, left behind. Momoye pinched her nose and swatted the air: it was the Man with the Terrible Smell. She laughed hard and so did he, in spite of his sore ribs. He almost peed in his bed. But when she drew her arms up into her sleeves to show him the Soldier Who Lost His Arms, he became sad and then frightened by the ugliness he imagined: the Peach Man with the tumour growing on his forehead, the Hunchback and the lepers. His mother had stopped laughing too. Frankie secretly envied the Sad Girl because, unlike him, she could shed endless tears. So many that salt dusted her cheeks.

"Did he help them?" Frankie asked.

The girls burst in.

"Tell us your secrets," little Augusta demanded, dancing around.

Aki, with her glistening marble eyes, glanced at Frankie. "Then they wouldn't be secrets."

She led the girls back outside. He heard them giggle, chasing each other around the edge of the house. Water splashed the window. He looked to his mother, waiting.

She shrugged. "He wanted to save them from suffering."

The house shook, the door flew open and Taiji stumbled through with Yas in his arms.

"Make room!" he shouted, and Frankie shifted aside as Yas was set down beside him on the bed. Aki rushed to dab the blood streaming from her brother's nose and mouth. Momoye and Taiji knelt beside the bed.

"Bring water," Taiji ordered.

Julia stood hushed beside Augusta, who murmured, incredulous, "He fell, he fell."

Yas fell. Frankie heaved himself up, his rickety breath,

arms and legs doing, surprisingly, as he told them. He fetched water and held it to Yas's swollen lips even as it dribbled down his chin.

He stood with the others encircling Yas, waiting, wondering. Hadn't he wished this on his brother? Frankie cringed with shame.

His mother bundled Yas in blankets, her prayer beads looped tightly around her fist. Yas was shivering, his eyes squeezed shut. Frankie lay down and closed his eyes too. Just hours ago he'd been the one doted on, fed and watered. He opened his eyes to find Yas gazing at him: his furious smile flashed with gritted teeth.

"Frankie," he rasped. "I caught an octopus."

Not a deadhead, not a goner.

That night, their mother lay in bed, snoring beside Taiji. Yas was asleep; they all were, except Frankie. He looked from Yas to Aki, Julia and Augusta, their faces lit by a fierce full moon. They all had the same straight slender nose like Taiji; the same proud rounded forehead. He pinched his wide flaring nostrils, rubbed his flat sloping forehead. Strangers. He threw his arms back and slept for a while.

His finger began to sting as if pinched between the logs. Julia and Augusta were giggling in their pillows.

Go back to sleep, hissed a voice.

A shriek: *His blood is black!*

There was a stain on his pillow, a trickle from his finger.

So it's true, Julia giggled.

I always knew, whispered Augusta.

The blood was as black as his spot. His spot: that splotch of spilled ink. Black blood.

He was sure he felt tears on his cheeks, down his neck. He reached up to touch.

"What is it, Frankie?" Suddenly Aki was there, surprising him, his hand held in hers.

He was sobbing his dry sobs.

"Crybaby," Yas muttered and went back to sleep.

"A silly prank," Aki told him. She showed him a needle and a bottle of ink by Julia's pillow. "You see?"

Frankie held his finger up: a drop of red trickled down. He was the stranger. The one with the spot that never went away; the tears that stayed stuck inside.

That was Yas: he might go down but he'd always bob up, faster than anyone. Yas got back on the logs again with Taiji in no time, cuts and bruises halfway to healed overnight by the same salt air and water that had made Frankie retch. Why was Frankie born this way and not that?

Momoye chose the fifth day of the month for Frankie to return to school. He needed protection from bad-luck number four. The day before, the two of them cawed once more; they hunched their backs and hid their arms, laughing again at the Priest's misfit followers. It was the end of their magic time of secrets, though Frankie didn't yet know how the whole story ended. He'd miss the Sad Girl and the Half-Lame Boy who followed the Priest. Frankie now counted himself among his flock, the strange and not quite whole.

"You are strong," Momoye told him, guessing his thoughts. "You are healed. You are healthy."But the followers kept following. Sometimes one or another of them declared themselves almost healed by the Priest, even though they smelled, wept or hobbled the same or even worse: the cawing louder, the lepers more scabbed and festering. They followed right to the dock where the Priest and his young bride departed for the New World.

Momoye mocked their cries: *Don't leave us! We're not healed!*

"They're still waiting!" She laughed then went silent.

"What happened to the Priest?" Frankie asked, though he wasn't certain he wanted to know.

"Gone," his mother replied, suddenly stern, her brows arched, like a warning.

"Did he go back to them?"

She nodded her head then, yes. "Back home."

"The brother?"

"Nobu?"

So that was his name, her brother.

She lifted her hands, swept them aside: *to the wind, to the waves.* She didn't know.

The next morning, Frankie was roused by his mother along with everyone else. "Time for school!"

He groaned. His body was more than healed; it complained at having been still too long. Frankie squinted at the bright morning sun. The salt air stung him all over, the breeze grazed him, yet when he breathed deeply his sides no longer hurt. Confident, he took the oars to row them all to shore, but never did the shore look so far off. His arms wobbled. He began to wheeze.

"It's all right, Frankie," Aki told him and took over.

At school, unfamiliar words awaited him on the chalkboard. Rows of numbers, equations he'd left behind. Girls laughed when he sounded out one new word, even the Japanese girls.

"The square root of sixteen, Frankie?" Miss McIntyre now asked. Frankie could not answer.

"The square root of sixteen."

He stuttered, *fffff.* Could not say it.

From behind him, a voice called out, "Four!"

Of course he knew. But he didn't dare say it. Death number four. The other Japanese in the class knew it, but they didn't care. They weren't afraid.

He was made to stay after school. The whole class filed past him.

The square root of sixteen equals four, he wrote as the clock tick-tocked in the empty classroom. Down the page across every line: *equals four, equals four. Four, four, four.* Nothing but bad luck when he'd already had his share.

On Port Alberni's highest hill, out past the sawmill, perched the biggest homes in town. Grand, like a waltz. The grandest he'd ever behold, he figured. Frankie walked briskly, head down. If anyone stopped him, he'd pretend to be there for a reason, running errands for some rich so-and-so. But he'd never been stopped, not once. He paused before the house with the turret at the front. The grandest of the grand houses, with a round room, no less. What was inside it? A round bed, a round table? What to do in it but walk in circles or play ring-around-the-rosy? Once he'd come after dark and seen it lit up as if for a party. He'd hoped to catch a glimpse of the pretty daughters up there, future queens of the Rose Queen Parade with their fair hair in waves and bows. He heard they went to some fancy school for girls only.

Roses climbed up the latticed walls of the house. Different colours of roses, from orange to coral to pink to red to burgundy to purple to yellow to white. Sometimes he ventured into the flower beds and squatted down to smell them, deep in their mysterious centres: they were sweet, spicy, bitter; some even smelled as if they were rotting, yet they were velvet. He was tempted to pluck one for his mother.

They'd had a garden once, not a bit grand. He was young then, but he remembered, or perhaps he remembered his mother telling him. It was on land, of course. A normal house like everyone else's, before they had to leave. The house he was born in. Purple irises spiralling around the house. They were strangely exotic flowers, purple petals furred with yellow, both upright and dangling. They recoiled into brown fists on their stems after blooming: dead wonders. His mother had wanted a river of them to circle their small house, like they would a temple in Kyoto, she said. One day he'd go there and see the Golden Temple.

Then the men had come. One worked, he said, in the office at the mill; the others were his friends—business friends. They warned Taiji that the City would be coming to chase him off his land because they didn't want Japs cluttering up the waterfront any longer. But this man would do Taiji a good turn and buy the lot from him before he got thrown off for a pittance. He was fair, he said, and generous—too generous, and too soft in the head—placing bills in Taiji's hand: fifty dollars. Taiji had never held that much at one time. The man pointed to houses of other Japanese down the way. The same thing was happening to them.

So Taiji said yes. He told the neighbours and everyone else sold their lots too, and started to pack up. Then one day, the City came with No Trespassing signs to nail to doors and two hundred dollars in envelopes ready to give to each family.

Frankie arrived home to find Aki lying face down on the floor. The others were outside, frolicking in the boat. He dropped the rose by his mother's chair. Aki tugged him down beside her. He felt the floor planks gape and strain like ribs against his own.

"We've been swallowed up," she said quietly, with a finger to her lips. She pressed one eye between the planks, cocked an ear to the slap of the water. Frankie felt his nostrils prickle.

"Frankie, look."

"Can I see?" Augusta had come in, hovering over them. Aki shooed her away.

Frankie set his own face to the dark crack; a cool draft stung his eye. "See what?" He couldn't see. He couldn't see anything. A wave carried them up, then down.

"The face there," Aki said, and instantly he pulled away. She pulled him back. "It just wants to say hello."

Not just the fish and the whale and the octopus, but the smallest pebble on the ocean floor, a bubble of seaweed could be peering up at you. "Even the sea has a face," she told Frankie. "You only have to watch and listen."

Frankie gave a laugh but shuddered to recall the murk he'd been pulled into between the logs, and the unseen sea of faces that had surrounded him.

In the morning, before the others rose, he watched Aki slide from the bed to the floor and creep again to the spot that was now hers. The house was rising and falling with the waves, more than usual, and she gave a little cry when water lapped up between the boards. She glanced over, grinned and beckoned, *Come look, Frankie*. But no: he didn't care to be greeted by any faces of the sea.

After school he found her there again. Alone this time because Momoye had met up with the girls in town and Yas was off with Taiji on the logs. She was lying so still, so patient, one eye pressed to the gap, until, with the sound of a tiny splash, she shrieked. Aki rolled back from her spot, her eye streaming red.

"Aki! Are you all right?"

Her hands flailed in the air. Her feet kicked. As she shrieked again, her one eye stared wide open without seeing him; the other was swarmed in red. She wailed and writhed on the floor, then lay still on her back, quiet.

"Aki." He crept forward. He bent down. The red that covered her eye and the side of her face was like blood, but thick and gluey. He was about to touch it when the whole mass slid off her cheek. He jumped back, and it slithered across the floor.

Aki did not move. Her eye was swelling shut between welts of red and purple. "Wake up," he whispered. "Aki, wake up!" But she didn't stir. He slapped her cheek, the untouched side, what he'd seen his mother do when Taiji drank too much.

She woke with a start. Her open eye rolled around, searching. It found him. He'd saved her, his sister.

"Yas!" she called, looking past Frankie. "Yas, where are you?"

"No, it's Frankie!" he shouted back.

Aki struggled to sit up. Beside her lay the creature from the sea that had answered her call. They watched it slowly inch homeward, its tentacles sprawling, then retracting, to heave its glassy red dome into the gap between the planks.

Frankie raised his boot to stomp it.

"No!" screamed Aki.

He would save her; he would save both of them.

"Stop, Frankie!" Aki was seeing everything at last.

Frankie's boot came down. But the creature escaped it and slipped between the boards, back into the sea.

A jellyfish, Yas told them. A red lion's mane jellyfish. He'd seen them while riding the logs. The fishermen warned they could sting even after they were dead. You might not die from it, but you could come close.

The doctor came and bandaged Aki's eye. There was nothing else to be done. Her face was mottled and puffy on one side. She wandered through the house without saying a word. Frankie offered her water to drink, food to eat; he even rowed as fast as he could, with Augusta holding a dripping ice cream cone from town. But Aki gave it to the sisters to share.

He offered to row her to shore to watch the sunset, but she said no. Not even Yas could coax her out.

Frankie lay in bed with his fists clenched at his sides. He should have pulled the thing from Aki's eye right away. Acted, as Yas would've.

After a week the bandage was removed, but Aki could not open her eye. The welts had sealed it shut. She'd become a cyclops, a monster from their school books, watching and listening to the world with only one eye pressed up to it.

Taiji and his friend Mr. Koga sat in the house, celebrating one more month lived through and gone. It was Thursday, payday. Yas was, as usual, out on the late shift after school, breaking up the latest boom come into the harbour. The afternoon rain was melting into evening vapour.

Aki lay on the floor, ribs to the planks, good eye to the crack beckoning to the creature that had visited her before. Frankie had given up trying to pull her away. Momoye sat in her chair by the window, gazing at the shore. That chair had become hers alone, and Frankie was sure she was pining for a proper house on land with flowers around her front yard. Augusta and Julia were reciting every line spoken or sung by Shirley Temple in *Little Miss Marker*, the one movie they'd seen in town. Taiji had succumbed to his Canadian Club whisky, muttering about a mountain and a lake he'd staked claim to somewhere on Vancouver Island.

Before leaving, Mr. Koga bent down to ask Taiji something he'd asked him many times before: Would he toss a coin or two into Mr. Koga's hotel?

"It's a long way to Tippelaary!" Taiji drawled.

Mr. Koga collected his bottle and headed out the door to meet his partner in the venture, Mr. Fung.

"Wait," Frankie called and scrambled after him.

Mr. Koga rowed a crooked line to shore under a waning moon, splashing Frankie now and then with the oars. Down a dead-end road they finally came to Mr. Fung's shabby lean-to. Before going in, Mr. Koga drank deeply from his bottle and handed it to Frankie. "Go on," he urged. Frankie held it to his lips and threw his head back. It scorched his throat on the way down, then set off a glow that warmed him from his ears to his toes. This was what Thursday tasted like.

Their venture would produce a hotel two storeys high with a potbelly stove and a wool blanket in each room. Visiting lumbermen needed a place to stay. Newcomers. People who couldn't afford to stay at the Arlington Hotel in town. So what was the problem?

"No land!" said Mr. Fung as he stacked a few coins on his kitchen table. "Cost too much! Pie in sky!"

Mr. Koga handed over his coins, which Mr. Fung added to the pile. "Payday!" Since Mr. Fung spoke Chinese and Mr. Koga Japanese, they met on rocky isles of English.

"Not enough." Mr. Fung slid a single faded bead to the near-empty side of his abacus.

"Float it!" Frankie blurted. Like his own house. Right now, he felt like he himself was floating. "Who needs land?" He'd learned that when the men had come to board up their house. Instead of letting anyone tear it down, Taiji had set it onto the water, anchored it on the inlet.

Frankie snatched Mr. Koga's bottle and took another gulp. He felt light but seaworthy.

A floating hotel. Guests could look out their window either to shore—like his mother did from her chair—or to the forest across the inlet.

"They could fish for their dinner!" Frankie cast a line across the cramped room and reeled it back in.

Mr. Fung squinted his squinty eyes at the boy. "How to build?" Mr. Fung was a land dweller. A farmer from Guangdong.

That was easy as pie. Build a house, only bigger, with two storeys instead of one. Put it on a raft and anchor it in the harbour. "Why not?" Frankie asked.

Now Mr. Koga narrowed his eyes at him. Not just a tag-along, he was supposing. The boy had more schooling than either of them. *Why not?*

Mr. Koga had ideas, then, too. He wanted it as fine as the Arlington Hotel, but at a cheaper cost. With a restaurant and a barbershop. And a beer parlour. People would line up for their ten-cent glass of beer.

And ice cream, thought Frankie. And a garden: a floating garden with flowers bobbing atop the sea.

Why not? The two men agreed. Fortune's cat was waving its right paw at them. They drank and passed the bottle. Frankie took another gulp or two. He was no rider of logs but he would not be felled. When the two men dozed off, he stepped out into the night and walked up the street. The ground was passing under him more quickly than he was passing over it. He could hardly wait to tell everyone that he was now a partner in a business. He'd help with the hotel, yes, but the garden would be all his: with irises for his mother, with roses of all kinds and colours. Sea Garden, he'd call it. Or Floating Garden. Floating Flowers.

He was still floating. Higher and higher, farther from the ground, from his feet. Spinning. A light up ahead was so white he couldn't see what was actually there. He knew he was heading down to shore, back to the boat, but where had Mr. Koga left it? Frankie's head was a top, whirling off into the air in the blaring light. He stumbled and fell.

Aki appeared above him, her cyclops eye catching the bright light. "Aki," he started. She reached down to take his arm. Then his other arm was taken too.

Mama. He was reaching for Momoye, his breath heaving. He couldn't help himself. Like a baby. He wanted to tell her about the hotel, the floating part that was his idea, and the garden. The flowers for her.

Aki was shaking him but he only wanted his mother.

Mama! He let his arms drop; he felt sick. *Let go,* he muttered and rolled half away.

Are you running from him?

From who?

She set the lamp down and the bright light flared beneath him.

CHAPTER 2

The Mongolian Spot

It was the stillness he noticed first. Then the air that was dry and warm in his nostrils and sweet smelling. Land air. He opened his eyes. He wasn't home. He wasn't even in his own clothes. Frankie was in a room empty save for the bed he lay in, a desk and chair, and a Jesus on a cross on the wall. *Shush*, the Jesus seemed to say as he hung there from his tiny hands and feet.

He tried to sit up but his head throbbed. His throat felt raw. Out the one small window he saw the sky that was his sky; his clouds too, and a peek of sun. Beneath wasn't sea, but a field. He looked to the door, and right then came a knock. Slowly, the door opened.

Two ladies entered, one smiling. "He's awake," she said.

"I am Miss McCracken. This is Miss Hawks."

They stood like sentries at the lower corner of the bed. He thought the sunlight might pass right through them; they were so fair. Their hair was white as clouds; their blouses too. Jesus dangled from each of their necks.

"Tell us your name, my dear," the first, smiling one asked. "Last night you couldn't tell us."

"Frank."

"We'll call him Francis," said the second. "He's not well at all."

"He must be hungry after all the retching."

They talked on as if he wasn't there. Was he?

"He must rest."

"And heal."

His head was stabbed with pain, over and over. He couldn't think. The smiling lady, who seemed the nicer, gently eased him back on the pillow. "Perhaps he should lie on his front," she said, wincing.

"Yes," said the second. "Turn over," she ordered. Which he did.

"When can I go home?" Frankie asked quietly into the pillow, which smelled of sweetness and powder. He glimpsed tiny Jesus out of the corner of his eye. *Jesus loves me*, he'd sung in school, just yesterday morning, it seemed.

"When it is safe." Seconds passed in silence. Then he felt the covers drawn back and the waist of his pants folded down. Cold stealing over his buttocks. A sharp intake of breath and a sigh. Then fingers probing there. He shivered. The eyes of tiny Jesus were cast down and away.

"Does it hurt?" a voice whispered, the nice lady's. He shook his head in the pillow.

"Barbaric," the other lady declared near his ear. Gently, his pants were rolled up and the covers tucked around his neck.

He didn't know what or where the Sisters of Mercy Mission was, but he soon learned that Miss McCracken and Miss Hawks lived in this humble home doing God's work however and whenever it was needed. The house was always quiet and no one came or went.

He longed to go home, but by the second or third night, the truth was he didn't want to go just yet. He was warm and dry, and cared for in ways he never had been. The Ladies fed him thick, meaty stew and there was always more, as much as he wanted. They bathed him in hot, hot water with lavender soap, being gentle but attentive around his backside, barely touching the spot, which they called a hemorrhage. They oh-so-lightly dabbed balm on the bruise as he lay on his stomach in the warm, dry bed he had all to himself.

"The hemorrhaging!" Miss McCracken softly cried. When she leaned down, the soft folds of her fell so close and her Jesus swung from the chain at her neck. "Who did this to you, dear Francis? Such a blow."

Frankie stayed silent.

"He's afraid to say."

"Was it your father? Were you running to escape him?"

"The dark of it means it's healing," said Miss Hawks. "The bleeding inside has stopped."

"You're safe here with us."

"We've told no one."

They combed his hair, exclaiming over its blackness and thickness. "Like a horse's mane."

What he liked less was the schooling, in all things. He was seated at a desk with a pillow on the chair for his backside and made to practise his penmanship and to read about Jesus who, like the Priest, could heal the sick. Frankie was also taught how to set a proper table, how to use a fork and a knife, and how to eat soup with a spoon without slurping. He cringed at the cold ting of metal on his teeth and tongue.

The days passed. A week. He missed his mother. She would be worried; Aki would be worried, almost as much as if it were Yas gone. The others might worry too, a little.

One night, Frankie awoke to find Miss McCracken kneeling by his bed, her hands clasped, eyes squeezed shut.

She was murmuring. *O heavenly Father.* She was babbling, like his mother clutching her prayer beads.

Watch with us over your child Francis. Grant that he may be restored to that perfect health which it is yours alone to give . . . through Jesus Christ our Lord. Amen.

"It's still there," said Miss McCracken the next morning. "Shouldn't we—?"

"We shall wait a few more days, then call the doctor."

Frankie had only once seen the spot's reflection in a small cloudy mirror his mother held for him. He knew it would stay, and blacker than ever.

Tiny Jesus on the wall was silent. Did not even shush Frankie now. Only the Ladies spoke to him. *Jesus died for your sins. God so loved the world that he gave his only begotten son.*

What did that mean?

Frankie looked straight at him, pinned there by nails in his little hands and feet. It was the Priest, the Priest who'd given up Frankie, left him to the world. Begotten. Forgotten.

In a drawer beside his bed, he found a round gold case. A compact with a mirror inside and a crescent of pressed pink powder. It smelled of sweet flowers that had dried in their vase. He stared at himself in the mirror. When would his mother come for him?

Now that another week had begun, he was ready to go home. When the Ladies left him alone, he took out the compact. He dabbed the pale powder with his fingers and then patted his backside where he thought the spot lay.

A knock came at the door and after a moment, the Ladies entered, followed by a man. A man with a doctor's bag, who removed his hat as he came in. It took Frankie a moment to realize he was Japanese. Better dressed than any Japanese he'd ever seen in Port Alberni, and taller, with a neatly trimmed moustache.

"Francis, this is Dr. Kuwabara."

The doctor gestured to Frankie at his desk to lie down on the bed. He felt his pants carefully drawn down and knew it was Miss McCracken's gentle fingers at work. He knew she was pointing with them at the hemorrhage, then covering her open mouth as she winced.

The doctor cleared his throat. "It's not a bruise or hemorrhage."

"Not a bruise?" Miss McCracken said. "Then what?"

Frankie straightened his pants and sat up. The scent of the powder filled the air.

"A Mongolian spot."

"Will it spread?"

"Is it contagious?" Miss McCracken took a step back.

Dr. Kuwabara donned his hat. "No. It usually disappears by age four or five. There is no injury, no internal bleeding."

"I've never heard of such a thing," said Miss Hawks.

"It only occurs among certain tribes," the doctor said.

"Mongolians?"

The doctor nodded. "And others. The boy can return home safely." He tipped his hat and went out, followed by Miss Hawks.

Miss McCracken bent down in front of Frankie. "Oh, Francis." She touched his cheek and left.

Frankie was surprised to discover that the house he'd been in all this time sat on a normal street with other houses nearby. He was in Alberni, Port Alberni's inland sister town.

Out they stepped, the three of them, Miss Hawks on one side and Miss McCracken holding his hand on the other. The air seemed warmer as if a season had passed. The Ladies looked different out in daylight: they were specked with bits of colour, freckles and moles under the brims of their hats. He wanted to free his hand, his hot hand from Miss McCracken's in its white glove. But she held tight as they walked. The odd person passed, some looking twice at the threesome.

The houses on the road grew farther apart until there were no more. They came to a school where children lived without their parents. It was set back from the road, newly built of orange brick, three storeys high.

Now a boy ventured near. "Hello," the boy said. He looked Frankie up and down. "Hello, brother." His white shirt was buttoned to the top the way the Ladies had dressed Frankie. The boy came closer to Miss Hawks with hand outstretched, tapping his palm with a finger.

"Shoo," said Miss Hawks. "Back to class. We have nothing to give you."

"Is it my brother?" Aki asked breathlessly, but the Ladies swept through the door with only a nod of their heads. Even after rowing halfway across the inlet, the sparkling brightness of their prim blouses and sweet lavender scent showed up the dank grime of the room, living room, bedroom, kitchen all in one. Entering behind them, Frankie smelled its odours as more pungent and sour than ever before.

"Frankie!" Aki hugged him tightly. Then Yas, Julia and Augusta. They looked at him as if he'd changed.

The Ladies removed their hats and gloves. "You are the missus?"

Momoye stepped meekly before the Ladies with bowed head, hands folded. Behind her, Taiji swayed a bit and rubbed his eyes. A bottle of Canadian Club lay in one corner. It was Friday morning after Thursday payday.

"Hanesaka," said Aki.

"Mrs. Handsacker," repeated Miss Hawks. Julia and Augusta giggled.

"We are from the Sisters of Mercy Mission. Do you understand English?"

Their mother nodded and shook her head at the same time. She understood enough to barter for eggs and milk in town, but that was all. How small and swarthy she looked before the Ladies. Her brows that could arch so sternly were still, even drooped.

"We found your son by the water," Miss Hawks said. "Unconscious. Smelling of liquor."

"And injured!" added Miss McCracken with a downward glance. "We fed him and bathed him. We took care of him." She was trembling beside Frankie, blinking.

"He come home," Momoye said, looking startled at the sound of herself in English. "Senku."

"She means, thank you," Julia piped in.

Momoye reached for Frankie and pulled him beside her, fingers biting into his arm.

"Your son," said Miss McCracken, taking a deep breath, "bears marks." She cupped her own backside lurking beneath layers of pleated cloth. "Hemorrhaging!"

Miss Hawks patted her friend's hand. "Yes, but the Japanese doctor says he's healed now."

"Yes, yes," said Momoye, gripping him tightly. His arm pinched.

Miss McCracken studied each child in turn, then cast a long glance at Frankie. "We are here for you should you need us." She placed a card on the table and her voice softened. "Goodbye, Francis."

Now Augusta waltzed before the Ladies of the Sisters of Mercy; she swept one leg behind the other and bent low for her audience. "I, Augusta Handsacker, a lady of the Sisters of Curtsy, thank you."

Momoye would not unclench her iron hold until the splash of the Ladies' paddles and the groan of their wooden boat faded into the distance. She turned to him, raised her hand and smacked him hard. "Stupid boy!"

He stumbled back.

"What if they didn't let you come home?"

Everyone was silent. He was grateful now for not being able to cry. He stayed close to his mother, his arm numb and cheek stinging. He was close enough to see the quiver beneath her eye.

"Yes, Mama."

He felt stranger in his family now than the stranger he'd already thought himself to be. Even with his mother. She had never struck any of her children before.

Momoye beckoned for him to sit by her chair. Augusta crouched beside him and touched his white shirt. He unbuttoned the collar and took a deep breath. It was made for a smaller boy.

"Were there lots of cookies to eat, Francis?" she giggled.

"We looked for you," Aki said, crawling to the other side of him. "All night and all day, then all night again, and all over again." Her eye rolled and glistened as if it could see everything. Yet they hadn't found him. He'd been sure that they would, that a knock would come at the door of the Ladies' house or at the window to his room. Or that his mother would barge right in without knocking and bring him home. He'd never panicked, never doubted, neither he nor tiny Jesus on the wall.

But they hadn't come. They hadn't looked hard enough. Not as hard as they would've if Yas had disappeared.

"Did they hurt you?"

Frankie shook his head.

Now he knew the name for it: Mongolian spot.

That night, Julia and Augusta folded down Frankie's bedsheets like nurses; they tugged his waistband and giggled away.

They scrubbed at the spot with a cloth while Frankie pretended to sleep. It was a well of blood deep down that couldn't be mopped up. It was meant to be and to stay. Just as Yas was meant to be free of it. That's why he was stronger than Frankie. That was how he could take more than two swigs of Taiji's whisky and stay standing, how he could ride the Colossus.

When they left him, Frankie twisted his arm around to touch his backside. It felt like the rest of him; no bumps or ridges. It tingled. Miss McCracken's gentle hands had exposed it to the cold air, she and Miss Hawks staring where they should not. He hadn't tried to stop them. In fact, he'd lain there with his face buried in the sweet-smelling pillow, on the soft bed, limp. He burned with shame, his Mongolian spot now hot with sweat. Beside and around him, his family slumbered on. Frankie slipped out of bed and went to his mother's chair. Why hadn't she come for him? He wept then, his kind of weeping, quiet and dry.

May Jesus walk with you, Miss McCracken had said; Jesus, who was pinned to a wall in an empty room. No, it was the Priest who walked with Frankie, another misfit follower like the Peach Man or the Hunchback. He was the one with the Mongolian spot that would not go away, and the Priest was with him as ever, in water and on land, maybe even through fire, for good or ill.

In spite of his mother, Frankie did go out after dark. He rowed off on his own whenever he woke in the night, which was often. He rowed past the shore where the Ladies had found him. He rowed with the sawdust burner eating fire in the dark by the mill. Each time he saw it, he was reminded of the Priest's fire-walking, his feet blackened but unburnt. He rowed, his muscles strengthened and strained, so as not to be pulled down between the logs again, and to never be so weak he could be carted off by two small ladies.

One night, as he rose to leave the house, he almost tripped over Aki lying face down to the floorboards. "Let me come with you," she whispered. He shook his head but she got up anyway, her Cyclops eye staring him down.

The waxing moon lit up the sky, the mountains under it a far-off rolling wave. Aki skimmed the water with her fingers and leaned over. "There are creatures so far down no one ever sees."

Frankie rowed for a time, then stopped. "That's where they found me."

"The Ladies?"

He nodded.

They pulled the boat ashore. Frankie held up the lantern as if to find the ghost outline of himself there on the ground.

They followed the road out of Port Alberni, reversing the steps he'd taken with the Ladies. Frankie swung the lantern from the road in front to the shiny black snake of a creek alongside it. A hum came from somewhere just ahead. Was it an owl, a wolf? No, it was a song that rose up and drifted down, a girl's voice that wavered and thrummed the air. The trees and bushes fell away on one side to reveal the school he'd passed with the Ladies, three storeys high. Windows glowed on the first and second floors. The humming girl sat on a bench outside.

She looked up when they approached. "I'm Mary," she said. Then she pulled her gown tight to her softly swelled belly. "This is Daisy," she whispered. She was not much older than Aki; she even looked like her but with two dark glistening eyes and straight black hair cut to her chin. She wasn't Japanese or Chinese; she was Indian. She was turning a piece of wood between her fingers. The wood was hollowed out with four nails tapped into its top. Bit by bit the girl looped red yarn around the head of each one, then hooked one strand over the next to release a web that spiralled inward. The wood turned easily in her hand, loops dropping; a knitted red tube emerged out the bottom from the hollow centre, worming into the girl's lap.

A bell rang and a man's voice boomed inside from above. "Lights out!"

Beside them, a window creaked open and three boys tumbled out, all barefoot in white gowns like ghouls of the night. Another window opened and they clambered in. The girl sprang to her feet and slipped through the same window the boys had come out from. The piece of wood dropped behind her, landing at their feet, its red tail in the dirt.

Frankie and Aki walked on. One house appeared set back from the road among trees, then another. Then more, side by side. Small frame houses. Was it this one, or that? A block farther, there it was: the window from which he'd watched for Momoye, framed by its lace curtains. No lights were on.

"That's the place?" Aki whispered. She took a deep breath. It was small but neat as a doll's house. And dark: no one home or all asleep. Frankie crept closer to the window. He wanted to see tiny Jesus on the wall, waiting. But Aki grabbed his arm and yanked him back, her eye fearful. "What if they take you again?"

Back in Port Alberni, they passed their school, Eighth Avenue Elementary. Their crisp steps echoed in the night. Argyle Street was empty and blank. They walked past the shop where, Aki explained, she and their mother once bought chicks in a little carton with a bag of feed. The chicks had squawked and squawked. Aki had put her finger to their squealing beaks. Two chicks soon curled into limp balls. "Mama tossed them into the ditch there," she said, pointing. *Left for dead*.

They went up the hill to the grand blocks where the rich white people lived. Frankie showed Aki the grandest house with the turret and the garden shrouded in shadows. He tried to tell her how glorious the flowers were by day, in sunlight: the colours and smells.

"They're asleep now," Aki whispered. Only she would think of such a thing, of flowers closing their eyes at night.

"If there's seven of us in our house," Frankie asked, "how many do you think could fit there? Seventy?" The two of them stared up at the darkened turret.

"One day, Rapunzel will let down her hair to you, Frankie," Aki told him. He turned away from her knowing eye.

Now the dark was tinged with more morning than night. Frankie led his sister to a maple tree that stood alone and above Main Street, whose thick limbs he'd straddled once or twice to watch the Rose Queen Parade. There were the lights of the Arlington Hotel and, leading from it, the path followed by the Rose Queen and her procession. The day of the parade was always sunny, and the crown glinted on a head of blond or brown curls like an eclipse he must not look at.

He hoisted his sister up. Some coins fell from his pocket. "Where'd you get those?" Aki asked.

"Never mind," Frankie said, scrambling to pick them up. He pointed out the fiery light of the sawdust burner at the mill. They watched the glow fade as the sun brightened the sky. He glanced back to the grand houses they'd passed. "The men who own the mill live up there." Though he didn't know that for a fact.

They turned to the crooked rows of shabby dwellings and bunkhouses below them.

"There we are," Aki piped in. Beyond the harbour, where the fishing boats were moored, their house bobbed all on its own.

"One day, I'm going to build a house with a turret," Frankie declared. He wanted to tell Aki all about the floating hotel and the flower garden. But no, he'd surprise them. He'd surprise them all.

CHAPTER 3

Floating Garden

"Lively Dancer," he shouted into the ear of one elderly bachelor. Frankie pranced in a circle, kicking his knees high. Then he reared his head up like a horse. "To win," he said, "to win."

The man slowly nodded. He dug into his pocket and tossed Frankie a coin.

Each week, Frankie visited the bunkhouses at the edge of town to offer newly arrived bachelor loggers and elderly cooks a list of horses to win, place or show at the racetrack in Vancouver. He pantomimed his best Quick Step or Lightning. He placed the bets and took a percentage if they won. The men could neither read the papers nor understand the radio, but they wanted to place more and more bets to double their chances to go home for good with pockets full.

"I can't promise anything," Frankie told one or two of them, "but I got a tip."

"Ahh," they nodded, their weathered faces brightening as they dug deeper into their pockets.

They trusted Frankie. So he let them bet on races that had already been run or had never taken place at all. Frankie felt good letting them win, though it was always less than what they lost. The men—Japanese, Chinese and Indians from India—worked and worked with no one to go home to; they worked on the logs, or inside the mill cutting or loading them up until they lost a finger or hand or got too old. But they never blamed Frankie for their bad luck. They squatted on their haunches outside the bunkhouses, smoking and clucking their tongues, telling him to try for a better life.

Frankie waited for word to reach Taiji of his bet-taking, waited for a scolding. At least a look cast his way—something of a father's disapproval for swindling the bachelors. Maybe even grudging approval for making his own way. But no, nothing.

Still, Frankie had his retort for Taiji: *What good is money if you don't know what to do with it?* Frankie was fourteen now, almost fifteen, and he knew. He knew not to do what Taiji did: waste a paycheque on whisky. Keep doing the same thing and never try for something better. Why swim upstream with an anchor at your waist? At least Mr. Fung was making an investment so that his wall of coins would grow along with the walls of the floating hotel.

Mr. Koga grunted as he hammered down a plank across a row of logs assembled on the shore.

"Shush!" Mr. Fung waved his arms emphatically. He feared someone stealing their big idea before they could get it off the ground and onto water. Mr. Koga resumed with a timid tap-tap-tap, but before long, his hammer was slamming down anew, echoing across the inlet. Sweat began to stream from his head. Mr. Fung slunk away.

"Give me a hand, boy!" Mr. Koga yelled. Frankie scrambled over to hold the plank in place.

Frankie took up a hammer and began pounding away

beside Mr. Koga, the force of his blows vibrating up his arm through his body.

"Are you sure this won't sink?" Mr. Koga asked.

"Sure." Frankie pointed to his house down the inlet. How puny it looked alone on the water. Far below the grand house with the turret and its neighbours.

Up there lived Mr. Bloedel, Mr. Stewart and Mr. Welch no doubt, owners of the mills. High in the sky, with a view of all who laboured on their behalf: the office men who made sure the logs kept coming and the buyers kept buying, who wrote the cheques though it wasn't their money. The foremen who were told what to do, and told others below them. Down lowest were those who were told what to do and did it. That was Taiji and Mr. Koga, the boom men who might slip from their logs, or saw operators who might lose an arm to the blade. Frankie and his family lived at the bottom of the valley, holding tight to Taiji, swinging like monkeys from his shirttails.

Frankie was born in the Year of the Ox, but his mother claimed he was a monkey, a good climber.

If the floating hotel was to float and stay afloat, the visiting lumber buyers, charged a lower rate, might sleep there instead of the Arlington. People would travel from miles around to stay in their hotel. And come spring, the Rose Queen might let down her golden stair and bid him climb up to her turret.

At Weaver's Dry Goods store, Frankie pored over an inch-thick seed catalogue from Victoria. Page after page of flowers. Who knew there could be so many? So many roses: red, coral, yellow, peach, pink, white. Climbing roses, hybrid tea roses, grandiflora roses, bred hundreds of years ago, with names Augusta would have a dance or a song for: Buff Beauty, Ballerina, Floribunda, even Kerria Japonica, the rose native to Japan. Mr. Weaver totalled his order and showed Frankie what he owed.

He didn't have it. Nowhere near. Who knew mail-order seeds could cost so much? Frankie fingered the coins and bills in his trousers. For all his wheeling and dealing, the earnings still fit into one pocket.

Mr. Weaver turned a few pages and slid the catalogue across the counter. "Here's what you need."

Flower seed for seaside planting. Pacific Beauty. Bronze Beauty. Victoria Sunset.

Not roses, but flowers still, in all colours and petal shapes, small and full. Snapdragons and others in the mystery language of flowers: *calendula, verbena, impatiens.*

"For ten dollars, you get thirty packets of seeds."

He chose his flowers like an old bachelor picking his horses to win. But he wouldn't be greedy. And very soon he would stop the betting and swindling too. Surely Taiji and others were beginning to think the worst of him.

While he waited for his seeds to arrive, Frankie planned his garden. A pathway of planks from the road through the trees and across the water to the floating isle. He'd paint the planks white so you could follow the path even at night. As visitors stepped onto it from dry land, they'd pass under an archway of wisteria. There would be blossoms on all sides with labels for each kind. A parade could lead there; a Rose Queen could be crowned there.

A floating garden. People from far and wide would hear of it and come sip fresh lemonade at a refreshment stand among the wisteria. He'd build a bench or two where people could sit and get comfortable so they'd buy more.

Of course, he'd have to charge admission like they did at Butchart Gardens. Not too much; a discount for locals, maybe. Once he paid for the logs and lumber, the paint and nails and such, and upkeep—which wouldn't be much because he'd be doing it himself—the rest would be profit. Then he'd build other floating gardens in Tofino, Ladysmith, Duncan; hire locals while he went from place to place, managing his enterprise. Who knew where else he could set up shop? Nanaimo and even Victoria.

Mr. Koga's head and neck grew bowed and bent from hammering. He stood in water day after day constructing a sturdy dock for the hotel. His skin grew scaly, moulting in the sun. He could hold his breath longer than anyone. Mr. Fung, charged with overseeing finances, grew forgetful of words, while numbers he could swiftly add and multiply on his abacus. The bachelors—who now laboured on the hotel—he designated by number instead of name, from one to fifteen down his columns opposite the hours they worked and the dollars they were paid.

Frankie worked on his garden early before school and late after. First he built three rafts atop old oil drums whose ends he'd sealed, then anchored and moored the rafts to the shore, side by side. Then he began laying down ten inches of soil in curbed beds he'd fashioned atop the rafts.

Each afternoon he'd check at Mr. Weaver's store. When Mr. Weaver shook his head through his storefront window, Frankie headed to the post office, just in case.

He could hardly wait. Yet he did, all the while tilling the soil over and over. One still morning came an unearthly crack that was not from a hammer. A heavy splash and a howling cry from Mr. Koga. Frankie ran to the hotel where Mr. Koga cowered, lower than ever. Above him stood the frame of the structure, eight posts with crossbeams between. He was looking down into the water that sloshed at his knees and gesturing a few yards out.

Fall down, Mr. Koga stammered. *Down.* He squeezed his head between his hands.

Frankie splashed into the water those few yards to one of the bachelors, face down and lulled by the dark water lapping at the body, the hair.

Frankie pulled the bachelor to shore. Mr. Koga was too weak to be much help. Out of the water the body was heavy—the skin slippery but warm. Shivering, Frankie squatted down.

Fallen off as he was hammering, cracked his head on a beam, explained Mr. Koga. The bachelor's neck was twisted and limp; his eyes were half-open, staring over Frankie's shoulder.

"Close!" Mr. Koga cried, turning away.

Frankie touched his fingertips to the bachelor's soft lids and drew them down.

Why had there ever been a Bachelor #4? The bad-luck death number; the man had had no chance. The other bachelors took his body to a clearing outside of town, blessed it, burned it, then collected some bits of bone to bury in a tin can. Frankie felt coins in his pocket, money the men had lost on horses that never ran. He'd never wipe his hands clean of bad luck.

One by one, they abandoned the hotel, even when Mr. Fung promised two, three, then five times the pay. Only Bachelor #13, whose digits added up to four anyway, laboured on, having nothing to lose. In Mr. Fung's ledger, he became Bachelor #1. When the outside walls were done, he went inside, dividing the space with Mr. Koga and Frankie, installing doors, nailing down floorboards and sanding them smooth. Whenever Mr. Koga left for dinner and Frankie went to build his garden, the lone, steady pecking of one hammer followed them into the evening.

Blooms in his garden: that was all Frankie thought of amid Mr. Koga's prayers to Buddha, and the click-click of Mr. Fung's abacus beads tallying their debts. Up on the hill, beneath the turret, roses were blooming red, rooted, majestic, tended by gardeners—when they should've been down below, blossoming on the sea.

Frankie could wait no longer. He made his way up from the water one night, up through the streets to the grand houses.

He plucked those blooms, one at a time, roots and all, beneath the turret's window. He filled in the holes and, by a full moon, he planted the roses in his floating garden.

All morning Frankie gave the roses sips of water and spread fresh manure. By nightfall, he put down his tools and went home, exhausted. He huddled in his mother's chair and slept.

The house swayed and rocked and the water rose up, frothing at the window. It was almost June but snow bounded wildly outside. His mother watched the storm too. Stricken, she began to babble, then fell back in bed as if she'd never wakened.

All night long, Frankie watched the snow whirl in patterns across the water and listened to the wind. He dozed in his mother's chair as it inched forward and back with the waves. The wind became a rasping voice in his ears. Everyone else slept.

In the morning, he pushed the door open and tiptoed out. Snowflakes melted under his bare feet; the air was already warming in the early sun.

As he rowed toward his floating garden, he could make out the rose bushes dangling with tiny skeletons now; he swore he could hear the tinkle of the frozen petals like icicles. He climbed aboard. The soil crackled, laced with ice and melting snow. The pecking of Bachelor #13's hammer echoed from inside the hotel thirty yards down the shore.

"No good! No good!" Mr. Koga approached Frankie clutching the newly painted HOTEL ON THE SEA sign that he'd hung in anticipation just two days earlier, though the hotel was months yet from opening. The wind rose and seemed to bluster with him. The sign must've fallen to the deck in the night. The remains of Frankie's pillaged roses and the ashes of Bachelor #4 now blew in their faces.

Frankie looked onto his garden that was now no garden at all. On his knees with a hammer, he pounded the soil and then tilled and tilled, relieved that he'd never told his family of his foolish scheme. He could imagine Augusta's giggles and his mother's brow.

A hand landed on his shoulder and he jumped: Bachelor #4 come back to haunt him?

"It's time to work," Taiji said, carrying a hoe and spade in his other hand. His friend George, a chip-and-saw operator from the mill, pushed a wheelbarrow filled with plants: wild-flowers. Wild roses, plucked from the roadside, roots and all.

Taiji drove his spade into the flower bed and dug. He stopped for a moment and handed the hoe to Frankie. There was nothing to say. Frankie nodded without a word, like he'd seen Yas nod to Taiji on the logs.

The three of them dug side by side. They planted the wild roses, small and low to the ground, setting them three deep in a wavy line—a river of roses crossing the island garden. The blossoms were wilted but sprang up with a watering, and their pink petals and golden yellow stamens brightened.

At the end of the day, all three stood back on solid ground and gazed onto the river of roses swaying with the water's rise and fall.

Before long, the wildflowers were blooming wildly, each blossom jostling with three others for sunlight and sea air. Frankie rolled his sleeves up still higher, and so did Taiji. They worked a two-man saw back and forth, without exchanging a word. They built an arbour like he'd seen in Mr. Weaver's catalogue. In no time, vines began to snake up with pink buds poking out every few inches. He built two more to frame the view of the water, a trellis and a giant basket brimming with more roses.

For the first time, Frankie felt a sureness—not underfoot as Yas must feel, but in his arms and hands as he sawed. He felt Taiji's shadow at his back.

Frankie kept his garden shipshape, pinching back wilting blooms and leaves as Mr. Weaver advised, to make way for more. Just before sunset, the river of roses appeared just right, undulating and bobbing on the water, pink bits catching light at the horizon. For that view, he charged five cents' admission. On the weekends, a small stream of visitors formed on the shore, waiting to set foot on the floating garden.

Even with its balconies overlooking the water, Hotel on the Sea reminded Frankie of his own shabby house: a rectangular box, a two-storey stack of cubbyhole rooms nailed to a rickety raft, pitching forward and back, side to side. For all their labour, the handiwork was not so fine. The hotel's wooden frame quickly grew warped. Its ceilings were high enough for Japanese, but no one else. It was nothing like the Arlington. When Mr. Fung applied to the City for a licence to serve beer, he was refused.

At first, only a few Japanese and Chinese on their way to logging camps stayed at the hotel. Then Mr. Koga and Mr. Fung decided to let the bachelors live in the hotel for a cut rate. The white men who came to do business at the mill stepped inside for a look, bumped their heads on the ceiling, then went to the Arlington or the Somass or the Beaufort. Anyone who came to Port Alberni by boat was sick of the sea; they chose to gulp their beer and fall asleep in a bed on dry land. But they did pay to see Frankie's floating garden of wild roses.

The hotel grew dank and rundown, only a little less so than the bunkhouses. But at least each bachelor had a room to himself and a balcony to sit on in the evening. In the early morning, Frankie let the bachelors onto the floating garden for free; they fished from among the flowers and plucked roses past their bloom to brighten their rooms. Indian bachelors soon joined the Japanese and Chinese at the hotel. The Japanese held diving contests off the balconies and before long, others joined in to perform backflips and somersaults, vying for the most applause.

Mr. Fung had given up on his gambling ventures and so had Frankie. The bachelors had grown wise to their diminishing returns. Mr. Fung contented himself now with beating them at mah-jong. He slouched behind the hotel desk, watching his coins sink lower and lower. Fewer visitors came to Frankie's Floating Garden. Julia and Augusta came by to sniff the flowers, and Aki to watch the sunset. But it was the same old view after all, and one look or two was enough, even with new pansies and calendula planted along each garden bed.

Until one afternoon Frankie glimpsed a ship anchored in the harbour. Yas arrived fresh off the logs, all lit up, just as Frankie rowed alongside the house.

"It's a ship from Japan, Papa," Yas called out. "The *Toyama Maru*." Toyama was Taiji's hometown.

"Let's go meet them."

Taiji shook his head.

The sailors loaded lumber onto the ship by day and come evening they fished and dove into the ocean. Yas jumped in with them. Augusta and Julia joined them on the dock, shyly trying out their bits of Japanese and feeding the sailors some English. Sitting just outside the house, Frankie heard Augusta warble "On the Good Ship Lollipop." Taiji stayed inside alone, not drinking, though it was a Thursday payday. Was he afraid they'd carry news of him and his shabby family back to Toyama?

On drunken nights, Frankie had heard Taiji go on to Mr. Koga about his rich samurai family in Toyama. If Taiji had stayed, he would've inherited it all, he said, being the eldest son. *You were a fool to leave!* Mr. Koga had snorted. Frankie had to laugh when he thought about what family fortune would be passed down to him now: a leaky home on water?

With the last of his earnings jangling in his pocket, Frankie headed to Weaver's Dry Goods the next morning. He eyed the suits and dresses for size and colour, following Mr. Weaver's advice. After everything was packaged up and paid for, he rowed home, warm and giddy.

"Oh, Frankie!" Augusta and Julia cried at the sight of their first store-bought dresses. They curtsied and sashayed across the room, admiring each other. His mother raised a brow at the money he'd spent but clucked approvingly when Taiji and Yas held their suits up.

"Why?" Aki asked when he gave her hers.

"Why not?"

The next morning, Frankie led the family in their new finery along Argyle Street, past Weaver's Dry Goods to Johnson's Photography Studio. Yas lagged behind, tugging on his sleeves and crotch, chafing in his suit. Frankie picked the snowy Rocky Mountains as a backdrop. The photographer, mumbling under his thick moustache, bade them position themselves in two rows, the men at the back.

"A picture to send home," announced Frankie, not daring a glance at Taiji.

"When the sailors sail to sea, sea, sea!" Augusta sang out.

Early the next morning, Taiji boarded a trawler heading for open sea. He didn't return until late that afternoon. He unloaded buckets of salmon, which he hung out to smoke, and seaweed laden with fish eggs, which Momoye pickled and dried.

Aki carefully wrapped the smoked fish, the seaweed and the eggs, and when the picture was ready, added that into a neat package tied with string. Taiji donned his kimono, set out his ink block, brush and cup of water, and sat himself down cross-legged on the floor. He held his sleeve as he dipped his brush, then drew columns of minute pictograms down the page, from right to left. Some resembled trees, some boxes inside boxes, some were simple strokes. He stamped the bottom left corner in red ink, an even smaller pictogram. "Hanesaka," he muttered. The family seal. Then he blew on the sheet and set it down to dry. *Dear Mother and Father*, Aki read haltingly. She was the only one learning to read and write Japanese.

> *It will soon be autumn in Port Alberni. The summer*
> *flowers are fading. My family and I are well. Please*
> *accept these gifts as humble tokens. I hope you are*
> *also both well and that we meet again in the future.*
> *Your faithful son, Taiji*

Augusta insisted on carrying the package to the sailors, who promised to deliver it to Taiji's family home. In return for their trouble, Taiji included a smaller package of fish and eggs for the sailors to share on their voyage home. Before they left, one danced a jig with Augusta and sang "On the Good Ship Lollipop" in sorry English.

Two officials from the City, the same ones who'd claimed the land on which Taiji had built their house many years ago, came knocking: now greyer; one fatter, one thinner. They asked for Frankie.

"Fu-ranki." His mother buttressed herself right up beside her son.

They demanded to see his land deed. The thin one gestured to the shore where the Floating Garden gently bobbed.

"I made that land myself," said Frankie in his deepening voice. "I don't need a deed to it." He sounded bold with his mother by his side. He allowed himself a smirk. "It's floating on water."

The man smirked back. "Then where's your dock licence?"

His mother's weight against him slackened.

"Nobody owns the water," Frankie retorted and shut the door. His heart was pounding like the lone hammer of Bachelor #13.

Augusta pressed her ear to the door and repeated what she heard: a sigh, a *damn Jap,* a bump-bump as they climbed into their boat, then splish-splash of oars as they rowed away.

Frankie was in his garden when Mr. Koga burst out of the hotel. "The Japs, the Japs!"

Inside, he found Mr. Fung staring at the radio on the counter, beside his dwindling coins. The announcer kept repeating: *The Japanese have attacked Pearl Harbor.*

Frankie ran and jumped into the boat. He heard his breath and the news wheezing out of his chest as he rowed, as if in slow motion. His mother was sitting in her chair by the window when he arrived. "The Japs," he panted. "The Japs."

She turned away with a sigh, unsurprised. "Now they'll send us back."

First, they were told to stay inside and not come out. But they had to: to work, shop for food, go to school. Then they could go out, but not at night, when they couldn't be clearly seen; they'd blend in too much with the bushes and shadows. They might sneak into the water and across the bay to where Jap submarines surely lurked. Maybe, Frankie privately mused, one was under their house right now to be spotted by Aki's one eye pressed between the floorboards.

Yas could not stay put. He could not stay inside. Even with the windows wide open, he needed open air and open water. He'd take off on the logs and disappear beyond the harbour, sometimes riding a log between his legs and paddling.

He'd drift back late at night, long past curfew, and sneak in through a window just for fun.

Mr. Fung sat nervously listening to the radio with not much to do. Many of the bachelors had fled while a few lay low in their rooms. He set to work. *How to Tell a Japanese from a Chinese,* he printed in large letters across the top of a blank page. He drew a Chinese face that resembled his own: *Honest and humble.* Beneath that face, he drew a Japanese face that resembled Mr. Koga's: *Sneaky Jap.* Then he drew a Chinese eye and a Japanese eye: one slanted down; one slanted up. One opened wider than the other. One with a fold and one without.

"To show I'm not one of you," Mr. Fung said when Frankie slammed a stack of flyers on the hotel desk. Frankie had torn them down from all over town. It was a wonder Mr. Koga hadn't yet been arrested.

By the following week, new signs appeared telling all the Japs in town to pack their bags, no more than what they could carry in two hands, and to be ready to move. When, the signs didn't say.

They huddled each night after dark. Taiji with his Canadian Club, Momoye with a bottle of sake, all waiting for Yas to come home. Each had their all-you-can-carry by their feet. They didn't have much, but it was difficult to choose what to take when they didn't know where they were going or when they'd be back.

Frankie spent every last minute on the Floating Garden, wrapping the climbers in burlap and covering the mounds with hay. Mr. Fung promised to look after it, but Frankie had his doubts. At Hotel on the Sea, Mr. Koga and Mr. Fung were arguing nearly every day. Mr. Koga wanted a share of Mr. Fung's wall of coins for all the hammering he'd done to build the hotel. Mr. Fung was not, he charged, being honest and humble at all.

But one morning, Mr. Koga didn't show up. At the end of the day, Frankie went to his house and found it padlocked. He looked inside. Everyone was gone: Mr. Koga, his wife, his two daughters. Pots, pans and dishes were on the table, blankets on the beds. Frankie went back to the hotel.

"The Mounties took him," said Mr. Fung, slouched behind his wall.

"But why? Where?" Frankie asked.

"He is national, not citizen." Mr. Fung shrugged.

But what did it matter? They were all Japs. All enemy aliens.

At last, in March, new signs went up. The Mounties instructed them to assemble at the train station in two weeks. They would ride the train overland, then board the ferry to Vancouver.

Then what?

Five nights before they were to leave, Yas didn't come home. The next morning, Aki walked the streets and avenues, up and down and up and down, peering into houses, shops, empty buildings. She came home to rest at night and then resume early the next morning. She didn't arrive home until just before curfew. She cried herself dry pining for Yas, while Taiji went on drinking. *Yas, please come home!* Julia and Augusta scribbled on a scrap of paper. They rolled it and poked it inside an empty whisky bottle and sent it sailing out a window.

What was to become of their house? Others on land, including the bunkhouses, had been claimed by the Custodian of Enemy Alien Property.

On the last night, fire broke out at Hotel on the Sea. Mr. Fung, drowsing at the front desk, was roused when his wall of coins, down to a few paltry piles, grew hot under his fingertips; he escaped easily. The balconies collapsed after the remaining bachelors dove off to save themselves. Only Bachelor #13 was unaccounted for, but he'd been hiding from the Mounties and hadn't been seen for some time.

When Frankie awoke the next morning, Aki was gone. He rowed the rest of the family to shore. Following signs, they began walking toward the station. At each block, others joined the growing stream along Main Street, arms straining with what they could carry. Frankie turned back to see his mother and Taiji slowly make their way along. Julia and Augusta skipping around them.

"Aki!" Frankie shouted and pushed against the crowd of people, past his mother, past Taiji, who looked up in alarm. He'd spotted his sister's thin figure heading away from everyone, on Gertrude Street leading out of town. He left his bags and started to run after her, skirting the crowd. He called and called but she didn't stop or look back.

Finally he was in reach of her and snatched at the tail of her coat.

"No!" she wailed, and tore free. "We can't leave Yas!" With a surge, he grabbed her coat firmly this time. They both tumbled to the ground. Aki's one eye was pouring out tears. The other had swelled up, bubbling inside its seal. "Please, Frankie!"

Frankie hung his head to his heaving chest. "We have to go."

Momoye and Taiji were waiting at the end of the street where Frankie had dropped their belongings. They were wearing the fine clothes he'd bought for them.

The six of them continued to the station. They passed his Floating Garden, its stems bundled for the winter to come. Then farther along, what remained of Hotel on the Sea, charred bones barely afloat.

CHAPTER 4

The Place Next to Hope

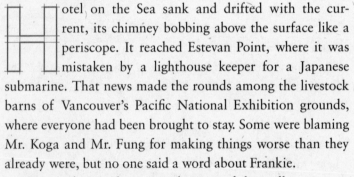otel on the Sea sank and drifted with the current, its chimney bobbing above the surface like a periscope. It reached Estevan Point, where it was mistaken by a lighthouse keeper for a Japanese submarine. That news made the rounds among the livestock barns of Vancouver's Pacific National Exhibition grounds, where everyone had been brought to stay. Some were blaming Mr. Koga and Mr. Fung for making things worse than they already were, but no one said a word about Frankie.

No one knew what was to become of them all.

Mothers and daughters and young children were made to stay in one building, men and boys in another. "It's so Mama can't have another baby," Augusta told them, holding her nose against the antiseptic used to rid the stalls of the stench left by the animals.

They lined up for food, holding out tin bowls as if the slop of porridge and prunes and watered-down canned milk was worth the wait. They ate at long tables and relieved themselves in troughs. There was no sunlight, no sea air, no lull of waves. Aki sat inside their stall for hours as if she were a sheep or pig or cow. Julia and Augusta played hide-and-seek among the sheets hung for privacy between families. Sometimes they ventured along the barbed-wire fence to gaze at a pond on the other side, and the ducks waddling across the grass. With no cooking, no brewing, no bartering, Momoye lay on her cot, lost without Taiji. No men and no house.

For seven months, Frankie hardly saw his mother or sisters. Then he and Taiji were dispatched with other men to set up camps in the mountains. Women and children would follow. The camps were beyond the one-hundred-mile quarantine zone. A Jap, even ones born here like Frankie and his siblings, could too easily lose their minds to the infectious Yellow Peril while anywhere within a hundred miles of the Pacific coast. So it would soon be No-Jap Land. The Land of No Return began at the 101st mile mark and extended into the mountains, where they all could be settled for their own safety and that of others.

Aboard a bus to the train station, Frankie and Taiji saw diners and a Woodward's store posted with big NO JAPS ALLOWED signs. On the train, they passed in and out the chambers of the mountains from daylight to darkness and back again. Jostled by the ride, Taiji sat silently, gazing past Frankie and out the window. Frankie had never been alone with his father before.

"How will the logs get to the mill now?" Frankie muttered as they passed a mountainside dense with trees. "Who'll they get to do it?"

With his face pressed against the glass, Frankie gazed up at the icy peaks that stabbed the sky and bled out the sun until each day came to its end. They were called the Cascade Mountains, but as far as Frankie could see they only went up and never came down. He thought of Yas, alone and left farther and farther behind with no way to catch up.

The train left them in the town of Hope; trucks let them off fourteen miles south on an open valley floor. The rundown Fourteen Mile Dairy and Livestock Ranch had been sold to the government. A few old barns were still standing and only a handful of workers remained. Stacks of rough shiplap lumber sat waiting for Frankie and Taiji and the other fifty men. Taiji touched one stack and shook his head. "Still green," he said.

The Mounties who'd brought them here set the men to work hammering the one-inch-thick shiplap and laying tar paper over that. Two families would move into each box, one side per family with no inside doors or plumbing. Outhouses behind every four shacks.

After days of work, Frankie looked over what they had built. Across the valley, identical boxes were forming rows; rows into streets into a town of identical shacks and plots. There would soon be ten avenues, from First to Tenth, intersecting with Tashme Boulevard on the south, and on the north, four bathhouses.

The government named it Tashme for Taylor, Shirras and Meade, the principals of a mining venture that had failed here half a century ago and had left behind a ghost town. Frankie craned his neck to see to the top of the mountains around it. You couldn't get much deeper down than this.

In his free hours, Frankie hiked north with the wind behind him, reaching the railway tracks. In school, he'd learned about the gold rush days. Prospectors came from far and wide to pan the rivers and creeks in the area but never struck it rich. Frankie wandered away from the tracks though thick forest, divining a path to their traces. With one step and another, the forest gave way.

It opened onto block after crooked block of gravestones. Some were plain and modest; others spread wider and rose higher than the rest and were fenced in with rusted iron rods.

Some were crumbling, some sinking into knee-high grass. Frankie went down the rows reading out the names to himself: *Creighton, Kingston, Stout, Willis, Stevens, Smith, Castle, Wooten, Pidwell.*

One stone leaned almost to the ground, spine cracked and bent. He squatted down to read it.

Sacred to the memory of Henry Blackwell who departed this life on the 4th of April 1870 aged 44 years with his wife Florence, aged 40 years and Child Mary aged 4 years.

Bad-luck number four over and over and over. Frankie pushed the stone back to try to right it, but it was stuck.

For what is life, asked another stone. *It is even a vapour, that appeareth for a little time and vanisheth away.*

A vapour, that was his life so far with nothing to show for itself. Everything sunk to the sea or into the ground. One day he'd lie beneath stones like these, only in a graveyard for Japs. He imagined these stones from high above, the plots in row after row, like this Tashme they were now building.

"It's recess all the time!" Augusta's clamour echoed across the valley floor. She, Julia, Aki and their mother had finally arrived.

Behind an old farm building, Frankie found a wooden chair: one arm cracked but solid. He set it by the window of their new home for his mother. When she first stepped inside, the cold blue light of the autumn sky was splintering through the slats. Taiji was right about the green lumber: it hadn't been adequately dried. Already the planks were shrinking back on all 347 shacks, leaving gaping cracks where not only the light but also the cold and wet entered and ice began to form.

Aki barely spoke to Frankie for making her leave Yas behind. She was pale skin and bones. Like Frankie, she walked. Sometimes he walked behind her without her knowing. She marked the perimeter of the camp with mud splattering her bare legs. She walked until the lights were snuffed one by one, wading through the dark mystery of the valley.

One night she did speak to Frankie.

"I saw Yas," she said, as quiet as a rustle of leaves. In another Tashme shack.

She had stood on one side of tinsel glass, the black sky flocked with stars overhead, clouds of her frantic breath in front. Then he, the boy whom she recognized, had come to the window and looked outside, right past her.

"I saw his face. It was Yas." Her lips trembled, her one eye quivering. "Please, Frankie, come with me."

She led him down the dark dirt street off Tashme Boulevard, clutching his hand until they arrived at a shack identical to theirs. Inside, he saw two boys. The smaller looked like Yas once looked, when Yas was a boy.

Frankie shook his head. She was missing Yas so much, she was lost in time. He didn't know what to say, but Aki let him take her hand and lead her home.

Weeks passed and early one morning—too early, now that no one had any place to go—a knock came at the door. When no one answered, the door nudged open. They appeared like returning ghosts, silhouetted in the early white sun: the Ladies. Frankie hung back. His mother began babbling, her brows arching. Taiji rose up beside her. Aki stood beside him, her one eye wild.

"When we heard what happened, we wanted to help," Miss McCracken sighed. She caught Frankie's eye imploringly. "Francis." She hugged her Bible to her breast. Both Ladies were altered, bedraggled ghosts of their ghostly selves, their blouses and hats wilted and frayed. Shrivelled weeds tucked in the bands of their hats.

Frankie pushed himself forward. "We don't need your help."

"He has been saved," said Miss Hawks, not seeming to hear Frankie at all. "Come in now, Jacob." Both Ladies turned to the door. "The Mounties entrusted him to us."

"Who's Jacob?" asked Augusta, sleepy-eyed.

Then there he was, just outside the doorway, a ghost too, with the morning sun behind him; a ghost grown tall and thin. Aki ran to him but stopped short. "Is it you? I can't see you," she said, straining on her tiptoes, her eye squinting.

He stepped inside. "I can see you," he said in a strange, deep voice. Yet it was Yas. So tall he had to bend down to all of them, even Frankie.

"Yasumasu!" Taiji fell to his knees and wept at his son's feet. He wailed, over and over until Miss Hawks urged him up.

"There is Sunday church service in the main hall tomorrow," she said, addressing Taiji. She pressed her Bible into his spindly hands while Miss McCracken left hers on the table. "You may give thanks to the Lord."

Yas was so tall that Aki had to start from the bottom of him and slowly work her way up through all the changes. One eye couldn't take in all of him at once.

Yas hardly spoke. No one was sure whether to call him Yas or Jacob. No one asked. He and Taiji didn't seem so much father and son these days either. Now Yas was the brother who seemed different, the odd man out. But there was no good feeling for Frankie in that.

Frankie sat alone in the graveyard. Beside him, the Blackwell family stone faithfully bowed. He sat night after night, hopeful for a tremor, a rumble, a message from the world under his feet. Even from the Priest. What came instead were scattered coughs throughout Tashme, then more erupting all around in a chorus.

The camps and nearby Hope were overrun with consumption. Tuberculosis was the proper name for it. The only treatment was rest; for prevention, attendance at Sunday service to pray for a cure. Julia and Augusta went for the milk and cookies, dutifully toting Bibles left by the Ladies.

Aki consented to being baptized. Not because of the tearful fussing of Miss McCracken; she dreaded being divided in any way from Yas—or Jacob—who'd been baptized in the Ladies' care. It seemed harmless enough, and it might bring added protection from consumption. So one Sunday morning in the building that was town hall, dance hall and church, they assembled, the whole family along with the Ladies, before rows of Tashme's newly faithful.

Do you desire to be baptized? asked the minister who travelled from camp to camp with his common prayer books.

I do.

Do you believe and trust in the Holy Spirit?

I do.

One after another followed: Momoye, now Mary; Taiji, now Samuel; Aki, now Anne; Julia and Augusta, still Julia and Augusta. Finally, Frankie, now Francis. Water was poured into a basin and each bowed before it. The water ran cool over Frankie's head, once, twice, three times and trickled down his neck as the minister waved his hand through the air, across, then up and down. *We thank you, Almighty God, for the gift of water.*

Frankie woke to such a flurry of hammering and sawing one morning that he thought he was back in Port Alberni with the bachelors. A hospital was going up for consumptives. The British Columbia Security Commission was paying twenty cents an hour to anyone who would get on the roof. Yas and Taiji, riders of logs, climbed up without fear. Frankie sat below, knocking old nails out of old beams. Father and son worked back to back in silence above him.

Day after day, the men came to work, sawing, hammering, planing, painting, grateful for something to do and for their twenty cents an hour. The hospital took the form of a cross upon the valley floor. Fifty beds in all, with separate wards for the men and women in the front and back, a morgue on one side and offices on the other.

On one of those days, Taiji stretched his bent back. The sun was glinting off the white mountain peaks. He leaned, then stumbled toward the edge of the roof. Frankie watched helplessly as Taiji flailed to regain balance.

"Papa!" Yas yelped and grabbed him.

The two steadied themselves in each other's arms and straightened. As if the roof was just another Colossus.

It's a long way to Tippelary! Taiji burst out and Yas joined in. They were riding together again, in tandem once more.

By winter, Frankie was bartering goods across the valley. His mother was using half the family's rice rations to ferment a sake more potent than any she'd made before. From one thirsty housewife in Hope, Frankie scavenged three pairs of strap-on skates and went down to the frozen Sumallo River, where he often found Aki sitting on the rocks with Yas in the evening. Frankie dangled the blades in front of them.

"Like this," he said. He balanced one boot over the base of the blade and buckled the worn leather straps tightly over the ball of his foot and at the ankle. He buckled the other and set off on the ice, wobbling at first but soon gliding around the curving banks. As he skated faster, the cold wind almost swept him up into the air. He'd gone far downstream. He turned back to wave.

They were gone. The blades sat on a rock.

They were too big for Julia or Augusta, and no one else wanted them; the housewife in Hope wouldn't take them back for anything. His mother raised her black brows in dismay. He'd wasted good sake in the deal.

When Frankie wasn't delivering sake bottles from his coat pockets or squatting alone in the graveyard, he sat as Augusta's audience of one. She loved to sing "Oh Danny Boy," but for him she sweetly warbled "Oh Frankie Boy"; she had a way of making fun of both him and herself that he liked.

He'd seen the Ladies on Tashme Boulevard, on occasion, coming out of the town hall, a spruced-up barn. He'd looked the other way, until one day they invited him inside, promising him milk and cookies, as if he were a boy again.

"How is Jacob?" asked Miss McCracken.

Frankie was confused for a moment.

"Is he cold to his own brother?" Miss Hawks hovered near.

"Of course he is," said Miss McCracken. "As he is to us. He says nothing to us, as if we were strangers."

"After the charity and goodwill we showed him," said Miss Hawks.

The empty barn echoed with every word and sound. He didn't dare say a thing.

"Come visit us whenever you like." The Ladies smiled and each patted his hand as he rose sheepishly to leave.

Frankie came back. Once a week at least, for a time. Miss McCracken shed tears, which seemed salted by guilt. *Irredeemable soul,* that was Jacob. After what they'd saved him from: the Port Alberni prison where he'd been held for days; abused, treated like a murderous saboteur and traitor, a spy and collaborator. *Who knew if he'd have ever gotten out?* The Mounties were about to send him far away, to a prison camp in the wilderness of northern Ontario, with the bachelors as it turned out, behind barbed wire, under armed guard day and night. Alone. She and Miss Hawks had vouched for

Jacob as a good Christian, as a loyal and patriotic Canadian; they'd put themselves at risk. Perhaps they could have brought him sooner to his family, but he'd needed rest and a good scrubbing. So they'd kept him in their home, where he slept in the same bed as Frankie had, in the company of tiny Jesus. Yet he'd shown no gratitude.

The longer Miss McCracken sat with Frankie, the drier her eyes grew, the lighter her voice. He remembered the softness of the bed in her home, the sweet scent of the pillow and her powder, and the softness of her touch on his back and behind. Now, she slipped him extra food stamps to use at the canteen, and occasionally a cigarette. He'd smoke it slowly and watch the puffs rise into the cold air. He'd smell the tobacco on his fingers for hours. But the cigarettes and Miss McCracken's powder began to nauseate and shame him. He stopped his visits.

Augusta squeezed his hand and then slipped a piece of paper into it. He glanced into his palm. It was a list: one yard of red satin, two spools of red thread, five pairs of white gloves, one jar of black shoe polish. He gave a shrug.

"Frankie, please," Augusta begged. She and everyone knew by now that whatever you wanted, Frankie Hanesaka could get. Pots, pans, string, nail clippers, nail polish, stockings, chocolate, chewing gum. He bartered, pillaged and sometimes swindled.

So he took what he could of his mother's sake and other items to town and traded them for the satin, the thread, the gloves and the shoe polish. Then came curtains, chairs, clothing, paint, wood: whatever was on Augusta's list. With inspiration from Shirley Temple and assistance from Julia, Augusta was pioneering the 3-T Club: Tashme Talent Theatre.

Then she added her oldest brother to her list. Augusta wanted Frankie to play a part in the opening pageant. How could he say no, with her hand squeezing his? He wondered what it would be like to stand on a stage, built with the scrap lumber he'd scavenged from a construction site. Frankie envied the dancing and singing boy who was to wear the red satin he'd procured.

Waiting behind the curtain the day of the show, he felt sweat clump the rice powder on his face. Down the line of waiting performers, no one else was sweating. They all looked giddy and happy. The grass skirt he'd been made to wear tickled and itched his legs. The curtain rose and he knew he'd made a terrible mistake. But the others were already swaying and singing, and he joined in, beating his chopsticks on the paint can strung around his neck.

> Like the beat, beat, beat of the tom-tom,
> When the jungle shadows fall.
> Like the tick, tick, tock of the stately clock
> As it stands against the wall.

At the frightened cries of babies in in the audience, Frankie glimpsed his mother's stern look. He burned with shame.

Augusta stepped forward with a garland of flowers around her neck. With the satin-sleeved boy, she twirled and sang "You're the Top." Frankie forgot his embarrassment. The audience laughed and smiled, and he brimmed with pride for his little sister. Then five boys, their faces smeared with black shoe polish, sang "Mammy" on their knees, waving their white-gloved hands. The babies cried louder.

They all came out on stage at the end and bowed, while the audience clapped. A girl in the third row clapped longer than most and stared boldly at him, then giggled behind a dainty hand. He burned hot again with embarrassment. Unbelievably, the girl had curls and bright red lips.

That spring, Tashme swelled from less than a thousand people to almost double that, while the number of shacks increased by only a quarter. Customers told Frankie it was happening in other camps as well, like New Denver, Sandon and Lemon Creek.

"These Japs are like rabbits," Frankie heard one Mountie remark to another amid the cries of a baby from a nearby shack. They were standing in their red serge outside the RCMP detachment as Frankie passed. "Jap-rabbits," the other laughed.

Frankie had noticed a girl younger than himself waddling along with swollen belly in winter; now she was strolling the boulevard, newborn held close. Frankie saw it all around him. Aging parents, even, were adding to their grown broods. In the dead of sleepless nights, especially in summer when windows flew open, Frankie caught wails and moans from nearby shacks and from inside their own, mingling with the howls of coyotes and wolves at the camp's edge. Some nights he got up to walk, but there was no escaping those sounds that pricked the yearning in his body.

The girl with the curls and bright lips approached him a few weeks later. Her name was Reiko; she was from Vancouver. She thrust out the hand that had hovered over her giggles and her small mouth. He noticed her fingernails were painted red too. From her wallet, she carefully drew out a square of paper with worn folds. It was a picture of a brooch in the shape of a rose.

She looked into his eyes. "Can you find me a rose like this, Frankie Hanesaka?"

He blushed. Her lips were the same velvet shade as a rose he'd plucked from the garden of the turreted house. She smiled, revealing a smudge of red on her front tooth. He stepped closer and took the picture—clipped from a catalogue—from her hand.

"I'll sure try." He nodded and, stupidly, winked.

Under a light grey sky, Frankie headed to the graveyard later that afternoon. Someone had been there: a rose lay outside the fence surrounding the Blackwell family plot, as if dropped by accident.

He sat down on the prickly grass, held the rose to his nostrils and drowsed, though his legs twitched, awake and running. When he opened his eyes, it was dusk and the sun, low in the sky, had brightened to cast every mote or bit of floating tree fluff in gold. Fairy dust, Augusta would call it.

The brooch Frankie found at a pawn shop in Hope didn't look quite like the picture Reiko had given him, but it was close. His mother approved.

"Oh, my!" Reiko gasped, carefully lifting the miniature rose of enamelled gold from the box he held out to her. He doubted it was real gold. She let it sit in her palm like it was magical and precious. When she reached for her purse, he held up his hands and shook his head.

"No, please," he said, refusing payment as his mother had instructed, to Frankie's surprise. She'd liked the look of the girl.

"Please accept our complimentary gift at no charge," he said awkwardly.

He took Reiko to the next dance at Tashme Town Hall. He pinned the rose brooch on her pale pink blouse, again as his mother had instructed. During the foxtrot, which Augusta had taught Frankie the day before, two spots of red appeared on each of Reiko's cheeks, matching the enamel of the rose pin. He dared himself to look into her eyes. Everything about her— the curls in her hair, the colour in her cheeks, even the smell of her—brought back to him the wildflowers in his floating garden. Perhaps he'd found his Rose Queen.

At Sunday service, Frankie introduced Reiko to Miss McCracken; he suggested—just as it came to him—that she take Rose as a Christian name. She was baptized soon after. Her forehead was dabbed three times and drops fell on the brooch pinned to her collar. When she raised her head, she was smiling at him, grateful, it seemed, to do this thing that pleased him.

The next day, late in the afternoon, Frankie took her to the graveyard. He'd never brought anyone there. They lay down behind the Blackwell gravestone. Reiko pulled him atop her body, the only body besides his mother's he'd ever held so close. It wasn't soft and giving like his mother's; its firmness strained him, while opening with ease. When he realized what he was to do, a mystery was laid to rest, the ache he'd haplessly circled round, relieved.

He felt like that sun dipping low in the sky, his body's heat and sweat lifting to a hazy vapour. Walking down Tashme Boulevard later that evening, his arm slung over Reiko's shoulders, her head resting on his shoulder, he whispered *Reiko, Reiko, Reiko*. Then *Rose, my Rose*. She giggled and shook in his arms. To hear his own voice say her name like a spell or a chant and claim her: that was certainly magic.

He and Reiko went to the graveyard, raced there, whenever they could; sometimes twice in a day, through spring, summer, fall and even winter; their breath rising up between the markers, their bodies pressing long grass or fresh snow under them. He spent every spare moment with her. He wasn't tagging after Yas and Aki anymore, a squeaky third wheel.

He came upon them one summer afternoon by the creek.

"This joins with a bigger river and goes southwest," Aki was saying. "I saw it on a map." She was sitting on a dock dangling her feet in the current. Yas sat on another.

"No, it just ends in some pond south of here," said Yas.

"All water wants to go to the ocean," Frankie chimed in, showing himself. He thought of the great Fraser River flowing south through the hundred-mile zone into the Strait of Georgia and back to the Pacific where their floating house must lie in splinters.

Without a word, Yas slid off the rock and sank into the water. Slowly, he was taken by the current. Frankie stretched to see his brother's head bob up and down among the rocks. Aki was up now, scrambling along the banks beside him.

"You come back!" she called. "You'll get scraped on the rocks!"

She stopped abruptly and hid her face. She was crying. Yas pulled himself from the water and huddled with her on the bank. Frankie turned to leave them alone.

Then came a squeal, a child's, but no, it was Aki in the water, riding the current just behind Yas. Frankie had never heard such a sound from her before, not even when she was little. He glimpsed her face, her eye lit up with delight.

The war did end. They crowded around a radio procured by Frankie to listen to the news and to hear what the Japanese people had heard. In the *Hope Herald*, they saw what the Japanese people saw. The divine emperor had taken the form of a bespectacled mouse of a man scurrying among the blasted ruins of the country squeaking at crippled soldiers, starving mothers and children and charred shadows: *Bear the unbearable, endure the unendurable.*

On the radio and in the *Herald*, they learned of the powerful bombs that had desecrated the emperor's divinity and melted his people. *Melted! Like the Wicked Witch of the West*, Augusta shrieked. Frankie had taken his little sister to see *The Wizard of Oz* at the Port Theatre and shivered at his memory of the witch, a hideous old woman who shrank away to nothing but her shoes.

Japan seemed not just one but many worlds away from

Tashme. Here they were safe in tar-papered huts thanks to Prime Minister Mackenzie King. On the very night the bomb was dropped on Hiroshima, the 3-T Club was performing *Yankee Doodle Dandy* with the satin-sleeved boy, now a teen-ager, tap-dancing in army uniform.

Still, it was unimaginable, un-dream-up-able: that flesh and bone might be melted by a ball dropped from the sky. Could the Japanese be so evil as to deserve such a fate? The people of Hiroshima, his mother's left-behind home? Could this evil have followed them here to the New World, to Canada, and survived the generations, survived in him?

Inside the house, they all sat close, waiting. Like they had when they'd gotten news of the Japs bombing Pearl Harbor. "What will become of us?" Augusta murmured, feigning a swoon. It was the same old question. Frankie knew that what Augusta wanted most was to keep playing leading lady in the 3-T Club to the satin-sleeved boy's leading man.

That night, his mother fell asleep in her chair. She woke him with babbling and chanting. He hadn't heard that in a long while.

The answer to Augusta's question fell from the sky in spring. Paper fluttered down from planes circling overhead telling the enemy aliens of Tashme and the valley the camps would soon close. They were free! Free to make one of three choices: They could go east in Canada. But the Mounties would tell them exactly where so there wouldn't be too many Japs in one place. But not west in Canada. Still no Japs allowed in No-Jap Land.

Or they could stay put and keep their shack and the patch of land on which it sat. A gift from Prime Minister Mackenzie King and the Canadian people. For the babies born here, now children growing up, Tashme was home.

The last choice was to go west but keep going, all the way back to Japan. Though it wouldn't be "back" at all for Frankie and his siblings, and all the rest of them who were born here. It was a foreign land with foreign people who might be evil-doers who deserved to be melted. The Canadian Japs might be hated for living in a country that had helped drop the bombs. Surely there was little left in that defeated land now; as new-comers, wouldn't they be resented for taking some of the last grains of rice?

"No going back," their mother declared. She held her prayer beads in her fist. She glared at Taiji and then Frankie. Then she returned to the business of brewing and selling sake; many in the camp needed a cup or two to help them decide on their fresh start.

Aki fixed her eye on Yas. Frankie knew she'd go wherever he went, with or without the rest.

They played rock-paper-scissors to help them choose. A clenched fist meant stay put; a splayed hand was go east; two fingers pointed like scissor blades was Japan.

Taiji wanted scissors. He wanted Toyama and the Sea of Japan. He wanted to claim the Hanesaka rice fields, his birthright as eldest son foolishly abandoned for New World adventure. But what remained to claim? He'd heard that parts of Toyama had been firebombed, paper and wood houses cindered.

Momoye again said no to Japan: no going back. Certainly not to Hiroshima, where her mother must surely have per-ished; their home had been close to the blast. For the first time in years, Frankie recalled the Priest's followers, and wondered what had become of the Sad Girl. Gone. Up in smoke.

Seasons passed. The camp grew quieter. Every few days, someone knocked on their door, arms filled with things Frankie had
procured for them. A rocking chair, a pitcher, a teapot—things
they couldn't fit in their suitcase or carry.

"You know what they say, Frankie. You can't take it with
you," Augusta laughed, quoting some movie. She'd begun
stockpiling things for a new stage production at the Tashme
Talent Theatre even though audiences had dwindled. Even
though the boy with the red satin sleeves who'd grown into
a handsome young man had left, boasting he was headed for
Broadway or Hollywood.

If Frankie didn't head somewhere soon himself, he'd be
a deadhead, a goner.

Momoye began packing up a good shirt Aki had made for Yas
and other items Frankie would need to wear or sell when he
arrived. She collected every last coin from everyone in the
family. They were pinning all their hopes on him, so it was
only fair. He'd send for his mother and the rest of the family
once he found a job and a place for them to live. He'd send for
Reiko too.

Two weeks before he was to leave, she told him she was
pregnant. *Should he stay?*

"Don't be silly, Frankie," she said. "We'll be joining you in
no time." Her cheeks looked rosier than ever. He looked down
at her belly. They married with the hasty scoldings and bless-
ings of Miss Hawks and Miss McCracken and Jesus, as well
as Buddha.

Frankie felt rich; richer than anyone else leaving the
camp—and not because of what others were giving him. His
riches were safely tucked away on his person. He felt the coins
and bills press into his side when Reiko hugged him tight
before he hopped into a truck. He was soon to become a man

with a family, not to be dogged by what lay behind him or daunted by what lay ahead, beyond the Land Beyond.

"My Frankie," she whispered in his ear, her curls brushing his cheek. Then she kissed him. More magic. "I'll miss you."

Once he got onto the train at Hope, he felt the engine reverberating through him, carrying him away from Tashme. He was going to the biggest city he'd have ever seen. Vancouver didn't count; all he'd seen of it was the PNE grounds and the inside of the livestock barns. First, of course, he'd have to check in at the police station in the town where he'd been instructed to resettle. He'd check in, yes, but then he'd board the next train to his true destination.

Frankie's legs twitched as he sat day after day by the window, watching the mountains and rivers give way to scrub and rock, to flat fields, then to leafy forests. Then to buildings and streets with cars and people. Finally, the train pulled into a dark tunnel and stopped at a place called Union Station.

TORONTO

CHAPTER 5

Under the Chrysanthemum Forest

By the time Frankie reached the Fujimoto house in the neighbourhood called Cabbagetown it was early—too early—so he settled himself on the doorstep. His mother didn't know the family, but had arranged for Frankie to stay here thanks to the Tashme grapevine that wound its way back through Port Alberni to Hiroshima and, now, to Toronto.

It felt good to finally plant his feet on ground he'd chosen. Frankie was no longer Jap nor enemy alien. After so many years, nobody—according to his mother—would tell him where he could or couldn't go.

Mrs. Fujimoto, her hair in curlers, cracked the front door to peer out suspiciously at Frankie. She looked him over with her tiny dolphin eyes, then finally opened the door wide. "Youkoso," she said. *Welcome.*

He met a familiar waft of smells: soy sauce, fish, pickled radish.

She led him up a narrow flight of crooked stairs, then up a narrower one to the attic and a tiny room with a tiny window, where she left him. He hung up the shirt Aki had sewn for Yas and his wedding suit, which she'd made as well. He emptied out his suitcase and found a small package at the bottom, tightly bundled and knotted with twine. It took some time to unravel. Inside was a figure the size of his thumb carved from ivory with a hole up its middle, something his mother must've packed. It was a homely, bent figure in speckled robes leaning on a stick, its face turtle-like. Was it a priest? Frankie propped it on the dresser beside his wallet and one set of cufflinks, but it toppled no matter how he placed it. He tucked the figure in his pocket and sank down onto the mattress, neatly made up on the floor. He was tired after the long walk north from Union Station.

Shortly past noon he woke to find an envelope slipped under his door. It was addressed to him in Aki's handwriting, and sent from Hope. He'd never received a letter before, nor sent one. It had followed him here.

> *Dear Frankie,*
> *We hope that you arrived safely in Toronto.*
> *I am writing with sad news. Yasumasu died four days after you left. Papa found him in the river.*
> *Mama reminds you to dress smartly.*
> *Your sister,*
> *Akiko*

He paced the room, lay down and got up, came back to the letter. How strange, the name, the words: *Yasumasu. Died.* The room began to slant ever so slightly; the floor, the walls, wherever he looked began to vibrate. He felt light, as if he were floating and couldn't touch bottom. He couldn't cry, tears or no. He opened the small closet in the corner of the room and curled inside, under the dangling tail of his brother's shirt.

He remembered Yas sliding himself in to ride the Sumallo River current amid Aki's warning cries. Then her delight when she joined him. It was always the two of them, Frankie the odd man out.

Four days after you left. Bad-luck number four again.

Frankie set off early each morning as if he had a job to go to: the job of finding one. Though he didn't quite know how to do that. Along the street, he passed houses filled with children, chins parked on windowsills, gazing out at him. Their homes were almost as shabby as the Tashme shacks, only made of brick; they'd crumble with age before being blown down by a winter wind.

Block after block drew him into the rumble of the city. Cranes criss-crossed above and all around, buildings being torn down and built up. He dug his fists into his pockets and walked, head down. He saw an Oriental or two on the street, but again turned away.

It was better, he decided, to be here instead of Tashme with the others, unable to match their tears. He had a job to do.

He walked south, retreading the path he'd taken from downtown the night he'd arrived; he bought a newspaper along the way, passing shops and restaurants but no HELP WANTED signs. By day, Union Station was huge and grey, a hulking mass. With nothing and no one to beckon to him, he soon reached the water; the sun sparkled over it. To the east or west, shipping docks, silos and smokestacks stood in his path. He found a way through to the east, until he reached a small stretch of beach, where he watched waves crawl onto the shore.

His mother would be sitting in her chair now, three hours back in time. She'd be praying for Yas's spirit; maybe thinking of Frankie too, worrying about him in the distant city. Her head would droop; she might start to babble or chant to ward off the same bad luck that had taken Yas from them.

At water's edge, Frankie wadded up the newspaper and sat down on it. More about the Tokyo War Crimes Trial; he'd read enough. What they'd done—he never knew a Japanese could commit such acts. That any man could. What they'd done to the captured British and American soldiers. Even to Chinese and Koreans. He'd heard of samurai in olden days beheading their enemies; his mother had even boasted of their family being samurai class. Was there something in him, in all of them, in the blood? He remembered Mr. Fung's posters showing the difference between a Chinese and a Japanese. Back in Tashme, they'd read about what the Nazis had done to the Jews.

The concentration camps, the POW camps, were nothing like Tashme. Tashme was summer camp that went on too long. Yet it was all war. Hirohito, the divine emperor, forced Americans to drop bombs on his own people: left them no choice, in order to end the war and save lives—lives that weren't Japanese. In the papers, the faces of survivors in Hiroshima looked not so different from his, from anyone's in Tashme. Like family left behind.

On the way back, Frankie caught his reflection in windows he passed. He thrust his chin forward and his shoulders back to make himself look and feel more at home. He missed Reiko. He missed her at his side as they walked Tashme Boulevard. He ought to be substantial all on his own, a man who had a right to be here and to stay if he so chose. *Someday,* he swore to himself. He clinked the coins in his right-hand pocket: these were nothing if not substantial.

The chrysanthemums in Mr. Fujimoto's backyard had grown nearly as tall as the Norwegian maple trees that lined the streets and reached up from the ravines of Toronto. Their stalks were thick as tree trunks, and the smallest petals clustered in their blossoms were plump as Frankie's thumb. Mr. Fujimoto showed

Frankie the chrysanthemum insignia of the imperial family on a coin he took from his pocket. In Japan, he'd grown flowers majestic enough to grace Yasukuni Shrine, where the war dead were honoured, he claimed. But he would never allow that now, not with Japan's war criminals exposed and the emperor disgraced. He shook his head sadly.

No one in Cabbagetown knew or appreciated any of that. The neighbours merely complained to Mr. Fujimoto that the flowers blocked their sunlight and radio reception.

"Ha!" laughed Mr. Fujimoto. "They need bigger windows and better radios!"

Through autumn rain and winter chill, the forest of chrysanthemums formed a canopy that held in warmth; it once sheltered a homeless family, undiscovered by Mr. Fujimoto until spring when they cheerfully relocated to the nearby Necropolis.

Mr. Fujimoto was as devoted to cultivating his chrysanthemums as he was to growing his own family. Fifteen Fujimotos were living in the narrow two-storey row house. Mr. Fujimoto had uprooted himself and his bride from Japan long before the war to start a strawberry farm south of Vancouver. He'd been canny enough to sell the farm before Pearl Harbor had been bombed and the Custodian of Enemy Alien Property came knocking. He didn't get a fair deal, but enough to bring his family east and buy this brick house in which to keep them safe and close; so close they slept head to toe on the floor of two rooms, three generations of Fujimoto family, including those who'd married into it. Some of his children had married in Toronto before the war, despite slim pickings. Each had shone as a beacon on streetcars, in shops and church, drawing to them their own kind from among the throngs.

"Tired," Mr. Fujimoto told Frankie with a weary droop of his mouth. "Tired and getting old." He lamented the five nights a week he slept uptown as a live-in gardener. He missed his family slumbering around him, their breath hovering together, another grandchild on the way. "Time is short," he told Frankie, and his work was shrinking it even more. That Friday evening, Mr. Fujimoto sank deep into his garden chair, longing to be settled there once and for all.

It turned out that the Tashme grapevine had also wound its way to Mr. Koga. As a Japanese national, Mr. Koga had weathered the war years in a prisoner of war camp in northern Ontario only to be deported to Japan with his wife and Port Alberni–born daughters. They'd joined his wife's family in Hiroshima Prefecture, outside of the city.

Frankie sat with Mr. Fujimoto after he'd finished watering his forest. "Burdock roots, flower bulbs," Mr. Fujimoto told him. Survivors and the repatriated were scrabbling for food to eat. There was little rice, little of anything growing. The earth was scorched. Mr. Fujimoto had just received a letter from Mr. Koga. He and his family were malnourished and painfully constipated. Mr. Koga's hair and nails had fallen out; his skin had flaked to a raw pink as if he too were sick with radiation illness. Mr. Koga's back was already bent; Frankie could not imagine him any more ground down.

"What little there is goes to anyone but repats," Mr. Fujimoto said. "They call them traitors."

Enemy alien here and there.

Mrs. Fujimoto brought cups of tea, casting Frankie a wary glance, just as she had when she'd first opened the door to him. She hadn't said a word to him since. Other family members slunk past, too shy to introduce themselves.

"Koga can't sleep, even after two bottles of sake," Mr. Fujimoto said.

"He needs Canadian Club," Frankie replied, and he and Mr. Fujimoto laughed ruefully. In his letters, Mr. Koga fretted about his daughters' chances to marry now that the family was more lowly than Untouchables. Yet they had to be wary of suitors with radiation sickness, for fear of deformed off-spring. Who knew how many generations would be tainted by the poison in their bodies?

That was the least of his worries. Japan was a country of limbless men. The suicide pills issued to soldiers to avoid capture often failed, leaving arms and legs gangrenous. Men hobbled home from all over Asia after Japan surrendered, a caravan of wretched torsos, never saying what they'd seen or done. Mr. Koga's youngest daughter had grown fond of one legless soldier who ground his knuckles along rubbled streets, riding at her side atop a board fitted with wheels.

Mr. Fujimoto began to hum the Kimigayo. Frankie recognized the Rising Sun anthem; Taiji used to play the record on drunken nights in their floating house.

"I am blessed by Buddha," Mr. Fujimoto declared, gazing up at his chrysanthemums. "The soldiers were foolish. They believed the emperor that they'd become gods in paradise." He sighed. "The cherry blossoms, the maple leaves, the chrysanthemums—these are the only benevolent spirits." Mr. Fujimoto got up and went inside. Frankie listened to the low rumble of traffic in the distance. Big as it was, the city was otherwise quiet. In the falling light, the chrysanthemums towered above, their heads held high, like nature's kind keepers.

WAITER WANTED read a sign in a diner window on Parliament Street. Frankie took off his hat, pushed open the door and set one foot inside. The diners looked at him, then looked away. No Japs—not in the booths and not behind the counter. The war was over but nothing had changed.

He walked on, westward until he reached a patch of Chinatown. He spent a few of his precious coins on a bowl of noodles amid the voices he couldn't understand. He envied them, together still like the Japs used to be. What had become of Mr. Fung? he wondered. Perhaps he'd live past a hundred and become, if not the richest, the oldest Asiatic in Port Alberni, as his father had.

By evening, Frankie found himself strolling the Cabbagetown necropolis. It was as quiet as the graveyard near Tashme, quiet enough that he could feel in his chest the slow thump of his loneliness. But then the blood flushed through him: *Reiko*. He'd barely let himself think of her since being away, their bodies in the grass, his sunk into hers. It hurt to be without her.

He'd been in the city for weeks now, wandering. His mother, Taiji, Aki, Julia and Augusta, along with Reiko and the unborn baby, waited at one end of a tipped scale, with him perched on the other end, alone. He sensed Yas there too, a shadow that weighted the scale against him even more. Mr. Fujimoto promised to find him work, but time was threatening to overtake him. His money would not last forever.

Marching past the grave markers, he felt something new and cold in his belly, gnawing him restless. He was afraid.

Another letter arrived from Mr. Koga. Mr. Fujimoto shared it with Frankie after dinner. They sat under the chrysanthemums. Mrs. Fujimoto brought tea, with her usual sullen glance at Frankie.

Strange stories were swirling in Hiroshima's black dust. "They're waiting for a shaman priest to come save them." Mr. Fujimoto half-smiled.

Frankie sat up. "Who?"

Thousands were suffering and dying most painful deaths. Now that the emperor was no longer divine, followers of this priest were praying for his return. "A healer," said Mr. Fujimoto.

Mr. Koga reported the believers walking on hot coals with

bare soles. It was the story Momoye had told Frankie when he was housebound: the Priest's miracle. Could it be?

"They say this priest brought at least one dying man back to life," Mr. Fujimoto read from the letter. "Then he deserted his followers and left Japan."

"Where did he go?" asked Frankie, though he knew the answer.

"Canada," Mr. Fujimoto guffawed. Mrs. Fujimoto returned to fill their teacups.

"The followers are waiting for another miracle."

Just as Frankie's mother had said.

The followers claimed that the man revived by the Priest years before survived the Hiroshima bombing and fled to join his mother in Nagasaki, only to die in that blast three days later.

"Foolishness!" Mrs. Fujimoto muttered from behind them. "Koga is drinking too much."

"Does he say if the Priest came back to Japan?" Frankie asked.

Mr. Fujimoto scanned the letter and shook his head.

Mr. Fujimoto did find Frankie a job. Then another and another. First, he washed dishes in the neighbourhood diner. He stacked the dishes too high and toppled them. Then he hauled buckets of pitch deep down to the basement incinerator of an eyeglass factory, but the fumes made him sick. Then he laid bricks for a building going up in the city. He told Mr. Fujimoto and the man who ran the construction crew that he knew how. How difficult could it be? He watched the bricks get buttered on their ends and tapped down onto the bed of mortar with the tip of the trowel's handle. *Like so.* The bricklayer was Italian, small and broad; he had been laying bricks in Toronto for twenty years and seemed to speak only these two English words: *Like so.* Frankie nodded, he nodded, then left.

Up went Frankie's wall, brick by buttered brick. By day's end, his back ached from bending down and he blinked away the mortar dust in his eyes. The bricklayer returned to inspect the work, scraping his trowel across the wall. Frowning, he raised his small, broad foot and gave a kick. Down it went, *like so*, lower than Mr. Fung's wall of coins before the fire sank the floating hotel.

The next morning, Mr. Fujimoto sat down in the kitchen beside Frankie and declared, "Today it is."

Today he would give notice to his employer of eight years, Mr. Uri Slonemsky. He would recommend Frankie to be the new gardener at the Slonemskys' Rosedale home.

He knew Mr. Slonemsky's dismay would be mild: lately he'd been unhappy with the way Mr. Fujimoto was cultivating his irises. Instead of sleek and slender, the blossoms burst forth thick and bulging but quickly withered. As the years went on, Mr. Fujimoto grew less inclined to restrain whatever seedlings sprang up from the earth. No bonsai for him. Mr. Slonemsky, however, was an architect: nip the buds, trim the roots and uproot what didn't conform. Keep life in check.

To help the ragtag groups of men arriving from the internment camps, Mr. Fujimoto had consistently turned to the Jews. No one else would hire the Japanese. Only the Jews extended a helping hand, having received so few themselves. Often Mr. Fujimoto had turned to a Mr. Gross, whose tire company now employed twenty Japanese, or to a Dr. Geist, who had just hired Mr. Fujimoto's youngest son (and Frankie, for a day). The nervous boy barely needed to speak at work, placing magnifying stickers onto bifocals with his dexterous fingers.

At his firm, Mr. Slonemsky now employed two Japanese apprentice draughtsmen, and at home a part-time housekeeper, in addition to offering room, board and pay to one gardener for a lifetime if so desired, as long as the dry garden remained dry and his irises flourished.

On the evening before Frankie was to begin his new job, his last under Mr. Fujimoto's roof, the two walked among the chrysanthemums. Atop their fibrous torsos, the petals were plump, and the filaments within seemed to pulse and hum as Frankie made his way below. Even the shortest flower in the forest stood just over the men's heads. He brushed aside a petal that drifted down to tickle his face, then another and another. One gigantic blossom quivered in the windless air and bent its head to Mr. Fujimoto's ear, just as a streetcar rumbled two streets away. Mr. Fujimoto quickly ushered Frankie out of the forest, as if an alarm had sounded.

Inside the house, he patted Frankie's shoulder. "Take good care of Mr. Slonemsky's garden," he said, "and you'll be set." His gaze wandered out the hall window. He hastily disappeared into the bedroom where six Fujimotos, including his wife, were already slumbering.

Frankie packed his few belongings back into his small suitcase. *For life.* Mr. Fujimoto meant Frankie would be set for life. On the floor below, all was quiet. But Frankie was too listless to sleep.

He took off his clothes and stood before the filmy mirror that hung on the closet door. A dark face stared back at him. He wanted to see his mother there but saw only himself and the Priest—at least what he recalled of the Priest in his mother's photograph. He'd always been darker than his mother or sisters; than Yas, even when he'd been out on the logs under the sun. Swarthy. This face was too big to go with his small, sinewy body. Frankie's penis was crooked, hung more to the left, his one shoulder fell lower than the other. Then he turned around and twisted to see himself. Was the Mongolian spot growing again, sprawling wider across his backside?

Since Mr. Koga's latest letter, the Priest had lurked in Frankie's mind. Wherever he might be. Frankie was waiting for him to show himself, just as his followers were.

He slipped into bed with a letter from Reiko. She chatted on about who else had departed the camp and who had stayed. Not much else.

How was the baby? Did she feel it inside her? he wondered. Was there pain? Itching? Was it heavy? How could one body stretch to hold another? The truth was, he was asking himself why it had to sprout so soon.

He wrote back that he was taking on a new job. A temporary job until he could find the right one. Regardless, he could save toward a down payment on a house and, soon enough, would send for the whole family.

Frankie had never met a Jew before. Mr. Fujimoto called them Ku-ichi, for the numbers nine—ku—and one—ichi—equalling ten, or ju.

Everyone in this big city seemed to know more than Frankie did. Even those he first sized up to be less than him. At the diner, the other busboys didn't speak proper English, yet they knew how to scrape and stack in one quick movement. The bricklayer knew how to butter and grout. In the butcher shop, there was a chart to show what cuts came from where on the cow. He saw the ads in magazines: *Here's How: Helps You Get Ahead by Showing You How. What Every Auto Mechanic Wants to Know. How to Become a Live-Wire Builder.* You had to have the know-how to get a job and make money. You had to have the know-how to earn respect, to be a man.

CHAPTER 6

The Iris Isle

In Rosedale, Frankie passed houses grander than any up the hill in Port Alberni or any he could imagine. They were mansions, really, sitting squarely and proudly on their sprawling trimmed lots, some behind iron gates. The Slonemsky house was different; it was from another time and place. From the future. He almost walked past it, set back as it was among tall cedars and birch trees. Frankie could think of no name for its shape. Its gold brick facade was rounded like ocean swells with double doors set deep in the centre. The roof slanted up towards the rear. Frankie stepped around the side of the house to glimpse the back, which rose up a storey and down a storey into a steep ravine.

A housekeeper let him in the front door. She was Japanese, he assumed, but would not look Frankie in the eye and said barely a word. She motioned for him to wait in the living room, which seemed also to be the dining room. The entire back wall of the house was glass framed within enormous wood beams. A wave of blue sky and greenery crested over him.

He sat down but then got up to walk around, taking the measure of the large, oddly shaped space. A curving ramp rose up to one level and wound down to another. He felt exposed and confined at the same time; with no corners he had no place to hide. Frankie went to the window and gazed down through the trees and up at the distant blocks of the city visible just above their leaves. He became aware of someone behind him: a fresh scent, faint humming. He felt grimy. Should he turn, offer his hand, say something?

"Come this way," the man said, opening a glass door onto a stone terrace. Frankie followed him out, across the terrace and down a sloping path. On one side was the dry garden Mr. Fujimoto had mentioned. On the other, a spacious lawn fringed by maple trees and a towering spruce. Then down more steps to a pond. A mass of bladed leaves budding with purple floated at the centre of it. Easily a hundred such blooms. Irises. Each regal and dignified as a queen. The same flowers his mother had planted in Port Alberni instead of roses, when they still lived on land.

Frankie felt the breath leave him: here was his dream, dreamed and brought to life. A floating garden.

Only now did Frankie let himself scrutinize the man. A trim figure in creaseless clothing—white shirt and grey pants; eyes carved far back beneath the overhanging cliff of his brow; thick coils of greying dark hair springing upward but precisely trimmed. Sandalled feet. He had to be a little younger than Taiji, though it was hard to tell. Mr. Slonemsky.

The man extended a long hand, smooth, unlike Taiji's weathered palms and scarred fingers. A hand that no doubt had only lifted a pen or pencil in its lifetime.

"Welcome, Frank. Uri Slonemsky."

Frankie took the hand, strong despite its slenderness. Of course his dream belonged to someone else—a man rich enough and smart enough to make it come true.

Not long ago, Frankie was patting his own back for coming out on top of old men with fewer chances than him. The reflection of the iris isle wavered in the pond. Here was his failure held up to show him he was worthy only of tending someone else's success.

"This was made for my wife." Mr. Slonemsky glanced back up to a second-floor window where a blind seemed to flicker. "She loved the irises in Kyoto."

To which Frankie could only nod. He knew so little of Japan.

"The whole house was for her. The rock garden was for me."

Frankie's eye wandered back up to the house.

"It's a kidney," Mr. Slonemsky said. "The house is shaped like a kidney."

Frankie had eaten kidney beans in the livestock barns on the PNE grounds in Vancouver. How could he forget the mealy tastelessness? A bean, an organ. Soon he'd be living and working in one.

Mr. Slonemsky, this man speaking with Frankie, was a Jew, the first Frankie had ever met. *Ku-ichi*. Germans had rid the world of millions of them; Americans had done away with hundreds of thousands of Japs. Yet Mr. Slonemsky owned all this, could build and plant and do as he pleased.

Jews didn't usually live in Rosedale, Mr. Fujimoto had told him. No Japs either, of course, unless they slept in the basement, attic, or if they were lucky the coach house, emerging to sweep and till by day. There'd be no bartering of fresh-brewed sake in this neighbourhood.

Back in the living room, Frankie began to notice the things inside it: miniature buildings with miniature people planted within. Might he one day be one of those busy people on his way in or out? Some buildings looked familiar, others he'd never seen the like of: a rectangle with clear glass on all sides. A tall, thin structure with rippling walls and tiny box windows. Two towers of pleated gold glass joined at the bottom. Then a kind of dome, a network of thin sticks with green nodes, like a space-age vessel just landed. He didn't dare touch, but he was tempted.

"Toothpicks and dried peas," Mr. Slonemsky said.

The morning after he moved in, Frankie ventured into the living room where Mr. Slonemsky was looking up to the second-floor balcony and the closed bedroom door, then at the watch on his wrist. "My Hannah, she won't come out today," he sighed to Noriko, the housekeeper. Then he slipped out the front door.

He did the same the next morning and the next and the next. Frankie had yet to meet Mrs. Slonemsky.

Frankie slept in a spacious room below, half sunken into the ground. Through the half window, he glimpsed the slender feet of his new boss—sometimes in fine shoes with leather soles as thin as paper—step past to the back garden on his return from work at dusk. Those feet would pause, sometimes rock from ball of foot to heel as their owner gazed down the slope, Frankie assumed, at the irises.

Mr. Fujimoto had left instructions for Frankie on the desk in his quarters. Frankie was to row out to trim the iris heads the instant they began to shrivel. Mrs. Slonemsky could not bear to watch them die. He was to tend the shrub garden, then the pond, and feed the carp. He was to keep the dry garden dry and free of any debris, to rake fresh circles in the gravel surrounding the rocks every morning. The large grey rocks sat like castaways within the waves.

He was not to alter anything without permission. The irises were in full bloom, lush and muscular, delicate and busy, sheathed in long, slender leaves. If only his mother could see this! But May was almost done. In the coming weeks, he would dread the first creep of brown into their dangling purple, golden-furred petals that might upset the unseen Mrs. Slonemsky. But for now, the tick-tock of time and season slowed just looking upon the flowers. Frankie imagined her gaze on him from her shuttered window, as he carried out his duties. Mr. Slonemsky assured him that the irises brought his wife pleasure. If only Frankie could prolong their blooms and coax her from behind her shutters.

In the newspaper, Frankie spotted an ad for a revolutionary new fertilizer: Miracle-Gro. He found the bright green box on a hardware store shelf. *Making miracles grow more beautiful each day,* it said.

Frankie's job was not undemanding. No sooner had he finished raking the dry garden than more twigs and leaves fell; a strong gust of wind could easily scatter the fine gravel across drawn lines. Every other morning, he rowed a small boat fifty feet to the isle and tended the irises without stepping ashore for fear of trampling the dense grove. He ladled water from the pond and reached in deep to nip weeds and debris.

In the evening, Frankie watched from his basement window, imagining Mrs. Slonemsky twinned with him two storeys above at her sill. Under a spotless full moon came a soft splash, then a sudden rustling on the isle. Blossoms shuddered, stalks snapped. Frankie rushed out with his flashlight. He'd been chasing away raccoons, foxes, stray dogs or cats since he'd started working here.

He grabbed the oar from the boat at water's edge and waited. A shadow slid across the water. Frankie waved the flashlight. Beside him, neatly laid out, ready to be stepped into, lay a shirt, suit and tie. A splash snapped his beam back to the pond. A head surfaced, silvery sleek as an otter in front of him. Frankie stepped back, not sure what he was seeing.

"Man overboard!" a voice called out. A white-haired man, stout, naked and pale rose from the pond, wading toward the bank. "Such a glorious night!"

Above them, a window scraped open. "Bucky!" called Mr. Slonemsky. "Good to see you!"

"And you, captain!" Blue eyes flashed in Frankie's light: round and magnified amid the midnight blue sky, water dotting the glasses the swimmer had just then put on.

Abruptly the light inside the window was extinguished. Frankie apologized, haltingly.

"No need," the man said. He smiled to reveal a chipped front tooth. "I was taking a midnight swim. I was homesick for my own isle." He paused. "I feel quite wonderful now.

"Would you?" The man grasped Frankie's arm and hoisted himself up onto the bank.

Above them, the moon hung full to bursting.

"There's the North Star." With his head tilted skyward, the man squared his feet wide apart and held his arms out from his bare sides. He gestured for Frankie to do the same. He closed his eyes. He seemed to lean ever so slightly to one side like a banking plane. "You'll feel it in a few moments, in your left foot, a slight pressure."

Frankie felt the cold sweep under his arms as he lifted them. He closed his eyes, and for an instant he imagined his left foot press down as the right side lifted ever so slightly. Did he feel it? He wasn't sure.

"The earth is moving with us aboard."

Frankie opened his eyes. The man was walking away in his shirttails carrying the rest of his clothes and shoes; he waved without turning back. "Goodnight!" He was heading toward the old coach house at the end of the property. Frankie had thought it abandoned.

In the morning, Frankie found the visitor sitting beside the dry garden in his rumpled suit and tie. "Pea gravel washes back if it rains," he said, turning a bit of stone between his fingers.

"Grit has square bits of granite. The patterns stays longer."

Frankie nodded.

"Bigger dowels, farther apart should do the job." Through thick glasses strapped all the way around his head, he studied Frankie's rake, then studied Frankie himself. "That way you could accomplish more with less effort." He held out his hand. "Call me Bucky."

After mowing the lawn in the afternoon, Frankie came upon Bucky with lengths of wooden rods strewn in the grass around him. He asked Frankie for a handsaw, a hammer and nails and a drill, along with some nuts and bolts.

Hours later, Frankie found Bucky balancing on a strange structure, a network of the rods, coming together in triangles on all sides, a latticed dome, three feet high. He held out a hand.

"Come aboard, my dear boy. It will hold."

It did hold: nothing but triangles of narrow wooden rods supporting three hundred pounds or more between the two of them.

"But how?"

Bucky's eyes grew larger behind his glasses. "Compression and tension hold it all together. The bending moments are negligible in such a structure," he said. He held Frankie's arms and began to bounce on the balls of his feet. The two bobbed up and down together.

"A spider web can float in a hurricane because of its lightness and strength."

Frankie lost his footing and tumbled off.

In the evening, Frankie found the two men lying on the grass amid a scatter of empty wine bottles, half-eaten bread and cheese. Side by side they gazed upward. Bucky raised a twig to the sky and the stars. He sat up and whittled some notches into it. "This is how the first navigators found their way home."

"You mean how they left home in the first place," said Mr. Slonemsky.

"The wind and the Japan current carried them away. Navigation brought them back, with into-the-wind know-how." Bucky waved his stick.

Mr. Slonemsky motioned to Frankie to join them, patting the grass and offering wine. It was bitter and dark, unlike the sweet sake he was used to. But it warmed him.

"Son, did the current bring you here too?"

Frankie shook his head. "It brought my father." He'd never before said *my father*.

"Are you a water or a land dweller?"

"Both," Frankie said, though he felt half untruthful. "Whenever we lived on land, they made us leave." He'd never uttered this before either. The bittersweet wine fuelled him. Bucky fixed his eyes on him, encouraging him further.

"Who are 'they,' Frank?" Mr. Slonemsky asked.

"Finance capitalists, of course," said Bucky, before Frankie could answer. "Those caring only for monetary gain. Am I right, Frank?"

It was the government, the politicians who called out the Yellow Peril, the evil Asiatics, the sneaky Nips, thought Frankie. But then there were those who wanted land cheap that had been owned by Japs. Land that someday could be worth a lot.

Bucky asked for Frankie's story. So he told it, from the house uprooted and set on water to the landlocked camp. He even described his garden of wild roses and the sinking hotel. Coming here instead of where the Mounties told him to go. Telling it like this, one thing after another, and to be listened to—he felt some bile in him stirred and stewed.

"He lived on the sea! You see, Uri?" Bucky's eyes ballooned behind his glasses. "Our Frank was pushed off by those vying for five per cent of the Earth—a few little dry spots. They devalue the three-quarters of Earth that is saline and fresh water."

"I, myself, am merely a dry-spot specialist," Mr. Slonemsky remarked.

"But the pond, the island." Frankie was looking in awe at the swell of water in the middle of this big city he'd come to, and the flowers floating in it.

"Bucky built it. With his land-on-water ingenuity."

"I'd like to learn that," Frankie blurted. Like a fool, he thought a second later, his face hot.

"Frank, you are a New World Man," Bucky said. "One of those able to establish himself on oceans. To navigate with anticipatory vision. We don't expect to own the water we sail through, do we? Do we have to own the air to breathe it? Why must anyone own the land," Bucky went on, "and then say who stays and who goes?" His eyes shone bigger and brighter than ever while blurring into two white flames behind his glasses.

Were they mocking him, Frankie wondered, or just drunk? But Bucky was right, he thought, cursing the men who'd demanded the deed for his floating garden and his dock licence.

Mr. Slonemsky sighed and downed his wine. "Too many questions."

New World Man? He'd start with Man of the House. A house of his own.

Frankie received a letter from his mother in her broken English. She had a new money-making idea. More families from the camps were making their way to Toronto, leaving the small towns where they'd been assigned to settle, just as Frankie had. They needed places to stay until they could manage on their own. His mother watered the grapevine that wound from camp to camp to Toronto, while Frankie contemplated how he would pluck the fruit.

That night, he slept fitfully. He was back on Alberni Strait, rowing toward the house from shore. Each time he neared it, the house was carried away from the harbour farther down the inlet until a wave pushed it out to sea, out of sight. Then, from behind a cloud, the moon appeared briefly, illuminating the house where it crowned the horizon. On he rowed through the darkness, each time to exhaustion, until the moon reappeared. He stood up, raised his arms and his whole body began to lift. When he woke, his arms ached.

He found Bucky exactly where he and Mr. Slonemsky had left him the night before. Lying down and looking up, still in his suit and buttoned white shirt. "We have more in common than one might think, Frank," he said, resuming their conversation from the night before.

"We do?" Frankie scoffed to himself. The two of them: he in his dirt-stained overalls, Bucky in his suit and starched white shirt and taste for fine wine. They couldn't be more different. Bucky was clearly a man who owned his life, whose ancestors no doubt had owned their piece of North America for generations.

Bucky jumped to his feet. He handed Frankie his old rake with a new rectangular base. "A remodelled tool for the New World Man." On the base were large tines of wood, spaced widely. Only then did Frankie notice a handsaw, chisel, hammer and crumpled sandpaper sitting among the empty wine bottles.

"In the future no one will labour in this way. Machines will carry out the work, and you'll be free to think and design those machines."

From top to bottom, Bucky's suit was coated with sawdust; there was the musty smell of sweat. He looked down and dusted himself off. "I never cared how I clothed myself," Bucky said, divining Frankie's thoughts. "Years ago, I decided if I dressed like everyone else, if I became an Invisible Man, then I would be better listened to." He tugged his lapels and buttoned up his jacket.

"Do you have a family to provide for, Frank? a wife, a child?"

"A wife," Frankie said. "A child on the way." It was good to declare that fact, to get used to it.

"A child," repeated Bucky.

An object came sailing out the glass doors and landed with a crunch at Frankie's feet in the dry garden. He dropped his rake and carefully lifted the object, like an injured bird. It was one of Mr. Slonemsky's architectural models, crushed: the towers of pleated gold panes. Now it was splintered, flattened, with a tiny person poking out of a cracked window.

"I hope it missed you." Mr. Slonemsky emerged from the living room holding a wine glass. His hair was not the usual neat hedge and his suit was rumpled, like Bucky's after he'd spent the night in it. "Sorry about that, Frank. I'm not quite myself today."

"No harm done, sir," Frankie said.

Mr. Slonemsky went inside, then came back out. "Will you have a drink with me, Frank?"

Frankie nervously made his way up to the house, proffering the damaged model to his employer, who set it on the coffee table.

"Thank you, sir," Frankie said, accepting a glass. He shifted awkwardly on the sofa in his dusty coveralls.

"Call me Uri. Or Captain Fincap, as Bucky does. He claims I'm a finance capitalist, enslaved to the whims of millionaire developers."

Frankie smiled. "He's an interesting man."

"So you agree?"

Frankie shrugged. Capitalists, millionaires, developers. What did he know? "You can't do anything without money," he said. That much he knew.

"We architects design the buildings, but someone's got

to pay for them. In fact, a millionaire developer has asked me to design a bank. As tall as possible. The tallest."

"In the world?" Frankie thought back to the turreted house in Port Alberni that, at three storeys, had seemed so high. A rope of hair dropping down for him to climb.

"Yes, but what I want is beauty. Glass and steel."

Frankie tried to imagine such a structure, its surface smooth and silvery, reflecting whatever was near. "Like the sky and the lake."

Uri looked twice at Frankie. "Precisely," he said, refilling their glasses. Then, with a long sigh, he lifted his glass in the direction of his wife's bedroom. "My Hannah, she's not coming out today. Or any day."

He drank deeply. "She doesn't approve of my building," he said ruefully. "She hates it." He glanced toward the heap on the coffee table. "Only this, the Kidney." He gestured all around. "She could stay here forever."

He downed his glass and refilled both of theirs again. "You haven't met her yet. But when you do . . . Well, then!"

Frankie sat back in the sofa. The wine was colouring everything a soft rouge. Mr. Slonemsky's face—Uri's—was pink. His eyes bloodshot. The sun cast an orange-red swath across the sky above the trees.

Mrs. Slonemsky had been watching him from her window, Frankie swore, while he tended the iris isle. "Yes," he said, "I look forward to meeting her." His lips and tongue felt slow and sloppy. He thought he should go before he made a fool of himself, and started to rise.

"No, stay a little longer," Uri said. "Please."

So Frankie stayed into the night. Another bottle came out, then another. Until he finally left Uri asleep on the sofa and stumbled down the stairs to his room.

He felt woozy, but his mind was a hive of thoughts—Uri's thoughts.

How do we better shelter the human body? Uri Slonemsky had asked. *How do we bring the outside in?* Frankie had to laugh. He knew a lot about that. The sea air rising between the floorboards on the inlet; the ice between the slats of their shacks in Tashme; the wind cutting like a knife through tar paper. The morning sun too, winking through the cracks. Really, it took only a few planks to shelter the human body.

Hannah, my Hannah, Uri had lamented. From the beginning, she'd been his inspiration. *She would hold me, curl around me like a vine. When I drew, she would guide my hand.*

But one day, she couldn't. She was too weak. After chasing ghostly aches all over her body, the doctors finally cornered her ailment: it was her kidney. Even a transplant—Uri's own kidney—would not be a cure.

Uri Slonemsky wanted not just to shelter, but to protect, even heal the human body with what he built. With this house, the Kidney.

From then on, she closed the bedroom door. He retreated into the study. *To no longer have her at my side! To be without her inspiration, her guidance.*

Every morning he looked up at the closed door, hoping it would open. He couldn't help wondering, he told Frankie. *Was she glad to be without me? Relieved? Was she suffering?*

Uri Slonemsky himself was surely suffering.

Frankie was not. He was practically penniless and uneducated, a citizen of nowhere in particular, but he wasn't suffering. His eyelids began to droop. He had a roof over his head, was now employed, and was strong and healthy, as was Reiko. How far apart they were from one another! Two thousand miles and then some. He missed the closeness of her body; the tickle of her curls against his cheek. Her scent. How little he knew of what she was feeling these days, with the baby coming.

At Union Station, he greeted the Honda family, newly arrived from Tashme. As promised, he met the mister and missus and their young son on the platform and helped to unload their suitcases and boxes knotted with twine, their all-you-can-carry.

"Ah, thank you so much!" the missus exclaimed. How relieved they were to see him, Frankie Hanesaka, who could get you anything in the camp, and now would do the same in the Big City! They gawked up at the columns of Union Station and across Front Street at the grand Royal York Hotel with its rich red awnings and gold-tasselled doormen. They cricked their necks to gaze up the thirty-four storeys of the Bank of Commerce. Frankie rode the streetcar with them to their temporary home in Cabbagetown.

When they handed him his fee, he carefully folded the bills into his pocket. The wad was thickening. He smiled into their uncertain faces. "Lay low, and everything will be fine," he said.

CHAPTER 7

Below, Above and Beyond

Fresh news slipped under the door. A letter from Reiko. The baby was dead. It had died inside her and been taken out at the hospital in Hope. *Taken out*. From inside her body, the *dead body, taken out*.

Frankie couldn't breathe. His throat, his chest clogged. Then his heart hurtled forward on its track, chugging, unstoppable. He pressed his head to the wall, then threw up.

The day after, a soft knock at his door. It was Noriko, eyes averted and mouth pursed, beckoning him to the telephone in the kitchen. He didn't want to answer. Still, he followed her upstairs. It was Reiko calling from across the country.

Frankie. He barely recognized her voice, arriving amid the rustle of Noriko in the kitchen behind him.

Yes.

I'm sorry.

It's not your fault.

Yes, I know. But—

They listened to the sound of each other, without much to say. She'd be calling from the camp canteen if it was still operating, or the post office in Hope. It would be early morning for her.

He wanted to ask for his mother. Instead he said goodbye, cradling the receiver at his end.

In the evening, he sat down to watch the irises, but their petals dangled too precariously in the breeze. He didn't know what to do with himself.

He jumped on his bicycle and rode south to the lakefront, then west following the water's edge as the road rose up. He glimpsed a Ferris wheel in the distance below, motionless in the falling darkness. A grand white building with huge columns and gaping walls. He rode down and parked his bicycle. He walked past shuttered booths and carousels with festooned horses, frozen and riderless. All closed down except for the lake and its waves slithering into the rock-strewn shore and slithering out under a feeble moon.

He rode back north and found himself in the old neighbourhood, walking his bicycle through the Necropolis. He sat among the gravestones. This—death—was the worst that could happen, and it had.

How? Frankie had cursed himself—that was how. For all along, wanting to be relieved of his burden and for feeling relieved now, in spite of himself. He sighed, then choked. As if he were sinking again, with no one to pull him up.

A week later, Frankie, to his surprise, received a letter from Bucky, mailed from Tokyo. It was typewritten. *Dear Frank,* it began and went on for pages and pages—

> *I find myself on the islands of your ancestors and thinking of your life experience so far. You have lived on land and on water, so you have seen that a house is not so different from a ship. In fact, houses may be considered aerodynamically as little ships whose standard cruising speed roughly equals the*

average speed of wind over the United States. If
accelerated, planking begins to fly off and flat
boards develop lift with the wind.

Frankie read the passage twice. Was Bucky saying that houses could not only float, but they could fly? Yes. Roofs of houses could be the keels of ships, paddling in air instead of water. If not to fly, then to be airlifted with ease from one spot to another, anywhere across the globe, from Lake Ontario to the Arctic Ocean to Tokyo Harbour. Frankie had asked to be taught, and here was his first lesson.

The letter went on with words that touched Frankie, yet dangled out of his reach. There was magic in them, and intelligence beyond him. There were words of Bucky's own making, Frankie was sure. Invented words. Bucky had sketched pictures of other worlds and creations: a house with the mast of a ship and an airplane in its garage, a shiny round aluminum dwelling with bubbles inside for washing and sitting. There was a strange three-wheeled automobile, and a city on water, a city on land, and one up in the air under a dome. The moon was a sky companion; the rotating Earth, a spaceship. He, everyone, was an *Earthian* aboard for the ride.

He wrote, too, of *priest-navigators,* wielders of magic and notched sticks held to the stars, who set out for distant waters carried by the wind and then found their way back.

Could the Priest be one of those who'd set out from Japan and safely returned?

Bucky had included an old photograph of himself as a young man standing high in the sky, taller than in real life, yet floating among clouds, it seemed, with a spired building rooted behind him. On the back, he'd written: *Guinea Pig B with Empire State Building, 1932.* Bucky looked strong and less stout, a young, smooth-faced self ready to climb the skyscraper behind him—a stairway to the stars.

Frankie pored over the letter. Especially the part that told of a daughter, Alexandra, who had died when she was four. Died because Bucky hadn't housed her properly, healthfully. His business had failed and he'd had no money. *Polio*, he wrote, and *meningitis*, which Frankie knew of because a boy had died of it in Tashme. *We aren't so different*, Bucky had said when they'd sat together in the yard. Now it was as if Bucky knew about Reiko and the baby.

Bucky had failed his family, failed in business, and one night took himself to the shores of Lake Michigan—one of the Great Lakes linked to Lake Ontario—to end his life. But instead, strangely, he resolved to make a lifelong experiment of himself, to see what an Average Man could do to help all of humanity. He called himself Guinea Pig B, for Buckminster, and declared it to all who would listen.

Bucky's letter—and the photograph with it—became the one thing Frankie could sit himself still to study, even when it confounded him. He kept it in a box. Whenever he brought it out, it was Bucky visiting him, teaching him to be smarter—better, even, than an Average Man. Bucky was no ghostly form flitting through his dreams, no Priest: Bucky was real, even as a memory. His eyes magnified by his glasses, his musty smell, the chipped tooth revealed when he smiled, the spittle on his lips when he spoke, even alighting on Frankie's own.

Already Frankie was using his new rake with greater ease in the dry garden, and already his shoulders ached a little less at the end of each day. He'd been ladling Miracle-Gro onto the iris isle and not a bloom had withered. He was carrying out Bucky's process of *ephemeralization:* doing more with less.

Seemingly impossible feats could be accomplished by humans if they simply joined hands, Bucky wrote. For example, all the humans on Earth could form a chain to reach the moon and loop back, nine times!

Could he, then, lowly Frank Hanesaka, do more with what he'd been given? Couldn't he be Guinea Pig F?

Frankie emerged one morning to glimpse a woman rowing the boat in the pond. Her fiery bright hair flew behind her as she circled the isle full of irises so perfectly in bloom they resembled a painting. He ran to the water's edge. Kimono sleeves of shimmering purple—the same purple as the flowers—flapped about. Uri Slonemsky waved frantically at her.

"Hannah! My Hannah!" he was calling, all creased and undone. "Hannah, be careful!" The woman stood up to wave to her husband but turned her eyes to Frankie instead. Even from shore, he saw their bright green with a dark flame in their centres.

Frankie eagerly called to her, "Good morning, Mrs.—"

"Good morning!" she replied, waving recklessly in his direction.

Mr. Slonemsky was already kicking off his shoes and heading for the bank.

"Uri, come help me," she shouted, just before she fell in.

It was a story told with laughter, a few tears, and jokes Frankie grasped only at their surface: Hannah's rebirth following her baptism in the pond. Her Blue Period had turned purple.

"Japanese believe the iris protects and purifies," Noriko told them.

"You kept them blooming for me, Frank," Mrs. Slonemsky told him. "Don't tell him but you outdid even Mr. Fujimoto." Frankie was grateful Mrs. Slonemsky thought he'd helped her recover. He imagined telling this story someday to others.

Hannah had emerged from her cocoon, and everything was changed. With Uri joining her in the bedroom again, laughter and exclamations of delight escaped the window at all hours. Both Frankie and Noriko were invited to sit down to dinner with the couple. Uri was there for all three meals with an expanding waist to show for them. He even let his hair grow.

Despite the pleasure and pride Frankie took in the company of the Mr. and Mrs. Slonemsky—or rather, Uri and Hannah—what he witnessed between them made him wistful; he winced with loneliness. The words and looks for only each other, the touching: it was another way of living.

"You've joined the Hasidim, Uri!" Hannah laughed one morning as she tugged at a curl at Uri's ear. "What will the neighbours think?"

"My lonely nights were taken up with only scripture until you came back to me."

Frankie had forgotten his own wife's face through his lonely nights. Reiko, his Rose Queen.

He came in from the yard one evening to find Hannah dancing with Bucky, who had just returned to lecture at the university. "Blue Skies" was playing on the hi-fi.

"Bucky!" Frankie burst out. He was in his usual musty dark suit and tie, swaying in those skies with his eyes shut.

"Do you foxtrot, Frank?" Bucky stepped onto numbered paper footprints he'd cut out and taped to the floor. He hummed, his foot sometimes landing where it should, and other times not.

"I taught myself," Frankie said, remembering the dances in Tashme Town Hall. Of course, Augusta had taught him a bit. He ventured a step or two as Hannah placed a martini in his hand. The green flame in her eyes seemed to flare in his chest as he sipped it, then explode behind his eyes. She clapped her hands.

"What is it that puts a baby to sleep?" Bucky asked, eyes still shut. "Rhythm. A rocking cradle. It's the melting point of the material and the spiritual."

Frankie's hand was grasped, Hannah taking the lead in a

brief waltz. "This hand does not belong to a gardener," she said. "Look at these blisters. Too soft. No calluses. Fujimoto's hands had soil in every pore."

"Tending the land is a worthy occupation," said Bucky, eyes still closed as he sashayed. "Land, water, air, wherever you dare."

It did not seem so worthy to Frankie. He'd dare elsewhere.

Bucky came and went these days without Frankie having a chance to speak with him alone. He was gone early in the morning and back to the tiny coach house late at night. Some nights he didn't return at all. Frankie was receiving little letters from his sister, Augusta, who was almost grown up now. He was grateful to have something cheerful slipped under his basement bedroom door. He was her audience of one again.

Dear Frankie,
Are you enjoying life in the big city? Are you lonesome? When can we come?

She wrote of more people leaving Tashme, loading their suitcases and scrambling onto buses. Neighbours were taking trains to catch ships to Yokohama, or come east. Either way, to who knows what. She and her friends hugged and wept as they said goodbye. *I'll be seeing you,* they sang to one another.

He wrote back of his plans—his big plans in the big city. To own property, to build them a house that was warm in winter and cool in summer; with a toilet that flushed, all to themselves. They'd each get their own room. A big living room where Augusta could tap dance for him and sing "On the Good Ship Lollipop" all day long if she wanted. He'd plant purple irises in front for their mother. They could own a view to the water, but not have to live on it.

By the time his letters travelled across the country, back through forests, prairies, badlands scrub, through mountain tunnels and back up their little dirt street in Tashme, her next had reached him in Rosedale.

A few letters on, she'd changed. Her handwriting slanted gracefully forward.

A room all to myself? For Julia too? How grand! They couldn't wait to visit. Especially once their mother, Taiji and Aki were living with him in Toronto as well.

You must visit us too, Frankie! The prime minister gave us the house in Tashme which we are fixing up!

Visit? He must visit?

No! Her home was to be here, with him and the rest of the family. Why else was he here, alone, working, scrimping— making plans? He wrote to tell her so. He tapped his foot impatiently for the weeks it took for his letter to reach her, and for her reply to come. Didn't she believe in him anymore?

Augusta hadn't let the grass grow under her feet; she'd mowed it. She'd taken the government's offer of their shack. She and Julia would transform the Tashme Talent Theatre into the High Hope's Theatre. Maybe even Miss Hawks and Miss McCracken would stay on to help.

Augusta's first play would be something called *Our Town*, the story of practically everyone in America, if not in Canada too. No one would mind that the narrator was Julia instead of an American gentleman, that Hope was to be Grover's Corners. There would be no Tashme. Augusta would play Emily, the girl next door. She still had to figure out who would play George, Emily's intended, since the satin-sleeved boy, all grown up, was now in Hollywood. The shows would be sold out, standing room only in the old hall turned new theatre. Augusta even changed the ending so that her character lives on, instead of falling sick and dying.

She told Frankie all of this, how excited and proud she was of herself and of Julia. And proud of Frankie. He was, and always would be, Man of the House.

Frankie ripped the letter in two and threw it away. The truth was, his little sister had no faith in him. The tap-dancing Augusta had built her own house and made herself the head of it. Broken up the family.

She and Julia could stay forever in Hope for all he cared.

The day after Frankie received Augusta's letter he noticed the first withering of an iris petal. After weeks and weeks of nothing but blossoms. It wasn't apparent to anyone but him, least of all Hannah. The isle of irises no longer preoccupied her. He clipped one dying blossom, then the next and the next and the next. Soon the isle had turned to green. Gone was the glorious purple. The magic was seeping away. One morning, Hannah noticed the change, simply held a hand to her breast, sighed and went on.

In his room, Frankie considered himself. The face in the mirror had become even more swarthy; his forearms were deeply tanned. He examined his hands: now they were calloused; now his palms were stained with dirt. Now, like Mr. Fujimoto, he had the hands of a gardener. He washed up and set out on his bicycle.

Frankie joined a line-up at Honest Ed's thrift store. Once inside, he pulled a plain dark suit off the rack, tried on the jacket and then paid for it. Back at the Kidney, Noriko pinned up the pants for him.

"How dashing you look, Frank!" Hannah said when she came in. He was still wearing the suit jacket but had put on his old pants. She cast an up-down glance at Frankie, her gaze snagging on a loose thread. She bit it off.

After Noriko left, they sat down before the fireplace. Uri was upstairs in his study. Frankie sat opposite Hannah, listening. She never posed a question to which she expected a response, so he was free to absorb his lessons without fear of being tested; her fluttering hand trailed cigarette smoke as she alighted on subjects he knew little or nothing of: *the sad delusion* of communism or *the democratic beauty* of Modernist art.

"Uri," she said, "has no delusions. He sees the future clearly, but only after it's passed. He's Mister Knew-It-All." She laughed. "You knew that, didn't you, Frank?" At birth and through boyhood, Uri Slonemsky had a patch of white hair at his temple. A glimmer of wisdom, of what was to come. Arriving in Canada, Uri Slonemsky's father had been urged to drop the last part from his name. The father had chafed; no -*msky* would amount to cutting off the nose to spite the face. He looked to his son Uri, who shrugged. The father shook his head no and there followed much grief: closed doors, failed businesses.

He knew his father should have packed up the family sooner than he had, sold everything in Poland instead of reinvesting. He knew not to trust the neighbour downstairs and the dog who barked at their comings and goings. By then, it was almost too late.

"Young Uri knew it all." Hannah smiled. "He tells me so every day." Yet here they were now, Slonemskys side by side with Smiths, in Rosedale.

"Of course, Uri knew the atomic bomb was coming," Hannah went on. "Would they ever have dropped it on the white race?" she said, exhaling. "No, not even the Germans."

Of course. Frankie choked, and Hannah's cigarette smoke swarmed him.

Hannah reached for her martini glass, then paused, stricken by what she saw on Frankie's face. "You know that's true, Frank, don't you?"

He burned with shame, all of him, to his bones. Hadn't he known what ugly yellow insects Japanese were to the rest of the world? Worse than Germans, than Nazis. Of course. He was lucky, despite everything, to have been in Tashme instead of Hiroshima. Lucky to be alive. He pushed his martini glass away, stubbed his cigarette.

Just then, Hannah glanced beyond him, stood up, and with arms flung wide, cried, "Annie! My Annie!" She scurried over to a girl standing in the living room doorway. Uri emerged from his study above and leaned over the banister. "My Anne," he said, his voice lifting. He came quickly down the stairs.

Hannah held on to the girl tightly, cocooning her in purple silk. She beckoned from across the room. "Come, come, Frank."

"Of course, Mrs. Slonemsky."

"This is our Anne, our daughter. Frank Hanesaka."

A daughter? A girl in trousers, with hair as full and wild as her mother's, but left dark and loose. Small and thin. Hazel eyes.

"I can't stay," she said. "I have to get back." Her voice was not a girl's at all.

"Why not stay?"

She shook her head.

No, she wasn't thin, not quite. Her blouse draped over full breasts. There was a slight sway as she held up her hands against her mother's tide.

She was Anne. A plain name, like his own. Sometimes Annie, it seemed.

She was returning by train from some kind of conference in Vancouver en route back to Montreal. Such a long journey, she had to get off.

"Yes, it's a long ways," said Frankie.

She turned abruptly to face him. "How long were you there?"

He was confused for a moment.

"Lemon Creek? Slocan?"

"Tashme." The first time he'd said the word to anyone who hadn't lived there or in another camp. That amalgam of a name that sounded, in a bitter irony, Japanese.

"Four years," he said, though it was more than five. He shrugged and glanced away. But she—Anne—would not stop looking at him.

"They couldn't hold you there. You had rights. You could've left."

Frankie shrugged again. It was true: others left long before war's end to join road crews, to work on the railroad so long as it was east and not west. It had never occurred to him to just leave; not until war was over, not until his mother sent him east.

Hannah stepped between them. She clamped their hands together in her pillowy palms. "What a treat to have you with us," she said, seemingly to both of them. He felt her hand pull away. He was something washed ashore with her mother's tide.

"Come, Anne," Uri beckoned, taking her other hand. "I want to show you something."

"You should call her Hannah," she called over her shoulder as she made her way up the stairs with her father. "And he's Uri."

"Frank knows that," Hannah called back, then whispered, "Now careful she doesn't make you a socialist."

When he took off his jacket, he noticed the price tag had been dangling down his back. All evening, they must've seen it but said nothing. He threw it to the back of his closet. Maybe Bucky was right about how a suit could make you invisible enough to fit in, to be respected like anyone else. But not a cheap Honest Ed's suit.

Lying in bed, he couldn't help but contemplate the Slonemskys' daughter—Anne, Annie: that thicket of hair, the deep angles of her face, her eyes set far back, almost another species. Her hand, strong, warm and dry. He was ashamed of the sticky dampness of his own. The way she'd spoken up for him as if he were a kowtowing house boy. It was his own doing, presenting himself that way. He'd never met such a girl: a woman. She was younger than him, for certain. She was a modern woman. His thoughts wandered to the breasts that had unmistakably swayed under her blouse; he now realized she hadn't been wearing a brassiere. He could tell her breasts were not at all like Reiko's, small and tight with brown crimped nipples. They'd be soft and white with pink tips, enough to spill out of his palms. He began to soothe himself, then felt ashamed of his dirt-stained hand under the sheet. He couldn't sleep.

He saw in his mind how she'd kept him at bay. She was at some institute of higher learning; he was an underling, not even a young one. He'd barely finished high school, if you could call the classes they'd cobbled together in Tashme school. He was forever lower, without institution; without the gumption to get out from under.

Waiting as always, was Reiko: his wife, his Rose Queen to lift them both out of dreariness. She was returning to him in bits rather than the whole: her small, widened eyes and the red in her cheeks when she'd first spoken to him. She'd seen him make a fool of himself in a grass skirt and face paint, and she'd wanted him. They'd made a baby in a graveyard of miners where it could be laid to rest. He didn't even know if it had been a boy or a girl, what had become of the body. Reiko hadn't said and he hadn't asked.

He smoked a cigarette by his window and was about to close it when he heard the shuffle of feet along the path, then saw a pair of slender ankles in mannish loafers; the shoes were scuffed and worn. He drew back but then her face appeared—Anne's. She squatted down, looking in on him, her hair falling across her eyes. She shoved it back and inhaled from her cigarette; the smoke rose like a veil between them.

"Frank?"

"Yes."

"Would you say goodbye to my parents for me? I'm taking the night train back."

"Why don't you?"

"They're asleep." She threw the cigarette into the darkness. He'd pick that up in the morning.

"You could wait till tomorrow," Frankie said.

"I know," she said. She left his window. After a moment, he heard the plink of stones tossed into the pond. She shuffled back past his window without stopping; seconds later he heard the glass door to the house slide open and close.

In the morning, Hannah and Uri were quiet over breakfast.

"That's all she said?" Hannah asked. "She had to leave?"

Later that day, Frankie met up with a family of new arrivals at Union Station. He found them on Front Street: husband and wife and three teenaged daughters with two battered suitcases and two boxes. There was the same wide-eyed look, scaling the tall buildings across the busy streets. They lit up when they spotted him.

"Thank you, Frankie," the man said, casting his eyes down. "So good to see you." The wife clasped her hands and bowed. "Thank you, thank you." The daughters stood shyly by.

They rode the streetcar into Cabbagetown and made their way to the Fujimotos' home. As the door opened, a whiff of soya sauce and fish and pickles took him back to his mother's kitchen. Mr. Fujimoto bowed emphatically, smiling: a warmer welcome than he'd given Frankie.

Just as he turned to leave them, the man held out a packet of bills neatly tied with the same twine that bound up their boxes. "Thank you again."

Frankie's hand burned reaching for the money in front of Mr. Fujimoto. He felt the man's glare on his back as he walked away.

In his pocket, the bills were light as air—lighter than the coins he'd amassed before, yet they weighed him down, made his walk crooked. He knew Mr. Fujimoto would not understand. It was money he'd earned. No one had met him in the dead of night in a city he knew nothing of, when he and the others were still, if no longer enemy aliens, then non-citizens. He'd walked the dark streets alone, found his way alone, waited on the street not knowing what awaited him. No, Frankie Hanesaka had earned his pay.

The next day's work seemed more tedious than ever. The weeding, sweeping, trimming. Even with Bucky's rake and the potency of Miracle-Gro, the energy he expended on the task felt more wasted than ever: wasting himself. Shrubs straggling: clip them back. Leaves fallen, twigs gnawed off: rake them up. Sprouted weeds: pull them up. When he looked out at the Slonemsky property, it was endless. Whereas the money he earned grew so slowly, even with his extra business.

He sputtered awake that night and looked out his window: the moon was waning. Under it was Bucky, standing in the yard quite still and alone, the prickles of his white hair glistening. A megaphone dangled from his neck. Abruptly, he began to flap his white shirt sleeves like a conductor leading a crescendo. Frankie waved instinctively, but of course how would Bucky see him at his dim little window?

In the moonlight, Bucky's glasses glinted like stubby antennae on his head, like some otherworldly alien. He raised the megaphone and spoke:

We are merely a statistical cartoon showing that if all the people of the world were to stand upon one another's shoulders, they would make nine complete chains between the Earth and the moon. If it is not

so far to the moon, then it is not so far to the limits—
whatever, whenever or wherever they may be.

Across the yard, Frankie saw what Bucky had been flapping
his arms at: a human pyramid rising into a tower alongside an
old maple. Several bodies at the bottom, and farther up, two
bodies facing each other propped atop those below: a totem
wobbling up, up, up into the sky, straining moon-ward.

Frankie might've hopped out his window and clambered
aboard.

We are not trees rooted to the land. We can conquer
the vapour sphere, expanding ever outwards. To the
moon and back!

Bucky let the megaphone drop and instantly the totem
toppled, leaving bodies strewn in the grass and one or two
hanging from a branch. Laughter broke out.

They were from the architecture school, all young men, all
younger than Frankie. He was struck by their erect posture.
They had long limbs; all tall and with good teeth, he was sure.
He'd heard somewhere that if you looked at the bones of an
Asiatic, they were different from those of a Caucasian. Asian
bones were flat and broad instead of round and trim. An
Asiatic's teeth were wide and hollowed out on their backside
for shovelling rice; yes, he could feel it with his tongue.

These young men—no one ever had to say to them things
like, *Chin up, look on the bright side.* No, their chins were
already up. They'd come into the world chin first. They'd
walked in their crisp whites and neat pleats on the swell, sunny
side ever since. They clustered around their teacher before dis-
persing into the night.

Frankie settled back to bed but Bucky's words floated up
before him, collecting at the ceiling of his basement room. It

was as true for him as for any of those students: he wasn't rooted to the land, to anything. He could climb, as his mother always said. He could ascend.

In the morning they were back with their notebooks and pens, clothes fresh and pressed, sitting before Bucky, who stood in his musty, rumpled suit with the megaphone still dangling from his neck. Frankie performed his usual duties but cocked an ear to what was being said, catching all he could, bundling it to sort later. He heard parts that were familiar: *Do more with less. I named myself Guinea Pig B. In and out, not up and down.* Ideas Frankie had thought were meant especially for him, to give him a leg up. Because he, Frank Hanesaka, was a *New World Man; son of a Priest-Navigator; able to establish himself on land and water through ingenuity*, unlike these young men of good fortune.

Frankie raked away at the gravel, digging too hard and wide into the dry garden as Bucky's lecture went on. By noon, it hadn't stopped. All morning long, the students had listened quietly, and now they were even more attentive, looking down only to scribble in their notebooks. What were they writing? Every last word was a lesson in itself. Frankie came closer. They began asking questions.

Bucky turned his megaphone around and out to the students, scooping up their words into its horn, funnelling them back into his ear through the mouthpiece. He called out a word: *anticipatory*. Frankie scooped that up and let it float in his imagination.

The next morning, Frankie emerged to find a giant net of bolted aluminum strips collapsed on the grass, flat, limp and glistening with dew. Beside it perched a miniature dome made of the same strips, like a robust baby birthed beside its spent mother. Bucky sat writing in a notebook, then staring at the inert web. He stood when he saw Frankie. His glasses were clouded, his clothes more rumpled than usual. He seemed not to have slept at all.

"You only succeed when you stop failing. That's what I tell my students. Remember that, my dear boy."

Frankie nodded.

"We'll call it the Supine Dome." Bucky patted Frankie on the back before retreating to the coach house, silvery head bent in thought.

Frankie did not believe for one moment in failing; nor, it had seemed to him, did Bucky. His successes were light, bright shining inventions conceived of nothing but possibility. His every word was blown up with success. He'd spoken and written of his early failure, but Frankie couldn't quite imagine it. Yet there was the deflated evidence on the ground. *Supine.*

Two mornings later, Frankie emerged to a strange sight. A webbed sphere, maybe eight feet in diameter, perched on the grass where the nest had lain, and inside, dangling like giant geckos, human bodies—the students—holding on to the bolted nodules, testing its strength.

"Frank!" Bucky called out. "Success, my dear boy!"

Guinea Pig F was not progressing well. Frankie didn't have enough money yet for the grand house, nor any house at all. But in April of the next year, he became Citizen F.

"You're one of us now, Frankie," Hannah said as they sat by the fireplace one evening. She raised her martini glass to his and clinked. "How will you vote?"

She spread the newspaper on the coffee table and showed him the faces of three men. "This one?"

He shook his head. He'd made up his mind weeks ago, even before he'd even seen the faces, heard the names that went with them, or even known there'd be an election.

"This party voted you into the camps. That one did the same and made you pay your way to boot."

Frankie knew that. But while the third might've kept him a free man, he would not help Frankie become a rich man.

On his lunch break, Frankie rode his bicycle downtown to watch construction crews with their jackhammers break up the road a few blocks up from Union Station. He'd read about it in the newspaper: they were building a new subway line. They were digging a giant tunnel under his feet while the city's one million bustled on the streets above, business as usual.

A giant digger lowered its bucket into a dump truck in the middle of Yonge Street as crowds tramped along the timber walkways framing the road. Amid exposed utility pipes and the muck of the city's crust, Frankie inched closer to peer beneath.

"Watch your head," a worker shouted out as the bucket swung near.

Frankie returned late at night the next week to find vertical pipes driven into the ground, steel beams lowered onto the piles below, timbers crossing the gap in preparation for the road to come. Cut and cover, cut and cover: that was the method. Below and out of sight, the rest of the work continued. Eight-car trains would deliver passengers from northern Toronto all the way down to Union Station at twenty miles per hour from morning to night. Like the train that had brought him here, tunnelling through the mountains, through darkness and out into light, only stopping at station after station instead of town after town.

The middle of another sleepless night, he was back. He hopped over a barrier and squatted to peer between the timbers under the street lamps. Soon there'd be a grid of crossroads and hubs down there. There'd be stands where people could buy newspapers and peanuts, stalls to get their shoes shined. Another city beneath this city.

He thought he heard a siren and quickly jumped out, immediately feeling foolish. No, the sirens were to the south, by the harbour. In the night sky above the buildings between him and the lake, smoke seemed to gather and glow faintly orange. He hopped on his bicycle and cycled toward the water and now the stink of fire. He rode faster as a keening hum opened to a scream of sirens. The air warmed and thickened with smoke and noise the closer he got, and above the sirens, human cries. It was a docked ship, a raging fiery spirit spiralling higher and higher out of its black billowing hull and all around, tufts of flames like giant fireflies swooped and dived that he realized were human bodies on fire, some landing in the water, some thudding onto the pier, not far from where he stood.

He was pushed back by policemen, told to leave as more firemen and trucks arrived. But Frankie could not look away.

He saw it in the morning paper. Over one hundred people— they were still searching and counting—mostly Americans on a leisure cruise along the Great Lakes, in the night while they slept. A ship, old but grand. It seemed all the more sad and impossible, water all around yet consumed by fire.

Reiko called. Her father was stricken with tuberculosis.

Frankie could not go back. He would not. But what could he say?

Frankie. That was all she whispered into his silence.

Mr. Fujimoto would fill in while he was gone.

Hannah squeezed Frankie's hand and gave him a hug, her floral perfume settling on him. Uri patted his back and shook his hand. "We'll see you before long, Frank."

He sat on the train and watched the city back away from him. As they picked up speed, tall buildings shrank away, flat ones sank into the ground until there was nothing in his view but grass and trees.

CHAPTER 8

The Place Left Behind

Tashme was a ghost of a ghost town. The shacks crumbling to the ground. The hospital deserted. There was no gate, no guard.

Stupid boy, his mother had called to say the day before he departed. To make him stay put, not waste time and money. Yet here he was: the first time he'd not listened to her.

He stepped off the bus from Hope and there was Augusta running down the dirt road to him, followed by Julia and Aki.

"Frankie, welcome home!" Augusta—a young woman now—hugged him, as did Julia. Aki listed toward him, took his hand and squeezed, her one eye meeting both of his. They walked up Tashme Boulevard with him, Aki on one side, Augusta on the other, both holding his arms, while Julia tagged behind.

"It's so good to have you back, Frankie." Augusta squeezed his arm tighter. "My, but you're looking swell." She was the same as ever, and then some.

Up ahead, Reiko was standing with an apron tied at her waist, her hands clasped, then waving, then clasped in front as she stepped forward. He dropped his suitcase, ran and then stopped himself, then ran right to her, picked her up and swung her around, surprising himself. She filled his arms and pressed into his body and that felt like the most natural thing in the world. For so long, she had been only feather-light words in letters and a mere voice on the telephone.

He set her down, both of them flushed and warm. Like salmon pulsing red as they push upstream, he thought and laughed.

"What?" She pinched him.

She was the same: her lips red, her hair wavy. Longer and less curly than he recalled but glossy as ever. He couldn't help but glance down at her belly, as if he'd see some trace of the loss there.

"Well?" Reiko raised a hand from behind her back and slipped on a pair of glasses. "I could barely see myself in the mirror," she said, peering up at him. "Do I look different?"

"No, no. The same."

"The same good or the same ho-hum?"

Good, of course. She was still his Rose Queen. She hadn't changed. Had he? He reminded himself that it was meant to be, his wife by his side. When she caught him staring, she leaned in to give him a kiss.

"Oh, Frankie. All this time."

His mother was bending down to feed the stove with wood as he came in. She struck him as a little thicker and just as sturdy. The shack was the same but seemed to him, after living in the Kidney, all the more a cramped, crumpled box. The old stove, the cots, the sunken armchair by the window, the dusty light streaming through. Propped on a small table was a picture of Yas, with a stick of incense, a bowl of rice and an apple in front of it.

"Mama."

At last she squeezed his shoulders with her strong hands. "Fu-ranki. You are too thin." Of course he wasn't. But only her cooking would do.

"Sit, sit," she said and Frankie did. It was Taiji who was too thin. His face gaunt, his body drooping from its bones. He paused with a hand on the back of Frankie's chair before settling into his own. Sighed *so, so, so* with a resigned smile. This was something new: parsing time between small actions.

From the far bed, a rattling cough that subsided into light snoring: Reiko's father.

"Come see our place after, Frankie," Augusta said. *Our place.* He'd set her straight on that when the time was right.

He was pulled along by her and Julia to Sixth Avenue, turning this way and that among old shells of the RCMP barracks, the nurses' station, the canteen. The look-alike streets he couldn't distinguish from one another even when he lived here, dwarfed by the green mountains. They pointed out the shack they'd begun to fix up with new curtains and such, but hurried him along to the old town hall.

"Stay here," the girls told him. Julia slipped inside to flick a switch and in a second, a string of Christmas bulbs lit up a lopsided sign: High Hope's Theatre. Augusta pulled him inside and tried the lights there, but they didn't work. No matter: he could see everything well enough, at least in his memory's eye: the dirt floor under their feet during the dances, the very ramshackle stage he'd stood on in his grass skirt, built with planks he'd scavenged.

"Frankie, you'll see. When the lights are on, when everything's ready," Augusta chattered on. To which he simply nodded. No lights and no Frankie to scavenge supplies. High Hope's was dashed. His sisters would be in Toronto just as soon as he could get his show up and running.

As they walked farther along past Sixth to Seventh and Eighth Avenues, odd sights began to appear. Two- and three-storey shacks, no longer shacks, but fortified constructions, built up into miniature mansions on the government-granted plots. They had front and even side doors, covered porches. Wood siding for warmth, even some brick here and there. Grand in their own way. It was near evening, but Frankie could still hear some hammers hammering and saws sawing amid a gramophone playing swing. There was free timber in the surrounding forests, as much as anyone could want, so the sky was the limit.

The sisters showed Frankie another kind of dwelling too, outlandish on this valley floor but familiar to him. Tall masts up the middle and each end of the house lengthened into bow and stern, atop trailer wheels. Augusta waved up to their owners, "Ahoy there!"

They belonged to the fishermen who'd lost their fishing trawlers and were now reclaiming them, even if on mountain shores. They reminded Frankie of Bucky's drawings, those strange vessels that were land-, sea- and air-worthy. An all-you-can-carry, in itself. Bucky would approve.

After the lights had gone out across the camp, and after Reiko had bird-bathed her father and tucked him in, she came outside to join Frankie. She hummed "Stardust" in his ear and they waltzed down Tashme Boulevard in the dark. He felt his heels sink into the dirt between the grass patches and the song seemed truer than ever. Lonely nights with only a dream of a song, a reverie; a memory. *A paradise where roses bloom.*

She tied her scarf over his eyes and led him along, step by step. Then *ta-dum!* They were on Pig Alley, where he'd rarely ventured, named for the pigs that were once kept and slaughtered there before Tashme became Tashme, when it was Fourteen Mile Ranch. The barn was a dilapidated, cob-webbed heap.

"What are we doing here?"

"Silly." She turned him to the doorstep of a cabin. "This is the where the Mounties stayed."

It was a log cabin, solid. He felt it under his feet as he stepped inside; he heard it when the heavy door shut behind them. Reiko lit the lamp. The floors were nicely finished, if dusty. No cracks in the walls. No outside let in.

This was how the other half had lived. There were counters, a sink and faucet. Reiko turned on the water to show him. Cupboards, a closet. And a big, high double bed.

"Just for one night. Nobody comes here."

Reiko had made up the bed with a quilt she'd sewn herself. He recognized one patch from a red polka-dot dress she used to wear. They fell onto it as if it were the grass in the graveyard. Her body was the same, her muscular legs curling around and gripping his thighs.

"Let's make another baby," she whispered. "A strong and healthy one."

Why had he waited so long to come for her? This unspent drive and haplessness had gathered in his core as if he were a teenager again: of course. All longing and mere consolation. How could he not have understood? He needed her—in the flesh. All along he'd needed her; just as Uri needed Hannah.

He woke in the night wrapped up in her, smelling his own stale breath. She slept on. He felt where their bodies came together and where they cleaved. She rustled. He remembered this sensation of being closer than close but sealed apart. The mystery of it.

In the morning, they lazed in bed as the sunlight glowed behind the paisley curtains. In the cupboards, Frankie found some rusted cans of beans, and at the bottom of the closet, a uniform. A Mountie uniform, ragged and moth-eaten with a sleeve dangling by a thread, no longer that proud, sparkling red. Frankie marched around the room in nothing but the jacket.

"O Canada!" he sang, clicking his bare heels and saluting.

"Oh, Frankie!" Reiko laughed.

They spent the day together like it was another time. They wandered to the graveyard, but when they arrived, someone was being buried. They crouched behind nearby bushes. A handful of mourners in black huddled amid the soaring mountains. A mound of dirt, a waiting coffin and a hole in the ground: a doorway deep into the earth, far beneath the valley in which Tashme sat.

"So sad." Reiko's lips brushed his ear. They both lowered their heads. One row over, there was the Blackwell grave, the old stone leaning as before, with its collection of bad-luck fours. Behind it, their special place. Glancing over, they began to giggle and then snuck away.

Frankie pictured Reiko in the Kidney. He pictured himself bringing her there, into the biggest room she'd ever lived in, no doubt. Even if it was in the basement. The half-windows allowing a slice of sunlight to shine on the waves of her hair as she lay on their bed. He thought of her on the grass with the irises behind her in perfect purple bloom.

He and his mother had come and gone to and from Hope so many times selling and procuring items, stopping in pawn shops, white elephant sales, wherever people left things to sell or trade. But why would people come from there to here, to Tashme to pay to sit in an old barn?

"To be entertained, Frankie," Augusta said. "For song and dance, adventure, romance and heartbreak!"

Frankie shook his head. Foolishness. "Who will get you your red satin and black shoe polish?"

Julia, who'd been playing the silent sidekick, stepped forward. "I will, and I do."

"By hook or by crook," said Augusta. Julia was tending gardens in Hope, tilling the soil to earn the money.

"I'm doing the same thing you are," Julia said.

"It's not the same," Frankie scoffed. "I've already got my eye on a big house where all of us can live." He was shrinking into his little boy self, back in the world where everything was big and he was small. "You'll each have a room to yourselves. There'll be a garden with flowers for Mama. A big garden."

No one said a word. Frankie looked to his mother, sheepish. "It'll be ready by fall," he assured her. "You won't spend one more winter here."

He sat in his mother's old chair that night, looking out the window at her view. It wasn't especially beautiful; it just looked onto other broken-down shacks and the base of mountains. Frankie felt as if he were alone with his mother despite Reiko's father lying nearby. The old man's groans had begun to mingle with the muted howls of wolves and coyotes.

He wondered where in the woods Taiji and the men of the camp had taken Yas's body to burn it.

"Mama." Frankie didn't have much else to say. He wanted to cry to her, to hold and hang his every need and worry of the past years on her and the word coming from his mouth. *Mama.* Momoye stood beside him, her waist at his shoulder.

The brows she used to arch in disapproval now draped tiredly over the corners of her eyes. It frightened him. Time was passing, life was passing. He owed her a better one.

He said his goodbyes. He even ventured into the dim corner where his father-in-law lay, though the man didn't remember him. He barely remembered Reiko from day to day. He rested under a layer of blankets, his head on a hill of pillows, his eyes sunken in their sockets. Everything shrinking back. Out of his mouth, a dark open tunnel, came that gurgling sound of faint life. Frankie didn't know what to say, but patted the mound where it seemed the man's shoulder lay.

Reiko came to his side. "Shush. Rest, Papa."

They walked the path from Tashme Boulevard to meet the bus. Taiji and his mother and Aki. Augusta and Julia trailed behind. Reiko walked by his side, arm linked in his, their footfalls dull in the hard dirt and still air.

Taiji patted his shoulder as he had at his arrival and Frankie was reminded that there was strength left in the old man, in spite of his withering grief.

The bus pulled up. "Frankie, you do what's best," Aki told him. Augusta and Julia each gave him a hug and a peck, more fleeting than when he'd arrived.

Then his mother, with whom he'd spent so little time, passed him a handkerchief of bills so that no one could see. She pressed it into his hand and at the same time pushed off from him, like a ship unmoored.

He embraced Reiko, wrapped his fingers in the waves of her hair. "I'll send for you," he said. "Your father too." Though they both knew her father could never make the journey. He'd have to die here before she could leave.

From the bus window he called out to all of them. "A room for every one of you! You'll see!"

He slept much of the way back, through days and days, and endless tunnels into night. He felt the train lift off its tracks, veering into the air like one of Bucky's strange vessels. He smelled Hannah's lavender perfume in his dreams, and rolled a pebble the shape of Bucky's tetrahedron, nature's building block, between his fingers. He woke with a start. Home, he thought, when he emerged onto Front Street with the solid edifice of Union Station behind him and the towering Bank of Commerce ahead. He held his arms out, closed his eyes, and imagined the tilting of the Earth on its axis as it spun, the slight pressure at the side of his one foot. Or maybe it was just the rumble of the night workers digging out the subway tunnel below.

CHAPTER 9

The Vapour Sphere

"Take hold and climb aboard, Frank!"

A pair of legs dangled from a cloud, low above the shore of Lake Ontario. Frankie grabbed hold of them just as the rain began, the wind lashing at him. The laced black shoes, scuffed, dusty; the musty smell of the wool pants: Bucky!

The head belonging to those legs wasn't in a cloud: it was inside a balloon—of sorts. The skeleton of struts the students had bolted together into triangles upon triangles in the Slonemskys' yard. A billowing sheath tethered to it. Bucky's Dome. Not supine. Alive, afloat, airborne!

Frankie felt the tips of his toes leave the sand. A gust of wind lifted the dome higher. He grabbed hold of a strut, let go of Bucky's legs and swung himself up. Suddenly there were the streets below he'd walked from Union Station; there was the gaping hole dug by the workers for the new underground city. "Join me," Bucky called.

Frankie stood and balanced gingerly on the lower frame, then hoisted himself onto the small platform in the middle of the dome where Bucky sat, cross-legged.

With a gust of wind, they rose up and away.

"Welcome to Cloud Nine!" Bucky boomed, his cropped white hair unmoving in the wind beneath the scaffolding of his glasses.

Frankie looked down as the Bank of Commerce shrank to a flat square. "But how——?" His voice was quavering; he was trembling. He'd never been up so high.

"We're aboard a geodesic floating sphere, my dear boy," Bucky said. "The air need only be heated one or two degrees." He pointed to the small gas stove sitting in the middle of the platform. "We could anchor ourselves to mountains and live up among the clouds. Or we could simply drift and see the world."

See the world. Yes, he was beginning to fathom how much there was.

"Have you ever flown before, Frank?"

Frankie shook his head. Below passed a city of more than one million and counting. He could easily fall headlong into it, spiral down onto one of those squares as it grew quickly under him, then splat.

"A famous architect once claimed that as long as humans can't fly, moving horizontally is natural. He built horizontal skyscrapers." Bucky laughed. "Man was meant to fly high as the moon. Higher."

They went with the wind. Why not? What was to fear? He and Bucky were Priest-Navigators.

"I took my first flight in 1922 and I've been to-ing and fro-ing ever since."

Frankie squeezed the aluminum bars in his hands. He could almost see himself in one of Bucky's drawings, floating just out from the planet Earth, rotating in tandem with it. There was no up or down. Just an in and out, as Bucky said. Of course: as they went up—or out—the world grew smaller, yet more vast and smooth across its surface.

From north to south ran streams like twigs, creeks like branches flowing into the trunks of rivers—the Humber, the Don—rooted in the expanse of Lake Ontario.

"The Earth is three-quarters water," said Bucky. "Yet ninety-nine percent of Earthians vie for five percent of land." As they dipped down again, Frankie could make out houses and caravans parked near the riverbanks that themselves were melting into the water.

"We could plop ourselves down right here, say, and float a city. Or in the Arctic, or the Amazon. We could live anywhere, on land, sea or air, serviced by planes and boats, connected as one world-around network."

Bucky patted Frankie's back. "Do you see that?"

The sphere caught a blast of wind that returned them to the east. Rain began to fall harder and the wind rose, but even as they were tossed about, Bucky seemed not to notice. Frankie tried not to stop looking down, or anywhere. The wind whipped at the lake as it rumpled and erupted. Its waves were churning high and fast, festering at its gashes, then gathering and rushing upstream along the rivers and creeks, engulfing the banks, sloshing over the land. The lake rose into a mountain of black water gliding across the land.

"To survive a hurricane, we need only follow nature's design," Bucky shouted. "A spider web can float in a hurricane. Compression elements in a sea of tension."

Hurricane? Below them, hydro poles toppling, bobbing like toothpicks, cars, houses crumpled and carried along, trees blown horizontal. People were clinging to the roofs of cars and houses, or whatever remained of them. It was a tide of things, the built world overtaken. Battered by the wind, Frankie and Bucky watched the furious undertow claw back chunks of the city. A firetruck overturned helplessly as its siren screeched then was snuffed as the men inside struggled to get out.

The sphere rocked and swirled but Frankie, shivering, clung to the aluminum frame more tightly than ever. He thought of Yas riding the river's current. He couldn't die, not yet.

"Hold fast, Frank," Bucky called out. He turned the flame higher and their geodesic airship rose above the brunt of the gale. They floated back over the thick of the city, over Union Station. Streets had turned to canals, cars and benches to rafts.

Then, abruptly, the wind died down. "Ah," sighed Bucky. "There now." He doused the flame and they began to drop, bit by bit. Frankie tumbled off onto a rooftop.

"I'll be on my way, now, Frank!" shouted Bucky with a salute. He tapped the third of the three watches on his wrist. "You'll receive a missive from my next destination." Bucky stoked the fire and Cloud Nine rose up and up and bobbed out of sight.

Frankie closed his eyes and opened them. The moon was high and bluish white. So close it seemed he could climb there and back all by himself. He was atop the Bank of Commerce, thirty-four storeys up. South a block or two, he saw, for the first time, Uri Slonemsky's partially built Towers of Finance, their steel beams reaching to catch and surpass the bank. A true Colossus, unsinkable.

Frankie was soaked to the skin but felt warm. All was calm. Distant sirens rang down the still waters of the streets below. He and Bucky had easily survived, like spiders in their webbed dome. He thought he glimpsed the constellation Lyra, which Bucky had once traced for him in the sky. There was its brightest star, Vega, one point drawn on the celestial sphere of the northern hemisphere, the Northern Triangle. When had the day passed into night?

A hurricane in Toronto? A tropical hurricane? Not in a hundred— two hundred—years, people said. But Frankie recalled Uri poring over the morning newspaper when a storm had first begun to stir in the Caribbean. He'd mentioned it in fact, how it was whipping itself up over land, gaining mass over the sea and ocean, gathering power. He showed Frankie a map or two, pointing out the changing form of the thing.

It had rained over Toronto the day and night before, but that was all. The creeks and rivers were rising, but they'd risen before; the ravine at the bottom of their property had grown soggy. Uri had gone to bed that night curled around Hannah.

But he couldn't sleep. That was a sign. He slipped away and sat down to sketch for the first time in years. The desk pressed into his newly acquired paunch; he felt the warmth of his flesh lap moistly upon itself and he was thirsty—he would remember those sensations. The cool, dry angles of perpendicularity between himself and the built world were no longer. He sighed. Nothing, as usual, was as it had seemed. As with this storm. As with Hannah's Blue Period. Of course, he didn't try to stop what he could see coming.

It had begun with what would be his first major building, the Towers of Finance. A modern building, one of the first in the city—in the country. But in order to build it, a block or two of storefronts needed to be done away with: a pawn shop, novelty shop, cigar store and others. A narrow huddle of decrepit buildings with slumping roofs and cracked, crumbling walls. Families ran the shops and lived above. Some were veterans come home from war, some were elderly; one was a widow with bedraggled children. Hannah had begged Uri to fix up the places and let the people stay: *People before buildings!* But Uri was not to be blamed or looked to for a solution. It wasn't him doing away with them. It was the city, the developers, the banks. He was no Fincap. He had been hired simply to design the building, to make something beautiful from this blight. Hannah befriended all forty of the residents, tried to find them homes. She did, for some: a Salvation Army shelter, and for the widow and her children, a caravan by the river. But not for others. She wanted to bring them home, to their home. They would come calling for some time after, knocking on the door of Hannah's heart at all hours, day or night. She couldn't sleep, couldn't keep up with all of them, their displaced lives a hive of stinging worry.

It was the first of his modern buildings, of his Alphabetical Architecture. U-Building, he liked to call it, would comprise two towers connected by a two-storey-high corridor across its base. His life's project that he could not relinquish, not even for Hannah. Before the bedroom door had closed and the great Blue Period had commenced, she'd sobbed to him: *We have so much, Uri, so much! Others so little!* What could he say? How could he answer? Still, work on the Towers of Finance started and stopped as the Fincaps hemmed and hawed at escalating costs. But Hannah closed her door for three years. Three years that had ended, thanks to Frankie and his wondrous ever-blooming irises. Frankie, at whose feet he'd sent the tiny model of the towers crashing.

The night of the hurricane, he sketched a bit of nothing, then climbed up the stairs to slip back into bed beside Hannah, curling around her, letting her hand clamp his wrist in her sleep. As usual.

He dreamed. The bedroom door was opening and closing rhythmically. *She loves me, she loves me not. She loves me . . .* The valves of his heart opening and closing. Was his heart giving out?

When he woke, fully, his mouth was dry and Hannah lay beside him, crooked in his arm, but he was cold, freezing: the blankets and sheets had been ripped from their bodies, their slack, middle-aged forms mercilessly exposed—to what? He looked up to the sky. For the first time, he could feel Bucky's universe in full motion: the tilt of the Earth as they turned and rotated around those stars that deceived with their own motion. Other things flew past, things that belonged to them:

papers, plans, books, a chair, Hannah's hairbrush, a rake and the rest of Frank's garden tools. Sucked up and out to the darkness of the night sky, and after it, improbably, a car bumper, a wheel, a small maple. Was he still dreaming? Were they leaving Kansas?

Hannah woke and cried out, trying to sit up, but the wind and Uri pushed her down. He held tight to her, climbed over her to shield her body. "Stay, stay," he bade her, and they burrowed into each other and watched all the worldly things swirl over and past them, disappearing into the night.

And that, he told Frankie in the morning as they collected his sodden belongings from the basement, was how the hurricane had lifted the roof off the Kidney.

The ravine was flooded, the dry garden no longer dry. With Frankie's basement apartment full of water, he moved into the living room. When he looked out the windows from the chesterfield where he slept now, he was at sea. The old dankness crept under his skin; he felt it in his hair, in everything he touched. It depressed him to be on water once again.

To Hannah it was a wonder. She was buoyed, even though her iris isle was submerged. In the mornings, she lit a cigarette and then cast a fishing line out the bedroom window. She reeled in a hat, a teacup, a toy train. Each item was an intercepted missive, a message in a bottle. Uri joined her, casting his own line out to sea. They called themselves *shipwrecked vagabonds*, never changing from their pyjamas and rubber boots.

Bucky's half-built dome had washed away. "It might make it out to sea," he brightly told Frankie.

"Maybe," Frankie said with a deep sigh.

"It can land where it pleases," Bucky declared, untucking his pants from wading boots. "No rent to pay at sea."

Upstairs, he cast a fishing line out the window beside Hannah. "An oceanic utopia—that's what we need. A community afloat with all essentials onboard, accessible by boat or front crawl."

Why not? thought Frankie. He'd lived in a house on the sea: he'd swum to it, rowed to it. But not for him. Not again.

Hannah's line snagged; she tugged and tugged until she reeled in a soggy iris bulb. She lifted it to her breast. "Remember how glorious they were, Frank?"

Temporary struts were installed across the top of the Kidney and Plexiglas sheets bolted on. Hannah wanted to see the sky.

Frankie was eventually given Anne's room while the basement dried out, though even the upstairs was damp. He stepped into a festooned wonderland of pink walls, pink bedspread and pillows. Shelves of dolls and teddy bears and books, ribbons and trophies. An outsized mirror cast back his reflection, startling him. Photographs lined one wall: Anne riding a horse, on a bicycle, in skates, in ballet slippers, posing awkwardly as a teenager. He studied her class pictures. How different she looked from the others: the untameable hair, the undainty features, the wary eyes.

When he slept between her rose-coloured sheets, Frankie dreamed his old dream of drowning in dark water. Of being taken to the other side and returned just in time. He lay in bed, later than he should, staring into the strange face of his mother's ivory carving: that half-human, half-feral animal face. He felt foolish and clouded by his mother's superstitions. Here he was perched in Rosedale. *What will you, Frank Hanesaka, make of Guinea Pig F?*

As if in answer, Hannah handed him the keys to the car. First, Guinea Pig F would learn to drive, with a little instruction from Noriko. As the flood waters ebbed, the need for countless repairs was revealed and there were errands to run.

How had this hurricane and flood come to be? How could such a force rise out of nothing to destroy houses and forests and lives?

Then, as if brought by the flood, a telephone call. Frankie heard the tinny ring. Somehow he knew.

"We're coming soon, Frankie," Reiko said. Her father had died. Her voice was different this time. Deeper, stronger.

"I don't have a place for us yet. Just a little longer."

"Anyplace will be fine," she said, then added: "Your mother says so." No more putting off what Frankie had been promising for so long.

The whole sky was pouring into the house. Soon the droppings of starlings and sparrows, robins, cardinals and blue jays cast splotchy shadows onto the living room by daylight.

One morning Frankie and Bucky looked out to see the larger rocks surfacing in the still-wet dry garden.

"The water giveth," said Bucky, "and the water taketh away."

A knock came at his—Anne's—door early one morning. It was Hannah, her hair and sleeves fluttering high and wild: she was properly dressed for the first time in days. She closed the door behind her and clamped his wrist. "I need your help, Frank."

He and Hannah drove along the lake, passing house after house whose walls were water stained halfway up or higher. Yards were muddy swamps strewn with debris and sand bags piled uselessly around them. Motley things lay on lawns and laundry lines in the weak sunlight: bits of furniture, books, clothing, blankets, stuffed toys.

They drove north into a warren of streets, still puddled here and there, where the houses were modest boxes. They slowed along a clearing where the land sloped down toward the Humber River. A footbridge lay on the grass twisted and splintered like a slain dragon.

"There!" Hannah pointed and stopped the car. She ventured down to the riverbank. Her mink coat grazed the mud and the wind caught her hair. A few caravans lay mired in the shallows. A truck pulled onto the grass behind them. Guided by Hannah, it backed up toward the only caravan still upright. It stopped and Mr. Fujimoto got out. With a nod, he handed Frankie a shovel and took another from the back of the truck. They dug a gentle slope out of the riverbank and towed the caravan to higher ground.

Hannah took hold of both Mr. Fujimoto's hands, the hands she'd praised for the dirt in their pores. "Thank you for coming to help," she said breathlessly. "The family has nothing but this caravan. Now they can clean it out and move back in."

Mr. Fujimoto's house had been mostly spared by the hurricane, but of his chrysanthemum forest only bent stems remained. He bent his own head now, in telling the tale. It was bad fortune, terrible fortune. He and his family would soon have to leave; their house was being bulldozed to make way for Regent Park— some new kind of Modern City Living. They could live in Regent Park once it was built, in a small apartment.

"Come back to us, Mister F, if you like," Hannah said, clamping his arm. "Take a corner of our yard to regrow your chrysanthemums."

Mr. Fujimoto shook his head and bent it lower. "Thank you just the same, Mrs. Slonemsky." As she turned to leave, he glared at Frankie, got into his truck and drove away.

When they returned to the Kidney, Uri was just home from his office.

"Thank you, thank you," Hannah whispered to Frankie.

"It's good of you," he replied quietly, his wrist gripped in her fingers.

"I'd do the same for you, Frank. Whatever you need."

Hannah sent him back to clean the caravan, along with Noriko. Miraculously, the inside was intact, though they would need to scrub away the muck and stench of old food and mould and a film of dirt over every surface.

Noriko picked up a photograph of a woman with a young girl and a boy: "Mrs. Slonemsky's friend," she sighed. The widow and her children.

Other caravans had been towed to the same riverside spot by the time the family settled back in. Within the next few days, they'd have to move again to a caravan park on the far eastern edge of the city. Frankie looked hard into the faces in the picture; they seemed worn, thin and sullen: aged—even the children's. He recognized the look: they were poor, cast out. They stared back at him. Is this how he looked to the world when he walked down the street? Even worse for being a Jap?

The woman in the picture appeared just then at the caravan door. Both Frankie and Noriko stepped back sheepishly.

"Please thank Hannah for me," the woman said brusquely as she climbed up.

"Mrs. Slonemsky's arranged for the electrical and water hook-up," Frankie told her.

The woman was silent for a moment. "Thirty-five people died here," she said. She flicked a chapped hand in the air. "Washed away."

Stories of these people had filled the papers, the radio. "But they'd been warned," Frankie said, repeating what Uri had said to him. "They knew it, but they went down with their homes."

Along the street, several FOR SALE signs had appeared in front of the water-stained bungalows. "Do you know how much they're selling for?" asked Frankie after a moment. He felt his heartbeat thicken.

"A pittance," the woman said. "They'll sell for a pittance."

City Hall came calling and the Slonemsky dining room table was soon covered with maps of all kinds. Historical: some twenty, fifty, a hundred years back. The streets, one-way, two-way, multi-lane; the topography. Another was a map with rivers, creeks, streams—above- and underground. Watersheds, wetlands, breakwaters, bridges. The table became the city in all its dimensions, with the shores of Lake Ontario dropping off its edge. City Hall wanted Uri Slonemsky's expertise, his foreknowledge—his anticipatory design sense, Bucky would surely call it—to help plan and rebuild, not simply in the wake of the storm, but with an eye to future comings. After all, he'd called himself a dry-spot specialist.

Uri's finger traced the waterways of the city over the high and the low lay of the land. Frankie's eyes followed.

"They built too close to the water," Uri concluded.

"Everyone wants to be close to water," Frankie said.

"Or course," said Bucky. "The water carries us to our destination, to our original home."

"Wherever that may be," said Frankie.

So the precious land along the riverbanks would become parkland, open to all and owned by none, so that people and their homes would never again be in peril. Uri's map of the city sat on the table with properties marked for *expropriation*. Frankie knew the word, and knew what it meant. Expropriation had sent his family from the shore to the strait.

"The City will pay more than fair market price," said Uri when Hannah protested. "Fair, as in before the storm," he assured her as Frankie listened. "You'll make sure?" asked Hannah. "Yes," said Uri, "of course."

Of course. Fair market price. Before the storm. Frankie took his bicycle out early the next morning and rode past the boarded-up houses, the downed fences, the abandoned chesterfields, tables, clothing, toys on soggy lawns and gardens. Cars. Splintered off bits of houses, STOP signs leaning or downed.

His heart was pounding, chugging.

So Frankie paid the pittance asked for one property, then another and another and another, until his bank account was drained. The worst on the street, closest to the creek, the lots Uri had circled on one of his maps. Four properties for less than it would cost him to buy one. Bad-luck number four, but he couldn't stop himself at three. He didn't even talk to his mother first; he didn't talk to anyone. He spoke only to the sellers, and as little as possible at that. Some were tearful, but what were tears, spent so freely?

"This was our home for twenty years," one woman lamented. "It's worth more." She held tight to his hand even as he slipped it free. He figured the woman lucky, all of them lucky. He was giving more than he'd ever gotten. Twenty years in one fine, spacious house!

He was using anticipatory vision, land-on-water/water-on-land ingenuity. He bought, and when City Hall came calling, he would sell it back to them. This time, he'd profit from expropriation. Ease the uncertainty of owners. He'd be saving these people time and worry, taking on that debt. In exchange, he'd be repaid once the expropriation went through at City Hall, just as Uri had described. Like a good businessman, he'd earn a profit for that time and worry taken on.

Frankie offered to help an elderly couple move their things.

"There's nothing to take," they said. They carried two suitcases each, their all-you-can-carry, and left the rest behind.

"Where will you go?" he dared ask. The man said nothing. "We'll be fine," the woman answered with a weak smile.

They would be fine, Frankie told himself. With better chances than Taiji, his mother and he had ever known.

As Uri's Towers of Finance went up, Frankie's houses went down. Waterlogged, they slunk and sunk until the ground froze. At night, Frankie rode his bicycle to see the progress of Uri's skyscraper. On days off, he rode through slush to the riverbank. He watched neighbours squint at the sky, praying for sun and dry winds while chipping away at ice frozen to their doorsteps. They shook their heads at him for his foolish investment. Water stains had begun to fade from their walls four, five feet up, but handmade FOR SALE signs were sprouting from the snow. He told no one what he knew of the expropriation to come, and began to wonder if men from the City would, in fact, arrive with cheques in hand. He didn't dare ask Uri.

The Towers of Finance rose into the clouds. Frankie watched in awe as each floor was topped by another, then another, each capped with snow, taller than the Bank of Commerce, with clear views to the lake. He felt dwarfed by the ambition of it.

"Twenty-four-karat gold baked onto its panes of glass," Uri told him. "You'll see. More glass than in any other skyscraper in the world, and more gold." Enough to dust the glass reflective and turn the reflected sunset pink. Something never done before.

The towers glittered like the light at dusk in the graveyard near Tashme that he swore was gold dust from the banks of the Fraser. Now, in the sky cast in the same magic hour, Uri Slonemsky's towers gilded the sky.

The Priest began to appear in Frankie's dreams, saying nothing, always in white robes. Frankie stood himself before the large mirror in Anne's pink bedroom and pushed back his overgrown hair. Was Guinea Pig F cursed or blessed? He slid down his pants and twisted to see the Mongolian spot.

It was as dark and unfaded as when the Ladies of the Sisters of Mercy first glimpsed it.

The next morning, Hannah sat Frankie down and gave him a haircut. Her fingers dug into his scalp one minute, then flew off the next. When she finished, she held her hands to his cheeks and made him look in the mirror. There was no turning away.

"How do you do, Frank!"

His face was not a handsome face or a kind face; it was neither this nor that. The Priest lurked there, not quite willing to show all of himself.

Still, with his hair trimmed away, Frankie was out of hiding. He looked fine; respectable, at least for what he was. No one would think twice except for those who already did.

A few days later, Hannah presented him with a suit, one of Uri's that she'd had altered. She made him try it on. A perfect fit.

"You see, Frank?" she cried, inhaling her own excitement. She smoothed his shoulders.

He thought of asking her, then and there, for the help she'd said she'd give him.

But then he looked in the mirror: it wasn't any ordinary suit. Nothing like the one he'd lined up to buy Saturday morning at Honest Ed's or the ones he'd seen in the window of Tip Top Tailors. The cloth was fine, inside and out. It was as if he'd stepped into someone else's sleek skin.

"Oh, Frank!" Hannah said again, clasping her hands.

Then she reached for his. "When you shake someone's hand, you give them something to hold on to. Not this." She let his limp, clammy hand drop.

"You give them your word." Now she gripped his hand again and held it firmly, squeezed it until he squeezed back. He listened closely to her for she was—wasn't she?—sharing with him the secret of the Jews. Be smarter. Do everything faster, better, cheaper than anyone else. From his mother he already knew to be a scavenger. From Bucky, he was learning to do more with that scavenged less.

Frankie practised handshaking with Noriko. Firmly and vigorously.

The day of a dental appointment, Frankie donned the suit and walked the Avenue of Finance. Past the Bank of Commerce, under Uri Slonemsky's growing skyscraper. Past the construction workers. No one shouted at him this time to get out of the way. This time was different. He was neither invisible nor alien. He strode taller, straighter. His gaze was met by those who passed, some with a deferential nod or tip of the hat; a woman with the slightest hint of a smile, he was sure. Doors were opened for him. In a restaurant, he asked to be seated by a window and he was, though he slipped out without ordering.

The suit was magic.

Bucky was wrong: a suit didn't make a man invisible. It made Frankie visible, important, or at least important enough.

He lay in bed in Anne's pink room, gazing up at the night sky through the splotched ceiling at the piercings of stars. His mother and Reiko would very soon be arriving. To what? Hannah had said they could all stay, but he could not imagine it. She had also offered Mr. Fujimoto a home and a garden plot—all in her Kidney.

She had looked into Frankie's hands and told him they were not the hands of a gardener. No, the future of Guinea Pig F lay elsewhere.

He'd been back in the basement for a week when he woke to shoes shuffling outside his window in the dark of night. Then the clatter of high heels. Was he dreaming? The bottoms of suitcases grazing the walk, the sound too grating not to be real.

At least they'd known to come to the back door.

He lay in bed for a moment before the knock came. Sharp, impatient raps.

He rushed up the stairs and opened the door, face burning. There was Reiko: cheeks as red as her lips, hair tightly crimped instead of waved, the clenched white-gloved hand ready to knock again. The brooch he'd given his Rose Queen was faithfully pinned to her lapel; it scratched his neck as she embraced him. Behind her, his mother stood; and behind his mother was Taiji, smaller even than he remembered. Aki peeked from behind; blinked to take him in with her one good eye.

They stared at him for a moment; the hair didn't cover his face as it used to.

"You took too long," his mother said, greyer but not so changed. She took hold of his hands and saw the dirt in his nails, then pushed them away.

"Yes, Mama," he said and sighed. He was relieved to see them here; more than he'd realized.

"I told you we were coming soon," Reiko said. She'd adopted some of his mother's sternness. She was tall in her high-heeled shoes, purchased on Hope's main street, no doubt. But then she glanced at him shyly, unsure; she slipped off those shoes and came down to size beside him. She slipped her hand into his.

"Welcome," he said, and led them down the stairs.

How good it was to hold a body—Reiko's body—close and to plunge inside. He was a man after all: still young, strong; an Average Man like Uri Slonemsky or Bucky or any other walking down the Avenue of Finance, and now he was reminded that Reiko could give him that feeling. Her eyes caught a spit of light in the dark between them. "I missed you so, Frankie," she whispered while the others slept—on the newly replaced carpeting, atop bedding laid out by Noriko.

The most glorious sight! Hannah fluttered her purple chiffon wings the next morning as she pointed out the window down to the mucky marsh that was once home to the iris isle. *The wonders your Frank worked! The gift of it!*

His mother nodded in return. Taiji stood silent behind. Reiko was quiet too, staring down at herself, at her dress and shoes and fingernails: too red; lips curling back from a red-stained tooth. Aki slipped outside to the edge of the murky waters and gazed up to trees she'd never imagined could grow so tall in the city.

Frankie did not belong there. Shame on him for the dirt under his nails, on his pants—dirt from someone else's land. He'd asked them to wait. Coming from the train station to this clammy basement, Momoye had seen men striding with purpose, in and out the revolving doors of soaring office buildings, fine hotels and automobiles.

Then he brought out the suit. "Look, Mama." He put it against him to show her the Frankie who was becoming Frank. Hmph. She fingered the fine cloth and studied her son, his short haircut and the chin he was holding higher than before. She saw the initials inside too: U.S.

Momoye pressed a satchel of bills and coins into Frankie's hand. He made a show of refusing it, but she muttered, *Take, take!* It was all she could give him: more, in fact, since in

addition to the dregs of the sake business, it included the earnings of Aki (for the sewing she'd continued to take in after the
camp canteen closed, and for cleaning the house of a family
in Hope), and of Julia and Augusta from ticket sales at High
Hope's Theatre.

"I have a plan, Mama," he assured her. "A fine home by
the water, high up. A room for just you and Taiji."

The next morning mother and son rode the subway. He
could see the strangeness of it in her eyes, riding to who knows
where as the lights flickered on and off in the dim tunnel. How
she stared at the other riders, looking them over, from their hats
to their gloved hands to their heels. When the two of them surfaced onto the busy street, she took a deep breath and charged
ahead; he saw her apart from the crowds and from himself. She
appeared small and hunched, whereas before she'd seemed
ample; now swarthier, weathered from the mountain cold; her
hair gone almost all white; and her clothes: he'd have to replace
her shabby coat and shoes. Of course: she'd never been in a big
city in her life. Now he'd have to look after her much more than
she looked after him. But she ably climbed up into the streetcar,
bandy calves as sturdy as ever. He led her along the lakefront,
in and out of rusted fencing to a piece of land he wanted badly
to anchor himself to. Massive old storage tanks occupied it
at the moment: sooty, rundown, empty and out of use, three of
them. He counted them out to his mother. "Look, no bad-luck
four." His breath cast a shroud around them in the chill air.

"What will you build, Fu-ranki?"

"A hotel. Or high-rise apartments. Modern. New City
Living," he quoted. He brought out a newspaper clipping he'd
been carrying for weeks in his pocket. He pointed his finger at
the big, bold letters there. *Apartments as Modern as Tomorrow*,
it said.

"New City Living," his mother repeated. Slowly and
silently, she walked the muddy width of the lot counting to

herself, then the length; Frankie followed behind. She looked across the water to the sliver of islands that faced her, not so unlike Port Alberni's narrow harbour.

The morning sun glinted on the lake. It was the last in the Great Lakes chain that flowed out to the Atlantic through the St. Lawrence River. It was the closest he could get to the sea. If he built high enough, the view would be perfect. They'd see over the islands, clear across to Rochester on the other side. He and his family would have the top floor with the finest view of all, windows on all sides.

"Lake of shining waters," said Frankie, "Lake Ontario."

"Shining water," his mother repeated, like a promise.

"Frank wants to make his mark," Hannah said, loudly and slowly, looking from Frankie to his mother to Taiji. "His mark," she repeated as she handed Frankie, his mother and Taiji each a martini.

Taiji nodded politely. When he moved, Frankie could almost hear the grief creaking in his every joint. There were no marks to be made after Yas's death.

"Uri and I know what it is to be singled out for the wrong reason," Hannah fluttered on with an inexhaustible sigh. "To have your life pulled out from under you. The doors shut in your face." She held her hand up toward where the roof once was. "The life you toiled for." She then raised her martini glass to her lips, and motioned for the others to do the same. His mother downed it in one gulp as if it were her tiny cup of sake. Taiji nursed a long, deep swallow.

As Hannah's eyes filled, Frankie glanced at his mother; she was staring down. Such nonsense. There hadn't been so much to lose to begin with. Then, abruptly, she spoke. "Fu-ranki need money. He will pay back." She added, "To make mark." She made a stroke on her palm.

How jarring to hear his mother through Hannah's ears. Her English never improving.

Now Frankie looked down, feeling Hannah's eyes brimming over him. He was abashed, red-faced. He never could have asked for himself. Yet he wanted the money. Didn't he deserve it for all he'd done? For the dirt on his pants and under his nails? The healing magic in the long-blooming irises? He'd been at her side, heeded her, received her wisdom, and now he would prove himself worthy.

An investment. He'd earn the money to pay her back and then some. He didn't need to hear the story, not from her, not from the Slonemskys of Rosedale; he knew something of it, the Jews' suffering through all of time. But thankfully, she merely lifted his downward jutting chin. It was his shame keeping it down but his pride too: he would not accept no for an answer.

After a moment, he looked up and squarely met her eyes.

"I'll give you the money," Hannah sighed, "but don't go buying a swamp."

Frankie laid down his money for that sodden skirt at the bottom of the city, including what still lay beneath flood waters. Not for long a swamp. The man who sold was relieved to be saved from bankruptcy though not overwhelmed by the generosity of the buyer. He left behind his three empty rusting oil tanks.

With the deed in his hands, Frankie sat down on his waterfront land. He sat until the seat of his pants was soaked through. Each night he sat, his pants were less wet by the time he left. Until finally, they were no longer; the water had receded and he sat atop solid dry land.

Sometimes, in bright morning sun, the lake took on an almost false blue-green shade like a tropical sea in travel brochures. A far cry from the sawdust-littered shores of Port

Alberni with its stacks of lumber and machinery, and the roaring sawmill planted wide and deep across the inlet claimed by Bloedel, Stewart and Welch. Frankie envisioned his high-rise apartments here, his Tomorrow Living for Today. First one, then another, then another, all across the waterfront, all with banks of windows to the lake and their backs turned to the city, hoarding their view. Then, like a beacon, a tower, his own Tower of Finance. So high, he'd call it Cloud Tower. Bucky would like that. He closed his eyes and envisioned its top lost in the clouds and its base buried in snow, so that it seemed to float in the mid-sky, untethered at each end.

Every morning he scanned the local news, waiting to hear of the City Council's decision to expropriate. Uri, Mr. Knew-It-All, could not possibly have been wrong. At night the engine racing inside of him started up, his legs twitching. Once Reiko rested her hand on his chest and recoiled, her small worried eyes fixed on him in the dark. "What is it, Frankie?" she whispered. He gave a stilted yawn and turned onto his side. It was just him waiting for everything to come true.

In the subway, Taiji jostled against his son as the train came to a jarring stop at each dimly lit station. It was hardly the sparkling underground city of Frankie's imagining. Words came into his head, talk that melted to nothing before he could speak. Words always came to nothing between him and Taiji.

How would it have been if Yas were with them? Would they be here or still back in Tashme, or perhaps Japan? Would he be in charge, looking after them instead of Frankie?

They transferred to an eastbound streetcar, and when they stepped off, Frankie didn't recognize the street. Mr. Fujimoto's house was gone. His block was gone. Children played where broken asphalt met newly poured concrete. Identical red-brick buildings squatted like pieces on a game board. A search for Mr. Fujimoto's new address led them along criss-crossing walkways over dry grass. There were no flowers in sight.

They found his address on the last apartment at the end of a long hallway. Frankie knocked and heard hushed voices behind the door. After a few moments Mr. Fujimoto opened it. Behind him, in a dim room, his family huddled, though they were fewer now. He and Taiji had learned of each other only through Mr. Koga and had never met.

Outside the window, a few chrysanthemums had risen barely a foot in their pots; weed-thin, most straggled sideways along the balcony. When the slightest wind blew, petals fell to the concrete, where only a few dandelions poked out between the cracks.

Mrs. Fujimoto offered them frayed cushions to sit on and set chipped teacups before them. She poured the tea and each of the Fujimotos sipped and squinted their tiny dolphin eyes into their cups for hope splayed in the leaves there.

They rarely went out, Mr. Fujimoto told them. The youngest son, the shyest one, employed for years in the eyeglass factory, had lost his way when returning home one day. He finally arrived after dark and never left again. The son who'd helped tend the Chrysanthemum Forest had grown pale and stiff from not enough sunshine and fresh air.

What about food? Taiji asked.

Once a month to the Japanese food store in Chinatown, Mr. Fujimoto said. The weather could turn at any moment. There were strangers all around.

Of course they no longer took in new arrivals to the city.

Mr. Fujimoto, Frankie noticed, was stooped. He gulped back his hot tea thirstily. His dolphin skin was crinkled and dry. His fingernails were clean.

He and Taiji could only nod sadly to each other.

"You helped Frankie," Taiji finally uttered and picked up

a large bottle of sake and a package of fish cakes that he'd set beside him. "Thank you." He held out the gifts and bowed his head low.

Mr. Fujimoto sat up abruptly as if doused with water. He folded his arms, refusing the gifts. "Frankie brought us bad luck." He seemed to shiver and shake off the last hairs clinging to his crown. "Your son," and he looked to Frankie.

Taiji dropped his head to ward off the bad luck; as if he hadn't had enough. He shrank away from Frankie. He looked into his cup. No good fortune to be found there. *This is not my son. My son is dead.*

Taiji did not say those words, but Frankie heard them. They left. Out between the buildings to the main street. Frankie following after Taiji, who strode ahead with the bag of fish cakes still in his hand. "No streetcar," he announced.

Fine. Frankie wanted to walk; he wanted to run and burn off the shame and dread he felt. He was bad luck; it was true. The chrysanthemums had wilted whenever he came near, just like the flowers he had planted in his floating garden. Even the irises, after their glory, were drowned.

They walked in silence, block after block until they reached the station.

"No train." Taiji pointed under his feet. He didn't want to go underground again.

Fine. Frankie turned toward the station himself, away.

But Taiji gripped his arm with surprising strength and pulled Frankie alongside.

"My father was rich," Taiji declared, his voice rising, insistent. He hadn't spoken much of his family to Frankie. Rice was their business. "A good business to be in over there." He slapped his knee, then laughed. Suddenly he was out of breath, and at the first bench they came to, he sat down.

His father had not been a generous man, except to himself and his mistress, he told Frankie. "He left my mother almost every night." She'd cry and cling to Taiji from when he was a boy. But his father gave him a horse to ride. Taiji had loved to ride all around the rice fields while the workers worked. He didn't care if the horse was tired or wanted to stop, or couldn't jump as far as he wanted it to.

One day he pushed it to leap across the creek on their property, but it stumbled.

"What happened to it?" Frankie asked.

"Leg broken!" Taiji rasped in English, and he jabbed at his chest. The horse had to be killed by one of their workers.

Not long after, Taiji decided to leave home for Canada. On his last night it began to snow. He went looking for his father and came upon him slinking through the fields. He tied his father to a tree to stop him from joining his mistress. Taiji knotted an imaginary rope now and grimaced, tugging each end as tightly as he could.

"He's still there!" he said, laughing as his eyes filled.

After the shacks in Tashme, Reiko told Frankie, she was happy with any ceiling over their heads that didn't leak. The indoor heating of the Slonemsky home was a gift: no more carting of wood for the stove. Luxury was an indoor toilet.

She tried not to dwell on the changes in her husband—his new ways of dressing, talking and even walking—though she did notice and remark on them. "You're a slick so-and-so," she teased. Whenever they found themselves alone, which was rare, she would love him as she had in the old graveyard. She wanted a baby: a live, healthy baby boy. But Frankie was always rushing off after his garden work to some other place she'd never seen. At home, he spent hours with his mother.

"It's not right, Frankie," Reiko told him. It was their life he was discussing without her. Whenever Reiko came near their huddle, she was shooed away by her mother-in-law while

Frankie looked on like a bystander. Almost every evening, he and Hannah sipped martinis, which Reiko refused to touch.

At night, after everyone else had settled in, he came to her in the basement and slipped into bed. Now he had time.

"What were you talking about?" Reiko whispered. Her eyes flickered in the moonlight through the window.

"Business," he said.

"Our business?" she retorted.

"What other kind of business is there?" He found her hand under the covers and shook it, firmly. "How do you do, Mrs. Hanesaka?"

"Stop it, Frankie," she hissed. She slapped his hand away. But as he took back her hand and led it elsewhere, she couldn't help relenting.

When Frankie had practised his handshake with Noriko, she had shared her own business ideas. One in particular seemed to be very, very good in a Bucky way: *anticipatory*, and *doing more with less*. Her brother-in-law, a Korean living in Noriko's hometown of Yokohama, wanted to sell the scrap metal salvaged from crumpled Zero planes and undeployed torpedoes, half-sunk ships and submarines bobbing bottom-up off Japan's shores. He would sell it here—to Frankie, in fact.

Facing the mirror the next morning, Frankie realized exactly what to do with the land he'd bought east of the city by the lake and highway. Scavenge and build, he told Frank in the mirror. As he'd always done. Then, with a firm shake of your hand, sell.

CHAPTER 10

After the Flood

Frankie found Aki a job. In a basement just south of Chinatown under a bare, hanging lightbulb, she cocked her one good eye to the thread unspooling under the foot of a Singer sewing machine and pumped its pedal. On her first day, he walked her there and waited for her in the evening. She showed him her work table, one of many in row after row, and the shirts she'd sewn, stacked beside her machine. When they emerged from the factory, Aki remarked that dusk on Spadina Avenue looked just like dawn.

At the end of the month, she went with Frankie to deposit her cheque in his account. Frankie knew money and knew what to do with it. He was looking after them all, as man of the house he was saving to buy them.

On his day off, he went to the other lot he'd bought for a song east of the city and surveyed the junk there. It was mostly metal, from railings to car parts to tin cans. The owner had left a contraption that crushed scrap. Nothing as big as a car, but if you broke it down into small parts, it could be crushed and cut into pieces of a size to be sorted, carted off in trucks and sold to a smelter. He hired men he knew from Tashme, and with axes, they set to chopping off car doors and hoods, like the branches of a tree.

He bought and bartered with his suit and his handshake. When that didn't do the trick, when someone didn't want to make a deal with a Jap, he signed off by mail as Frank Hanes and pretended to be the truck driver at delivery time. When business picked up, he hired more men.

But still, at night, he was sleepless. When would the expropriation arrive? In Port Alberni, it had arrived, the bad fortune of it, unsummoned, all too soon. This time, Frankie told himself, good fortune was simply making him wait. Wide awake, he slipped upstairs in the middle of the night. He found Hannah sprawled on the living room floor studying a book cracked open under a lamp. Her hair was tied back and a pair of reading glasses was perched on her nose. She started at first. "Ah, Frank. Come sit with me."

She showed him a page lined with symbols and a language that looked like nothing he'd ever seen.

"Do you know what this is?" Hannah asked. Of course he didn't. She spoke quietly.

"The seventy-two names of the Hashem, of God." She ran her hand over the page as if it were Braille. "Touch it," she urged and watched him. "Close your eyes." Surely this was the true secret of the Jews. He placed his fingers on the paper and shut his eyes. He kept them closed, awaiting further instruction.

She drew him closer, her lavender and iris breath. Her face this close, without makeup, was almost unfamiliar, its fine lines an obscure map. "Let the words enter into you. Feel their energy," she whispered. "Can you hear them?" He nodded, though it was not God's words he heard, but Hannah's. "These are the words God used to create the world. The code." Her purple silk skimmed his wrist. It was like the hush of the Ladies' prayers asking that his spot be healed. For him to be forever returned from the other side, out of the dark, into the light.

The air grew cool and stale; he opened his eyes. Hannah now sat apart from him.

"You don't have to mention this to Uri," she said with a finger to her lips. "He disapproves."

Her husband was a man who had anchored his feet in the concrete foundations of his work. "Not that he has feet of clay," she explained. Above the ankles he might sway with the wind. The seeming whimsy of his alphabetical buildings was not whimsy at all, but the impulse for order.

Of course Uri loved beauty but his beauty was scientifically, systematically constructed. Only through form and order could something so much taller than wide be engineered to remain standing. In the modest instance of the Kidney, it was simply the order of flesh and blood to which he'd adhered, a schema of renal physiology.

"Uri doesn't believe in the mystical," said Hannah, "not the way we do." She sighed and flapped her silk sleeves. Her hair fell loose. "The world is nothing if not mystery. You and I know that. Bucky knows it: the sun, the moon, the stars. Bebop and jitterbugs." She squeezed Frankie's hand.

"Uri says a building earns its aura, or doesn't, by the hand of its creator—not the Creator." Hannah sat back in her seat.

It was true: Frankie believed in mystery, even if he didn't want to.

On a visit to check on his houses, he spied envelopes poking out of each rusting mailbox. The notice had arrived: expropriation. Then, not long after, four cheques, each made out to Frank Hanesaka. He handed over his deeds and deposited his windfall. Now he could invest in a proper metal shredder.

And from that, he'd soon have enough to finance his high-rise apartments: his Tomorrow Living for Today.

In the marshy backyard of the Kidney, miraculously, the irises began to poke their heads above the pond, gulping the air and sunlight. In a week or two they were sprouting anew. "Lovely!" uttered Hannah, squeezing Frankie's hand. He'd almost forgotten the rich purple of them, how regally they stood. It was as if the flowers were assenting to his plans.

Then one morning, Reiko gave him a look that said yes. She was pregnant again.

He told his mother. She studied Reiko's walk, looked her over. Hannah, in her way, did the same.

"Boy," his mother announced.

"Frank, it's a boy!" Hannah declared.

"A boy!" Frankie repeated. The feel of it bouncing from his mouth, the sound of it in the air! A body was sprouting—a being—and he'd planted it.

Guinea Pig F wasn't just going round on his exercise wheel. He was climbing, rung by rung.

Frankie surfaced from the basement to find Uri Slonemsky bowing repeatedly. "Frank. Just the man I need," he said as he straightened up. Would Frankie help smooth the path to a deal with the Japanese manufacturing firm, Minamoto Electric?

A little instruction, a few words in Japanese?

"Yes, sir!" Gladly!

The project on which Uri Slonemsky had set his sights suited the architect to a *T*, if not an *M*: a building to house the first Canadian office of Minamoto Electric. As an admirer of Uri's gold-dusted skyscraper, Mr. Minamoto contacted him from his Tokyo headquarters. Mr. Minamoto had adapted the company's wartime munitions production to the manufacture of small appliances. Japan's postwar rehabilitation under American occupation was complete, and Minamoto Electric was ready to expand into North America with an arsenal of shavers, steam curlers, toasters and transistor radios.

Frankie bowed low to Uri—low enough to expose the back of his neck. *Like so.* "The samurai demonstrates trust and honour in this way," he told Uri. Trust that his counterpart won't behead him.

"Eyes downcast," Frankie instructed.

"Ah, yes."

The two men took turns bowing to one another. "You've been a help already, Frank," Uri said with a final bow.

But it was Uri along with Hannah helping Frankie, laying down stepping stones for him to climb up from the basement.

Frankie's rusting Japanese had very little metal left under its tarnished surface. He practised some phrases and bowed to himself in the mirror. But no matter: he and Mr. Minamoto were in the same business. The business of making livingry out of weaponry, as Bucky might say. Frankie's yard was now brimming with scrap recovered from the South Pacific. The metal arrived by ship, departing from the same Yokohama dock as Frankie's mother and the Priest did all those decades ago. The foundation of his enterprise and now Uri's had come to rest on the rubble of Japan's defeated military: its rusting flying contraptions for suicide missions with their piggy-back cockpits for the doomed pilots. Salvaged from land, sea and obsolete hangars throughout the former empire. The machines would be reincarnated as the suicide pilots had hoped to be, but in the forms of fuse boxes and money boxes, girders and railings, street lamps and smokestacks, bicycle frames and elevators, even airplane parts—anything made of metal.

As it turned out, Mr. Minamoto spoke excellent English. When Frankie and Uri bowed, he stepped forward and held out his hand to shake—to Uri, but not to Frankie.

The *M* in Minamoto, he explained, stood for *modern*. Japan had long led all of Asia in modernizing its people and industries. This was why he had chosen Uri Slonemsky to be his architect. He'd seen photographs of Mr. Slonemsky's soaring Towers of Finance with their shimmering panels of gold glass. He wanted modern, sleek and streamlined with the soaring possibilities of a new postwar world.

It was the future that Mr. Minamoto wanted. Frankie understood: Tomorrow Living for Today.

What Uri Slonemsky proposed was a form that was neither up nor down nor across, but angled skyward, outward. Like a jet plane taking off. Ascension.

Frankie found a suitable lot for the offices of Minamoto Electric in the northwest end of the city. In summers past, you could pick your own strawberries there. The farmer had left his berries to rot in the autumn sun; too many planes were streaking too low overhead in and out of the nearby airport. Frankie offered the old man his handshake, an invitation to sell, and his new business card. There were no impressive initials after his name, but with a new career launching, the card felt substantial in his hand and in his wallet.

"Hanesaka," the farmer pronounced slowly and studied Frankie, looking him up and down. "What kind of name is that?"

"A good name," Frankie said, forcing himself to stand tall in his suit and meet the farmer's eyes. "The name of a man who stands by his word." The farmer shook his head and crossed his arms. No. He wanted to sell to someone who'd farm the land just as he had and his father before him. And he wouldn't sell to people who'd nearly starved his brother in a POW camp.

Uri visited a week later. The farmer scrutinized his card too. He hemmed and hawed until Uri increased the offer. Then he accepted.

When Reiko introduced Frankie to his newborn son, he imme-diately peeked under the baby's diaper. There it was, of course, faint but unmistakeable: an inky pool between the buttocks. Surely his son's Mongolian spot would fade and shrink as it should.

For weeks, he delayed naming the boy. Until one morning, he brought his mother to Reiko's side.

"Uri," he announced. The sound of it embarrassed him at first, and it dismayed Reiko as she held the infant in her arms. Momoye snorted indifferently. He was more creature than boy: tufts of hair sprung from his head; forehead to ankle, his body was furred. But his eyes: his eyes were wholly human—round and searching. Reiko kept nudging his chin, meeting his eyes with hers as if to say, *Here, look here.*

The thought of their son being Uri Slonemsky's namesake—would people call Frankie a kowtower?

He didn't mind being a kowtower to Uri Slonemsky; he was envious, yes, but he'd learned so much in the man's wake. He'd once watched Mr. Koga and Mr. Fung, who knew little and did more wrong than right. But Uri Slonemsky did things right, and knew it all.

Frankie said his son's name aloud, this time tapping the *r* and with a *Y* in front to make it *Yu-ri*, a Japanese name. For the boy's second name: "Richard," Bucky's first name, which might in time become the name printed on Yuri's business cards. Frankie patted the bundle in Reiko's arms.

He named himself too. Already Hannah had christened him Frank, a man, not a boy, nor anyone's servant. On his newly printed business card, raised letters that he could feel with his fingertip made it official:

FRANK HANES
Slonemsky & Associates Architects

He'd severed the "aka" from the end of him, the tail that would drag him down.

Construction began in late summer, the ground broken by dinosaur backhoes with long necks and gouging jaws; cement poured out of churning mixers to fill the gaping hole.

Mr. Minamoto returned to Toronto, this time with his second-in-command Mr. Yamamoto, who walked the perimeter of the base with its protruding steel rods, stomping the concrete as he went.

"Very good," he said. The man gave a wide, crooked-toothed smile to Uri and Frankie. "The meaning of the last half of my name is *foundation*, so I have made this my specialty." He gave a little laugh.

Mr. Minamoto was pleased with the progress of the construction. "Thank you very much," he said, bowing deeply to Uri Slonemsky, who bent awkwardly in return. Mr. Minamoto was saluting Uri's intelligence and talent, and his being a Jew. "Jews survive," he said, "as do Japanese." He himself had survived the war and prison. His family survived the atomic bomb. When he emerged, he understood how the world had changed, and he would survive that too.

"There is a new war to be waged in the marketplace," Mr. Minamoto declared.

"A war?" Uri raised an eyebrow.

Through fall and winter, the two towers rose quickly. By late spring, they were linked by two glass-enclosed escalators, each slanting down at forty-five degrees to meet at the base. From the nearby highway and intersecting concession road, one could see the giant letter *M* forming, sunlit by day; by night, lit up and down each of its lengths.

Mr. Minamoto and Mr. Yamamoto returned months later to survey the progress. At the end of the visit, Frankie drove

Mr. Minamoto to the airport, leaving behind his second-in-command. Mr. Minamoto turned ruefully to Frankie. "It's regrettable that your family left Japan."

To which Frankie could only nod.

"Our country will be strong again." Mr. Minamoto instructed Frankie to pull over. Through the window, Mr. Minamoto gazed back across the razed strawberry field at the new Canadian outpost of Minamoto Electric.

"What do you see?" he asked Frankie.

"*M*," Frankie said. "Minamoto. Your name."

"Do you know the name?"

Frankie didn't but he nodded dutifully; no doubt it was a prominent clan in Japan.

"It means the source. The origin."

The building was rising with steel beams and cased in glass. Far from the wood and paper dwellings cindered during the firebombing of Japanese cities. Across the field, a pictogram was taking shape in the deepening dusk. What Mr. Minamoto saw was two men bowing deeply to one another. Over the coming months, he would return with his lieutenants, the salarymen, who would work quietly, dutifully, to ensure Japan's new rise in the years to come.

"Drive on," he told Frankie.

Then it was Frankie's turn to lay a stepping stone at Uri Slonemsky's door. He drove Uri to the foot of the city to show him the lot at the shore of Lake Ontario. Uri paced its perimeter just as Frankie's mother had.

"You own this?" he asked.

"Me and the bank," Frankie answered. He didn't mention Hannah, though she was the bank. He presumed it to be another something kept between them.

Uri studied him, as if in a new light, then turned to the

lake. The bright light turned the water tropical sea blue, and the trees on the adjacent islands were a lush emerald. Yet to the east of the lot were the dirty silos of the flour mill and the sugar refinery. Farther along to the west was an old fishing boat and dock whose owner wouldn't sell, then the ferry terminal for the islands. And there were the three rusted tanks on the lot itself.

"That's a lot of land to garden," Uri remarked. They both laughed.

"What do you see here, Frank?"

"Tomorrow Living for Today," said Frankie. He bounced on his toes just as Uri would, but nervously. Held his arms out toward the water. "Apartments. With a view." Frankie had been reading about the city Chairman, a man bent on skyscrapers and expressways. High-density City Living! A bold man.

Uri studied Frankie ever more closely. Was he seeing through him? Seeing what he shouldn't see, or should see: that he wasn't just a gardener, he was a man with ideas and gumption.

"The zoning would have to be changed," said Uri.

"Yes."

"I could talk to the Chairman. Just to feel things out."

Of course Uri knew the Chairman. *Big Daddy*, as he was called, even in the newspapers. The way could be paved; investors could be convinced. After all, shipping was moving to the bigger suburban ports, out near Frankie's scrapyard. This could all be a new neighbourhood for people to live and work. More than a neighbourhood: a city within a city.

Frankie held out his hand to Uri Slonemsky to shake on their partnership, and all his practice made it the firmest handshake of his life.

The Chairman was a metropolis of a man, sprawling and dense. He pulled a flask of whisky from his breast pocket.

"You see that?" the Chairman shouted, pointing at nothing in particular across Frankie's empty lot.

At his side, Frankie nodded emphatically, dizzying himself: *He saw it, yes siree, Mister Chairman!*

Port Alberni had never had a chairman. Its two-bit mayor had only given Frankie the time of day to herd him and his kind first off the land, then off the water, and then out of town.

The Chairman held up his arms to embrace the breadth of space on either side of them. "The Yanks will see our scrapers clear across from Rochester. Lit up at night, on fire!" He slapped Frankie hard on the back, whisky-breath gusting him forward.

Back at City Hall, the Chairman reached low into his desk for a bottle of single malt Scotch whisky. Finer stuff than Canadian Club, Frankie guessed.

"Frank, my boy!" The Chairman clinked Frankie's glass hard.

The Chairman spun round and leaned in. "The city's shrinking at the core and bursting at the seams. We have to build up and then out," he declared. He spread his arms even wider to be understood. "That's the master plan."

"Up and out," Frankie echoed after catching his breath. He downed another glass. Inside the ice cube crackling at the bottom, he thought he saw his reflection.

"It's like a garden here at City Hall, Frank," he said. "It'll need a little fertilizer to get things growing."

After a top-off and then the one-for-the-road presently raised to his lips, Frankie was red and tingling, and swaying. The Chairman's eyes were a colour Frankie couldn't name, between brown, green, even yellow under his thick, flaring brows. The Chairman rubbed his thumb against two fingertips. Then he winked. "Fertilizer," he repeated.

In a second, Frankie was ushered out to the bright, garish hallway. Others were waiting for their audience.

The Chairman leaned out to give a thumbs-up sign before slamming the door.

Frankie wended his way up Bay Street, fists tight and thumbs up, fighting to keep himself on the straight and narrow. He could see it in his mind's eye: before long, trunks of concrete would rise higher and thicker than any forest, foundations riveted deep in the ground so they couldn't be felled. One next to the other, unmovable, unshakeable. Instead of Bloedel, Stewart and Welch on Port Alberni's waterfront, it would be Frank, Frank and Frank on Toronto Harbour. He laughed and snorted on the dark, empty street. He could hail a cab, like Uri did: a flick of the wrist in the air. Let someone else do the driving; the wrist-flicking too, for that matter! He had enough bills in his pocket—not nickels and dimes. He had deeds. Up and out. Yes siree!

But he reached the Kidney the way he'd gotten most places—at least without his bicycle: one foot in front of the other. He headed to the basement without a stumble even when he hopped from the third step to the fifth to miss the bad-luck fourth. In his new home, he laughed to himself, there would be no fourth step.

Uri and Big Daddy Chairman did pave the way. Like the mill owners, the Chairman was a top-rung man who could corner the market, pile the timber high and keep the workers working below. Before long, the backhoes and diggers and bulldozers and cranes came in, the dump trucks hauled away the scrapped tanks to Frankie's warehouses, and the foundation was laid. Salesmen spread out their wares of tiles and carpets, countertops and panels of wood before Uri and Frankie, sealing their deals. Frankie wore a hard hat with his name on it and inspected the site at Uri's side, every detail big and small as the building went up, so nothing would come down.

Tomorrow Living for Today High-Rise Apartments was not quite as high or as tomorrow as Frankie or Uri had hoped. But its simple, sleek form rose alongside the silos and rubble and a lone, stranded fishing boat. Bucky suggested a revolving dome perched on its roof, to house a restaurant, perhaps, something like a circular house Bucky had once designed around a single mast in its centre.

"A dizzy notion," the Chairman snorted when Frankie mentioned it. Frankie knew precisely what Bucky would say, giving back a snort of his own: *But Mister Chairman! Spaceship Earth is spinning at its equator at a thousand miles an hour and orbiting the sun at one million miles each day. Are you dizzy now?*

It was Frankie's idea to present a rose to every lady who attended the opening of the sales model of Tomorrow Living Apartments. "A corsage," insisted Reiko. "A rose corsage."

The renting, however, was left to the real estate agent. It wouldn't do for Frankie to show his face there. The morning of the open house, he spread out the newspaper for his mother. The advertisement took up a quarter of the page, with his tower sketched at water's edge. It had cost him a lot to buy that quarter-page, but the Chairman had insisted.

His mother touched each word there with her calloused fingertip, as Frankie read it aloud for her:

NOW RENTING:
Tomorrow Living High-Rise Apartments
Canada's Largest Apartment House Project!
Combine the Pleasures of Suburban Living with the
Convenience of the City and Beautiful Lake Views
Open House Today 2 to 5 p.m.

She sighed deeply, and murmured out the rest, each word in her English broken in two or three: "Mar-ble walls and flo-ors." She laboured on through "air-conditioned laundry rooms with automatic washing, drying and ironing machines. Rooftop sundeck overlooking lake."

It took a long time for her to be done, but when she was, she patted her son's hand.

Frankie moved his family in first. Every unit was rented. There was now a waiting list. Concrete and sawdust was everywhere, unsettled, but it was magic dust and the magic light streaming in over the lake held it afloat. Frankie guided his mother to the large windows Uri had insisted on and watched her take in the view. Reiko followed, with Baby Yuri in her arms. Momoye glanced down at the old fishing boat whose owner would not sell. "Who lives there?"

"No one," he said hastily. Instead, Frankie steered his mother toward a view of the new expressway rising in the west. "Mama, look at that!" It was an unravelling ribbon: that unobstructed strip for only cars was a manmade miracle, a miracle made by the Chairman and named after himself. Frankie had never seen anything like it: six lanes hugging the lakeshore, then rising above it, an archway of asphalt and concrete, speeding people in and out of the city, lit by night with lamplight torches.

"Oh, Frankie," said Reiko, overwhelmed at his side. She bounced Baby Yuri to get his attention. "Your daddy built this."

The Chairman kept paving the way for more of what he named Harbour City, spreading west along the lake in tandem with his unfurling expressway. Frankie and Uri kept building, one tower financing the next, each the same as the tower before it. Uri admired the uniformity of them, he told Hannah and Frankie. *Like sentinels guarding the shore identically at attention.*

"Build 'em!" the Chairman liked to shout while slapping a back or two. "Build 'em high!" He'd down a gulp from his flask and offer one to Frankie and Uri.

The streetcars to and from the quays were full each morning and evening, office workers elbow to elbow with the dock, factory and construction workers. Cars rumbled past fresh excavations with cranes perched high above them, and in front, large signs read HANES DEVELOPMENTS.

Business was booming, and yet Frankie's coffers still needed filling for the next project, and the next. It was the way of the world, he'd now learned. At the end of each month, Aki brought to him her earnings from the garment factory, as always, and his mother deposited High Hope's Theatre's profits. Because only Frankie knew what to do with money: he was growing it, every last penny.

Baby Yuri was not growing. It seemed to Frankie that the Mongolian spot had sprawled wider while the boy's behind itself had not. He rarely walked. He gargled words but never spoke them. Momoye and Reiko both claimed to understand him, but hardly ever agreed on what was being said. The doctor referred them to specialists who told Frankie and Reiko to be patient and let nature take its course. But where would nature lead?

"Bad luck, bad luck," his mother fretted. A bad-luck number four must have figured somewhere along the way to stunt him. That was her reasoning for everything that didn't go the way it should. Yet they'd been blessed by the slimmest of margins: he'd been born early in the morning of the fifth of May.

"He's just stubborn," Reiko said. "He doesn't want to grow. He wants to stay on his mother's lap."

"Nonsense," Frankie snapped. As the years passed the boy still preferred crawling to walking, babbling to talking. His gaze was forever darting, never resting eye to eye with any-one's, not even Reiko's. In their spacious apartment, Frankie heard his mother chanting at all hours behind the door of the bedroom she shared with Taiji. She mumbled calculations of dates and times and other numerical factors, multiplying superstitions he could not keep up with. The small altar in the corner of the living room became more and more cramped with oranges, pears, cups of tea, bowls of rice and flowers offered to Buddha. Behind its photograph of Yas, Frankie discovered, lurked the Priest in his robes, snipped from the old picture of him and Momoye as a young bride. The room began to smell briny, sour and sugary all at once.

The small compact case held a crescent of pale, sweet-smelling pressed powder inside, instantly familiar when Frankie opened it. It was the scent of the Ladies: he was stepping inside their house once more, with tiny Jesus on the cross above his bed, and the view through lace curtains of the road home to Port Alberni. It felt heavy in his hand, but he suspected it was only plated in gold.

In the bathroom, he slid down his pants and bent forward, twisting his neck to see the compact mirror behind him. Yes, there was spot, the same, it seemed, no smaller, no larger. Maybe a shade lighter, something that happened with age, he'd heard, as the body starts to run low on its resources. He smelled the sweet—sickly sweet—powder and remembered the Ladies' hushed breath and soft touch as they examined the spot.

The door cracked open door and there was Baby Yuri, standing, his fists bunched, his nose scrunched at the sight of his father, pants down, hunched over. The boy's eyes fixed brightly on the compact in his father's hand. He grabbed the compact in his own quick paw. "Mine!" he gargled and scooted away.

Frankie hitched up his pants and scrambled into the hallway, shouting after him. "Come back!"

He found the boy in a bedroom corner behind his crib among a growing collection of balls, twigs, leaves, stones. Toy cars, tiddlywinks. He was trying to pry open the compact with his chubby fingers. Frankie tried to take it from him, but Baby Yuri wriggled under the crib and out the door. Frankie had never seen him move so quickly. "Give that back!" he called. Finally he cornered the boy and yanked the compact out of his fingers, but it slipped and fell open to the floor, splintering the glass and sprinkling the powder like pink snow into the air. "No, no, no!" Frankie cried. The boy's face went pale and frightened and he scampered away.

Frankie gathered the bits of glass and the compact, now unhinged in two. The smell was everywhere, sickly sweet. He nearly gagged as he was cleaning it up. The powder covered his hands, making them pink and pale. He remembered discovering the compact in a drawer beside the bed in the Ladies' house, how he'd used the powder to try to cover the spot. To make the Ladies believe the bruise had disappeared.

"You see there, my dear boy?" said Bucky, leaning over him toward the airplane window. "More signs of humans' colonizing activity." Again Frankie was rising into the sky with Bucky over Lake Ontario, taking off to the *out there*. His first plane ride. He spied his own Tomorrow Living high-rises shrinking, as if into the long ago and far away.

On a napkin, Bucky quickly sketched the sphere of Earth with spikes and boxes jutting out from all along its rounded surface. He scribbled a plane, a bird and inexplicably, a baby hovering just above the planet. "Your child already sees planes crossing the sky as natural to him as birds."

The lake shimmered and then melted under clouds that hid everything below, and the plane passed through them like nothing. They must be impossibly high up—or out, as Bucky would say. Frankie could almost believe that heaven—the heaven the Ladies back in Port Alberni had spoken of, where Yas, his first baby and Bucky's child might've gone—was not much farther out.

"Here you are, Frank, with a young child. As I was. A chance to look after this new life. This is the beginning of impossible things happening. Where people live now needs attention. The way we build. We don't have to build with tons of heavy bricks and mortar compressed into earth. We can use the kind of technology that we use at sea and in the sky and see how it works on land. We can build houses so light they can be picked up and carried wherever, whenever we want.

"Here's the real news, my dear boy," Bucky said. "It is feasible to take care of all of humanity at a higher standard of living than anybody has ever experienced or dreamt of; to do so without having anybody profit at the expense of another."

Bucky stared at him for a long moment with his big, blurred-behind-glasses eyes. "Now, is Guinea Pig F going to make money or make sense?"

Frankie didn't know quite what to say. He wanted to make money; that was truer than ever. He never wanted to be told where he could or couldn't live. Didn't that make sense? He turned to Bucky, but he'd already settled back in his seat, closed his eyes and spread his hands to meet at their fingertips.

Frankie closed his eyes too.

Moments later, it seemed, there were domes flying this way and that outside the plane window, Bucky's domes, each dangling at the end of a line suspended from helicopters, one after another along a vast white plain. A reverie, straight from one of Bucky's letters. *You see, my dear boy? Lightful houses. Stepping stones. Set down anywhere.*

One newspaper called him *Frank Hanes, Rising Son on the Waterfront,* brightening the blighted shore. Another warned of the *Concrete Wall* he was building with his high-rises in a row. It was true his buildings hoarded their view of the lake, but why not? Wasn't that view what his renters' money was buying them?

Storeys below along Lake Ontario, Frankie surveyed the giant cranes perched over holes gouged in the ground lifting great and unwieldy loads made possible by Bucky's octet truss invention of some kind of triangulated tension. The high-rises were being rented out faster than he could build them.

Frankie opened the drawer in which he stored everything Bucky had ever sent him and took out the napkin. He carefully smoothed out the rumpled Spaceship Earth sketched by Bucky's hand, fringed with his own high-rises and one lone spike jutting farthest out: the Empire State Building. Frankie riffled through the drawer until he found the old photograph of Bucky in 1932 atop a building in New York City with that tallest of spires behind him. Who had taken the picture and from where? His face was tilted to the sky, open to the future.

And yet, Bucky confided, he'd felt unmoored at the time. His significance in the universe still obscure to himself.

Up they went, all of them rising together. It felt like the elevator was inside him, instead of him inside it. Like a rocket about to tear through the top of him, soar out of the building, into the sky. Frankie looked to his mother and Taiji. They both stared at their feet, as if unconvinced they could be rising so rapidly when the floor was staying put. The doors opened. One by one they stepped out, Reiko tottering on new, higher-than-usual heels.

There was New York City, the mighty megalopolis, spreading out, growing on every side of them, even as they stood there. If you watched carefully, you might see movement in each square inch of space way down there. People inside buildings and on the streets; machines starting, stopping, carting, dumping, all below the drifting clouds. And to think, all the while the whole ship rotating at a thousand miles an hour and, as Bucky would say, *as all the while the quadrillions of atomic components of which man is composed intergyrate and transform at seven million miles per hour.* You couldn't see it, but it was happening. He felt it inside himself. The roiling in his head and his belly, the tilting and pressure on his one foot. He was movement, like all Earthians: a verb sailing forth, as Bucky wrote, not a noun.

But was it all mystery or all knowable?

Reiko held tightly to her husband as the crowds jostled for a position at the perimeter. It was like they were on a ride at the old amusement park at Sunnyside, thought Frankie. She smiled at him, her teeth chattering, though it wasn't so cold. Her Frankie had brought them on this adventure and wasn't it something, she was surely thinking.

After she'd gone inside, he walked around the observation deck. On an adjacent building a short distance below, he saw a man standing on the rooftop, looking up. Could it be Bucky, the young Bucky in that old picture? Younger than Frankie was now, but already a father who'd lost a child, yet determined to make impossible things happen. Suddenly, the man moved, appeared to twist as if about to dance, then dropped out of sight. Frankie's heart froze. But in a second the man reappeared, walking toward the rooftop door.

When they arrived back in Toronto, Frankie took the napkin with Bucky's sketch and carefully drew another building on Spaceship Earth, a tower dwarfing his own high-rises, climbing out over Uri's Towers of Finance and the Empire State Building. The spire reached beyond the clouds, and there he saw himself, at its peak.

=====

Give me something to do, Taiji's drooping face seemed to say after he'd set a fresh orange and a bowl of rice in front of Yas's picture. Now that there were no logs to roll, no sawmill or hungry mouths to feed.

Of course he'd never ask that of Frankie.

Not in those words, at least.

Taiji surprised him that afternoon. The new tower was almost finished on the outside, but inside, much remained to be done. Frankie had already set up his office. The site at ground level was busy with trucks rolling in and out. The foreman had sent Taiji straight up in the elevator, tote bag in hand.

"We're higher than the Empire State," Frankie said proudly.

Taiji sat himself down by the window. He silently gazed at the lake far below.

Ahh! He remembered why he'd come. He wanted to show Frankie the book he'd brought with him, but the bag was no longer on the ledge beside him. He glanced around in confusion. It was still on the ledge where he'd left it, but the room, with him and Frankie in it, had rotated forty-five degrees. The view out the window now faced southwest instead of south.

"The room is moving," Frankie explained. Rotating like Spaceship Earth itself. One could enjoy the view, all 360 degrees of it, without shifting seats. He couldn't wait to bring Bucky aboard.

"Can you make it slow down?"

Frankie laughed. "It's not going that fast."

Miraculously, Taiji had found this book in the library. He'd never known there were such places freely lending such a book. He opened it in front of Frankie. There was Canada. There was British Columbia. There was Vancouver Island. The north of Vancouver Island. The scratches of rivers and creeks grew larger on each map. Taiji traced his way from the capital city, Victoria, as he had those years ago, to the upper reaches of the island. He turned the page to one on which the creek and river, mountain and valley were large on the page.

"See?" he jabbed at the book four times.

Frankie turned the book to see. "Yes, yes, Papa," he said. "I see."

"Mine. I own. I claim." Taiji jabbed his thumb at his own chest. He watched Frankie's face.

"Are you sure, Papa?" Frankie said. They both looked at the map and the name: Hansoke. Hansoke Creek, Hansoke River, Hansoke Mountain, Hansoke Valley.

"Yes! Before you were born." *Didn't Frankie see?*

But he wanted to tell Frankie more, to warn him to be careful, as he had not been.

On the island, he'd followed a small creek through towering forests to the foot of a mountain. He found the nearest town and hired the only men who understood him: young Japanese loitering in the local bar, some gambling at cards. A few others too, local Indians who resembled untouchables back in Japan.

He found a Japanese bookkeeper who knew English well. The man had been in Canada for years. Smart man. *Stake your claim,* he said. At the registry office they took it all down: the creek and river, the mountain and the forested valley. Hanesaka Mountain, Hanesaka River, Hanesaka Valley. He wasn't the first to discover these places, but he was first to claim them.

The camp prospered. The men were happy; women arrived and one-room cabins were built in Hanesaka Valley for young families. He was saving his profits to take back to Japan.

The bookkeeper danced down Hanesaka Lane with the ladies on their way to the bath. The way to keep the men working hard, he told Taiji, was to spark the spirits of their women.

The forests were endless; no sooner had the men felled them than another leafy wall rose before them. Taiji rode his horse among the workers, just as his father had ridden in the rice fields.

The trees kept falling. The men kept chopping until one day the ocean was before them. They dropped their axes and saws. The endless forest had ended. Taiji was scaling his mountain at the time, and watched from above. The wall had been shaved bare.

The men were dumbstruck, but quickly began packing up their homes. *Where next, Boss?* they asked. Taiji ran down to see the bookkeeper. The bookkeeper would know what to do, where to go.

But he was gone, along with his wife. The book was blank save for a few scribbles. The lacquer box where the bookkeeper kept the money was empty.

Taiji stood abruptly, straightening himself. "Be careful of this man you think you can trust."

"Mr. Slonemsky is a good man. I know," Frankie said.

"Yes, yes," Taiji nodded thoughtfully. "Probably so." He put the book in his tote bag and got up.

"Just remember that if you keep building, the land will run out."

It was beyond Modern, beyond Tomorrow: it was The Future. Once completed—which it almost was—it would be the tallest in the world. Cloud Tower would be 117 storeys tall (a number to which Frankie's mother did not object), including a broadcast tower and antenna. Higher than the Eiffel Tower, Tokyo Tower, and one storey higher than the Empire State Building. Beyond *-er*: it was *-est*. He and Uri had found the best engineers to design the tallest, sleekest tower; its elevators zipping up the sides at 1,200 feet per minute: the fastest. They could take you highest quickest, surpassing take-off in even a jet plane. You'd have to swallow the most times during the seventy seconds of the longest elevator ride of any elevator ride in history. It would have more stairs than any other structure: 2,570.

From the highest office suite, Frankie saw the lake as a great sea. Soon he would hear the city loud and clear because of the broadcast tower and its signal bringing news of the world—of the universe!—to everyone.

Uri Slonemsky was, of course, its architect. If Cloud Tower was to tower over his own Towers of Finance, his U-Building, he didn't mind. It was new ground to break and a vital addition to his modern lexicon: a towering, unequivocal, singular, self-declaring, capital *I*. There were the construction triumphs: the hexagonal concrete shaft at its core, the tapered contour. *The engineering wonder! Marvel of telecommunications bringing the clearest reception of radio and television in all of North America.*

On the observation deck level, a solid glass floor would overlook the ground from 110 storeys up. Whoever dared could cross the floor with only a pane of glass between them and a plummet to earth.

The Chairman was proclaiming Cloud Tower soon to be the World's Tallest Free-Standing Structure, a boon for tourism, a landmark to stand the test of time. Again, it was the Chairman who had spread the loam at City Hall. No roadblocks so long as 1,500 workers were working twenty-four hours a day, five days a week. With half the country watching on television, a giant helicopter flew into the city to lift the forty-four pieces of antenna into place.

If he could, Taiji would chop down Cloud Tower, and in its place, plant a forest of spruces. Frankie had asked him and the rest of the family to meet him there on a Sunday afternoon, for a private tour before the building opened to the public.

Taiji had gone first to shop in Chinatown. Now he waited at the lobby elevator, and waited. The place was empty of workers, who often rode the elevator with him. The building site was quiet with only the occasional rumble and hiss of trains pulling into nearby Union Station. It was some special holiday, and for once Frankie had given them the day off.

The elevator didn't come. Taiji waited for several minutes with his bags of groceries balanced in each hand, then made his way to the stairwell. He began to climb, slowly. From the bottom, he shouted out each number to echo and spiral to the top. He would make sure Frankie hadn't been cheated of even one of the promised 2,570 steps.

He climbed on. Surely he had stepped this many steps and more while rolling logs; surely he had walked more steps from Hanesaka Mountain to Desolation Sound to Port Alberni. Surely, he had balanced as many footsteps on rooftops in the camp. This was nothing to him, he thought, climbing faster, if only one step at a time. He pushed himself faster yet, not noticing that the egg-plants and cucumbers and rice cakes were tumbling from his bags. Down they rolled as he rose, first to land on step 4, then 44, then 444. Taiji was toting nearly empty bags at his sides, lighter than air as he climbed. *One thousand!* he shouted up. Everything was growing lighter. The air in his lungs he could barely feel; there was nothing to breathe, it was so light. Each heartbeat touched the other so that there was no beat, just a hum in his chest. He must be travelling downstream instead of up; this must be how Yas had felt, carried along the current.

When he reached the top, he called: *two thousand, five hundred and seventy-two!* Two more steps. Momoye wouldn't like that, he chuckled to himself. Digits adding up to sixteen, divisible by four. But he'd have to tell Frankie, who was always after a good deal: he had gotten two extra steps for his money.

CHAPTER 11

Up and Down

It was Frankie who found him. In the foyer near the stair-well door. He crouched down and tapped Taiji's cheek. His eyes were open, looking beyond Frankie, much as they always did.

"Look at me!" Frankie whispered. He touched Taiji's neck: cold and slack. He drew a tremulous breath and passed his hand before the eyes: gone.

He closed the lids; that was what to do, he knew. Cold stole up Frankie's middle and burrowed in.

A Buddhist prayer came to his lips, then he crossed him-self; then, remembering something Hannah had told him, he rent Taiji's already frayed collar. Or was it his own he was to tear?

Taiji was wearing the same shabby coat he'd worn back in Tashme. Frankie should've bought him a new one long ago.

He thought to drape his own coat over the body. To call whoever was to be called. Then the elevator doors dinged and opened: his mother stepped out.

Her eyes went to the floor, to Taiji. She dropped to her knees, her mouth open for a few seconds before a wail rose up.

She fell atop Taiji wailing, pounding at his chest, locked and still. She wept and cried out. Each time she grew breathless and quiet, she started up again, howling.

"Mama!" Frankie couldn't bear to see her in such anguish. He squatted helplessly among the torn shopping bags. She howled and howled, not to be consoled. That she'd let so much out!

"Shush, Mama," he said, coming near. He patted her shoulder, pulled her to come away, gently at first, then more forcefully. She pushed back, shielding Taiji's body from him. She glared fiercely.

A swish and click-click started up. Was it Taiji? Body parts could tick on while the rest expired, couldn't they? Underfoot, nearly tripping him, was Baby Yuri, knees swishing, the buckle on his shoes clicking, but not crawling: he was swimming across the unfinished cement floor, raising his short arms, taking gulps of air with a gaping fish mouth.

"Oba, Oba," he called. When he reached his grandmother, she pushed him back too.

Frankie was no consolation; nor was Baby Yuri.

Frankie picked up his son and left to call an ambulance.

As the tower neared completion, noise from above and below thinned. Fewer trucks rumbled over the site; workers who remained wielded screwdrivers, wrenches and whirring drills to render finishings. When Frankie looked up from his desk to gaze at the lake, he heard for a while the tapping of a lone hammer.

He came home to find his mother lying on a rattan mat. Frankie carried her to her room, her arm flopped over his shoulder.

"Fu-ranki," she murmured, suddenly squeezing his neck, in gratitude or protest. He took in her musty, sour scent—no

longer the burnt sweetness of brewing sake. Splotches darkened her cheeks.

"Did you count the steps? Did you?"

"Yes, Mama," Frankie said, as he'd said a hundred times
before. "There was no bad-luck four."

"Count again," she muttered. "Again." He set her on the
mattress and box spring he'd bought. She'd find her way back
to the mat on the floor in the middle of the night, he knew.

In the few months since Taiji died, the fleshiness of her body
had seemed to dry and harden without him. In her head, always,
endlessly: numbers. But not as before, calculating shrewd bar-
ters and Frankie's odds of success. No, the numbers—however
random, however sky high—nowadays and -nights came tumbling down the steps Taiji had climbed, dwindling in seconds to
four. She only glanced up to pull the miniature Baby Yuri to her
breast. The boy could wrench her back to her old cares. She held
him in the sunlight streaming through the front window to see
whose traces he bore.

But there were no traces. He was like none of them. Still
as small as a three year old; still nothing the doctors could
point to or treat. He stared too long but never into anyone's
eyes, and barely blinked; he stood and swayed as if at sea,
pinned to the bow. Momoye liked to bathe him; at eight he
was too old for it but not too big. Recently, Momoye had
noticed something else strange about him: he liked to pull
himself under the bath water and stare up from the bottom
for long spells of time. When she tried to haul him out, he
stayed under water, bubbles escaping between his few teeth.
Minutes ticked by, it seemed. When he surfaced, his breathing
was calm and even.

Now Momoye insisted on bird-bathing him, scrubbing him
down with a washcloth in the sink. But one day, she found
him with his head in the toilet, his legs kicking high in the air,
trying to tunnel through. She hauled him up and smacked

him—she still had strength enough for that. Baby Yuri simply giggled and pinched her cheek.

"Mother, he smells," Reiko declared one night as she was preparing dinner. "He needs a bath." Reiko dropped the knife with which she'd been slicing radishes. She held out her arms for her big baby.

Momoye whisked him away.

"Give me my son!" Reiko shouted as Momoye disappeared with Baby Yuri into her bedroom.

Frankie rushed into the kitchen. Reiko's entire body was arched with a fury he hadn't seen before. Her lip bled from her own teeth biting down.

"I am the mother!" Blood trickled to her chin. She approached the bedroom door. "She is not!" Reiko shoved it open. Baby Yuri lay on Momoye's big bed beside his grandmother. A plank of light crossed his face.

When Frankie took hold of her arm he felt the current surging. That first time in the graveyard he'd seen it in the air around her; it had spread to him from inside her and onto the grasses on which they'd lain. He'd forgotten.

"I am your wife, Frankie," she said now, bristling in the narrowing light, her small, bright eyes flaming. She turned abruptly and disappeared into their bedroom and in he went after her. That night, they lay down on their queen-sized bed from Eaton's department store as if it were the prickly grasses of Tashme.

The next day, Frankie ordered an apartment in the building vacated for his mother. Aki would join her.

"I'll take care of her," his sister told him. "Don't worry, Frankie." He expected his mother to resist or scold or shame him, but she didn't. It was the second time he'd taken a side apart from her, even if it was just across the hall and down.

———

Frankie placed his mother's chair by the window and there she clung to it like a snail in her shell. She sat jittery and lonely for Taiji and only Taiji. She barely looked up when her son came in with Baby Yuri, who immediately dropped to the floor.

"Get up!" Frankie commanded. The boy knew how to walk, to run, to jump, yet he was crawling like a sand crab. The boy was not right. Frankie yanked Baby Yuri to his feet. "Time for school." The boy rose only to drop back down once his father's back was turned. Frankie could barely look at him. It embarrassed him, the boy acting like a dog or a monkey. The teachers at his school didn't know what to do.

When Momoye dozed off, Baby Yuri climbed onto his grandmother, straddling the single mountain of her breasts and belly. He bounced and yelped and she began to babble, first in hoarse whispers, then in a deep, guttural growl—sounds, Frankie realized, mimicked by Baby Yuri. The boy paused to listen before climbing down and crawling toward the bathroom.

She woke startled, and her hand flew to her mouth. Her hair, turned snowy in the season since Taiji's death, fell over her eyes even as she pushed it aside.

Number four?

She was lost.

"No, Mama, it's thirty-eight," Frankie said, choosing a safe number. He left her to add digits, divide and multiply her Old World worries.

Frankie found Baby Yuri in the bathroom, gurgling, just as Reiko had reported: head in the toilet with his legs bouncing. Baby Yuri raised his head with a giggle upon hearing his name called, spewing the toilet water. Frankie wiped him roughly and scooped him up in his arms, only to have him wriggle free and bound back to his grandmother's lap.

Momoye held tight to Baby Yuri until the last possible moment. She babbled furiously even as Frankie led him out the door.

Lately Reiko had begun to feel the oddest sensation of their apartment building leaning to one side, maybe even toppling. *Just what was anchoring it below?*

"Don't be silly," Frankie said with a laugh, as he put on his new silk tie. Tonight was the opening of Cloud Tower. "It's steel and concrete."

"You know I never liked heights."

Did he know that? He did notice that his wife quivered with each creak or whistle of wind at the window. That she rarely stood at the window, and she often rapped her broom on the floor and walls at echoing voices and footsteps.

Frankie had shown her pictures of sprawling, luxurious houses he was building in the suburbs, the winding, irregular roads they sat on with wide drives. She didn't want that either. She'd have to learn to drive, and the lots were too big, the houses, big as they were, marooned within. *Oh, so lonely.*

She missed Tashme. She missed her father, whose spirit lingered there, she was sure. She did not like this big city where there was no place to feel sameness and order; no Tashme Town Hall, no Japantown, as in Vancouver. Men on the streets careened too close with grimy outstretched hands. She had always been a no-nonsense kind of girl, and Toronto held too much nonsense for her to bear.

When she walked down the street people stared, not admiringly or with envy. At the corner grocer's, the man spoke loudly and slowly, as if she weren't Canadian-born and bred, *as if she couldn't understand English just fine, thank you very much.*

She had thought of Frankie as no-nonsense, like her father, like herself. But he'd changed. Changed his name—and hers. *She didn't look like a Mrs. Frank Hanes!*

Before it had been Momoye, now it was the Jewish woman filling him with this nonsense. She who sat in her purple pyjamas never getting properly dressed day or night, who stroked his hands and called him Frank.

"Please," Frankie said, with a hint of pleading. He wanted her by his side this night of all nights, high among the clouds. He looked into her small, bespectacled eyes and touched her curls. He carefully led her to the window where Cloud Tower was lit up. "Look how far we've come," he said.

It was true. She was proud. But then she'd felt proud parading down Tashme Boulevard with Frankie's arm around her shoulder. She'd always loved to dress up, especially in the camp. The rose pin Frankie had given her on her collar, lipstick from the drugstore in Hope, red on her lips.

"Whose silly idea was it to build the tallest tower in the world, anyway?" she said.

So they set out, Frankie in his finest tailor-made suit and Reiko wearing a dress made of jade silk her father had brought years ago from Japan. Though Tomorrow Living for Today Apartments were walking distance from Cloud Tower, they arrived by limousine with Momoye and Aki and Baby Yuri.

Inside the tower, Reiko's high-heeled foot wavered over the elevator's threshold. She could not step on. She insisted that Frankie, Momoye and Aki go on while she collected herself.

Frankie watched her seat herself on a bench opposite the elevator, holding on to their son. But just as the doors were closing, the boy bounded aboard.

It was April and all day the sun had shone, but by evening, the sky had knit up with clouds. Guests stood on the revolving deck, clinking their glasses beneath the broadcast tower as blackness pitched back their reflections from the windows.

Frankie cued the dimming of the lights so that the city sparkled back to a collective *ahh*.

He settled his mother on a window seat. She accepted a glass of wine from him. Beside her on the ledge sat purses, while the ladies who owned them rotated ever so slowly past. Filled with strangers, Frankie's office was transformed. As was the foyer where Taiji had died. The floor he'd fallen to was now laid with polished marble. Momoye held onto Frankie's sleeve for a moment, then let go. She shooed him off to attend to his business.

Frankie headed into the press of guests, his face shiny and sheepish. Uri Slonemsky was on one side, Hannah Slonemsky on the other, enfolding him in her purple wings. They seemed about to carry him up into the sky: their Rising Son!

"*I!*" Uri Slonemsky was declaring above the din to whomever would listen. "The tower is an *I!* Ninth letter of the alphabet."

Frankie looked back to his mother. Nine, she was sighing with relief, no doubt. She cupped her hands around her eyes to see out onto the lake. He caught a glimpse of Baby Yuri standing at the glass near the door. Uri saw him too, and met Frankie's eyes. The strange boy was bumping up against it, gently, rhythmically, refusing its existence. But for that glass, the boy would slip over the tower's lip and down. His small, round face with its round eyes was pressed to the window; his open mouth, a hot circle on the glass. He was staring, like his grandmother, at where he thought the water was down in the darkness. To Frankie's relief, Aki pulled him aside.

The muffled din of the party went on. The door to the stairwell squeaked. Aki just missed noticing Baby Yuri vanish behind it.

Down, down, down Baby Yuri flew, his legs cycling, then flying over steps at a time, and spiralling from the two-thousandth step to the thousandth and then hundredth, round and round, his giggles ricocheting against the cement walls. It was better than a train ride. When he reached the bottom step, he bolted out into the night and the cold wind.

As soon as Aki realized where Baby Yuri had gone, she stumbled into the too-bright stairwell. The stairs went on and on. Her one eye couldn't locate him, but she could hear his steps, or was that the echo of her own? She could hear his burbling, or was that the muted roar of the trains nearby? When she burst outside, the wind blew snow into her face. She could barely make out a figure in the distance that had to be Baby Yuri. She called his name but the gale tossed her cries back to her. She tried to run but was pushed back and back again. Yet the tiny figure inched forward, snow collecting around it. Baby Yuri? How could it be? Finally the wind pinned her to the concrete wall that rose more than a hundred storeys above her.

Momoye had not stirred from her spot at the room's perimeter. She glanced at Frankie every so often, straining her neck to find him rotated to a different point, still guarded by a Slonemsky on each side. Outside, a sudden dense curtain of snow closed over the window all around, only to clear momentarily into blackness.

Frankie joined her at the window. Snow in April! No one else seemed to notice.

Reiko had not come. Had she gone home? And where was the rest of his family? Where were Baby Yuri and Aki?

He recalled glimpsing them near the door to the stairwell, or maybe it was Baby Yuri crawling alone there, grabbing at the handle. He'd thought to stop his son, but Uri was introducing him to someone. Surely Aki with her watchful eye was hovering close by. But a security guard was approaching him now. The man reported an alarm had sounded at the base of the tower: someone had gone down the stairs and out an emergency exit. The room stopped for a moment, then swirled faster and faster in its rotation. Frankie wheeled to face the window, but it had turned to a skyline of buildings. He ran to the elevator and pounded the button with his fist, and miraculously it came. The doors opened and swallowed him up and the descent began, too slow into the night.

When the snow stopped falling as quickly as it had appeared, Frankie found Aki a short distance from the tower. Squatting, praying. Her rapid breathing pumped steam from her lungs. "No, no, no," she was crying.

Once the wind had subsided, she'd come to where she'd last spotted Baby Yuri. But there was nothing there. All signs had vanished. Had the snow tricked her? She'd run around and around, searching.

Frankie slumped down in the dusting of snow and looked up to the tower. *Mama!* he cried, but nothing came out and no one came down. *Help me, Mama!*

Hannah appeared, pulling him under her purple wings. "Oh, Frank," she whispered. "They'll find him." There was a swarm of people now, policemen, firemen.

But still no Yuri.

Mama, he cried again, eyes dry as bones.

Momoye had given up waiting for the elevators. So many people were trying to leave. She went to the stairwell and began to climb down, as quickly as she could, which was slow, and counting each step. Down, down, down the same steps Baby Yuri had descended and Taiji had climbed. Finally she reached the bottom: two thousand, five hundred and seventy-two. She knew right away, no matter how the numbers were added and divided, four was the answer. Outside was her Frankie, lost in the night, calling after Baby Yuri. The boy would not be found. He was gone.

The search went on all night, circles of light flashing over the open terrain around the tower. It was broadcast on television and radio, more clearly than ever before, images and voices unghosted by shadows or echoes, because of the tower's 350-foot-high antenna. Frankie sat with Aki in the tower as it turned, waiting for news they knew would not come. They sat like rags hanging onto the last rung, though they sat high in the sky.

Police came on horseback, scouring bushes and deserted waterfront lots to find the missing boy. But his footprints in that one night of April snow had immediately melted away, sunk into the earth. The newscasters could not help but remark that the rich and powerful Mr. Industry had not been able to keep his son safe.

Frankie was cursed. Cursed. Twice over; maybe more.

CHAPTER 12

Man in the Tower

In autumn, migrating birds flew into the sides of Cloud Tower every night: swallows, starlings, pigeons, seagulls, blue jays. Hundreds dropped from the sky to form a garish carnival feathering the base. They'd been confused by the powerful lights shining out from the tower.

In the spring, the search was officially abandoned and Reiko returned to Tashme. She left only a note and the rose brooch; its red glaze had completely peeled away.

Good bye going home, she'd written in her childish hand. He could not blame her.

Frankie looked up from his desk in the rotating office, and there in the clouds was Baby Yuri: his tiny eyes peeking out. Two round cut-outs of clear sky through cloud. There'd been nothing of Frankie or Reiko in the creature, no reason, no self-discipline: mystery was all.

It was late afternoon and Frankie was overtaken by exhaustion. He let his head drop onto his desk, cheek and palms resting on the ledger sheet. He was sure he could feel the tower rotating with the Earth away from the sun. Since meeting Bucky, he'd banished from his imagination the foolish idea of sunrises and sunsets that all the world embraced.

Frankie roused himself, slapped his cheeks and noticed the rows of numbers blotted onto his hands. Out the window, the view had turned ninety degrees.

Frankie's blocks of high-rise buildings weren't growing as fast now. The Chairman was gone and so were his old associates. It wasn't as easy to seed a path past permits, zoning restrictions, union regulations. Below, his wall of high-rises was broken only by that narrow strip of land belonging to the old fisherman who wouldn't sell. His decrepit boat leaned at water's edge. An eyesore: Uri's word. Frankie's eyes smarted from all the looking at it and willing it to be gone.

Even after some years, Cloud Tower was still the tallest structure in the world. With Reiko gone, he'd moved himself in, setting up simple living quarters. It was and would be, as Uri pronounced at its opening, majestic and lasting.

Behind Frankie's stacks of accounts payable, accounts receivable, forms and contracts lay a batch of unsorted letters, one of which was from Augusta, on behalf of herself and Julia. Aki arrived that afternoon to fish it out for him and make him open it. He stood up when he saw her, thought to embrace her but stopped himself. He surprised himself how happy— relieved—he was to see her. It had been months. He thought to ask about their mother but didn't.

The letter—addressed as it was to Frankie Hanesaka, someone he no longer was—had been buried, willfully passed over. The letter was dated almost a year ago.

"They'll be arriving next week," Aki told him.

"To live?" Frank asked. At last, to live. He let out a sigh, some small part of him longing for the days when he sat as his little sister's audience of one.

"To visit," Aki said. He looked over the letter, which was written in a graceful hand. At the end it read:

Dear Brother, Can you please pay us back our money
as soon as possible?
  Your loving sisters,
  Augusta and Julia
  p.s. We saw your Tower on the television.

Below that, a sum written out carefully in dollars and cents. As if he hadn't grown that little molehill into a mountain. As if he hadn't done that for them, for the whole family. As if he weren't their brother, their flesh and blood.

But the money, they claimed, was needed now that High Hope's Theatre was sinking. It was not a large amount, and interest was not requested. Merely a shoring up of hopes for the theatre to continue. Repairs to the roof and stage were needed as well as new folding chairs for a new season that would include a production of *Three Sisters*. They were thrifty enough to get their wardrobes from the local Sally Ann, but both Julia and Augusta needed special orthopaedic shoes because of painful bunions.

Frankie folded up the letter and put it inside his desk drawer. He resisted the impulse to tear it up.

"You will pay them back, won't you, Frankie?" Aki asked with her one good eye fixed on him. "It's not very much. Not for Frank Hanes."

After Reiko left, there'd been no reason for his mother and Aki not to move in with Frankie. But they had not, and he had not asked them to. And though he kept paying the bills, Momoye refused even to stay in Tomorrow Living for Today High-Rise Apartments. Where would she go? Back to Tashme with the girls? Back to that ghost town?

She had ventured out with a shadow of her old gumption. Her pigeon-toed steps had grown shorter without Baby Yuri to chase. Her handbag swung from the crook of her arm. There was nowhere to plant her feet, except on the road hugging Frankie's wall of high-rise after high-rise with their gated drives. Its end was out of sight. He hadn't even thought to build sidewalks. Cars honked and swerved around her. She kept on; after a while, it was difficult to tell how long she'd been walking or how far she'd come: what time of day was it? Her shallow gumption drained with the daylight. She remembered marching into Port Alberni to barter her bottles of sake for food. The shame of it all. What would her mother have said, seeing her like this? An old woman long past her time: a few coins jangling in her purse, a son and grandchild gone, and no one to look after her. Her brother had deserted their mother for New World adventures. Frankie had done the same.

Taiji had often scolded Momoye for giving Frankie more than his fair share. *He's worth more than the rest of them put together,* she'd once retorted. The girls had heard; Yas too. It was the truth and she couldn't take it back.

Then, a break in the wall: no gate, no high-rise wedged against the next. A lake breeze and opening of light. She stepped off the road. Before her lay a stretch leading down to the lake strewn with rocks and sand, chunks of concrete and asphalt, and bits of garbage. Not so different from the stretch on the Alberni Strait the day she and Taiji had cast off in their house.

There at the shore, alongside a dock half sinking into the lake, was moored a small ship with a rusting hull. A man with a whorl of white hair sat on its slanting deck. He waved as she stepped closer and uttered something she couldn't understand. It was English dipped in a strange sea. He was an old man, older than her.

"Hello, there," he beckoned, and slapped his palm on the side of the ship. Jim, he called himself, Captain Jim. He was a fisherman. Momoye knew fishermen, of course; she'd grown up by the sea, lived on it. Fishermen didn't talk much, which suited her. He limped to greet her, inviting her aboard.

The ship had once been a fire tug, he explained, then part freighter, part passenger ferry. Inside was different from the rust and flaking paint outside: larger, grander, straight up and down, level, over and across. It had last been a restaurant with its kitchen in its middle, and all around, from bow to stern, stood tables plated with dust, candles burnt to stubs. There'd been music and a dance floor pocked by ladies' high heels.

"Nobody comes now," he said. "The party's over."

He set out a chair for her on the crooked aft deck, facing the lake and the setting sun. He sat on another chair and cast a line into the harbour. Every day, he told her, a trout or a walleye. By sundown, he was grilling fish for the two of them.

"This," Momoye said, pointing to the wall and then to the tower above, "my son make."

Frankie waited by the elevator. He was nervous. He hadn't seen his youngest sisters in years. Augusta, his tap-dancing, singing Augusta who'd kept him company when no one else would. Yet when it counted most, she'd left him. When he'd done so much for her, for all of them.

He paced the floor in circles. They were late.

He paced over his glass floor. Tempered glass, two and a half inches thick and a layer of air inside. One thousand, one hundred and twenty-two feet up and he could see dots below that he knew were the tops of children's heads.

Two columns on the newspaper's Metro page and a picture of three bandy-legged girls at the foot of his tower. Some woman they interviewed claimed the children were suffering from rickets in the shadow of his buildings: tired and listless, failing tests in school from not enough sunlight. He and his sisters had been bandy-legged, but no one had cried out for them. Everyone was blaming everything on his buildings. Others built tall buildings, yet he was the one they singled out. Trees were tall; mountains were tall. He'd been the city's Rising Son; now it was back to *Jap, go home*.

Maybe Reiko was right to leave. Way back when, bony-ankled little Augusta would tap her tap shoes together on the floorboards of their Tashme shack, chanting *There's no place like home*.

Frankie squatted down on his glass floor. It was solid, unbreakable. Down below him, the dots dispersed, and he saw a sleek, white head catch the sunlight. Could it be? Bucky? A thousand feet below? Magnified as if by the thick lenses of his own eyeglasses. He was holding his blue megaphone.

Julia and Augusta stood at the base of Cloud Tower, where Aki had brought them. "At the feet of the giant!" said Augusta. She backed her heels against the tower and stretched herself tall. "How many of us would it take to reach the top?" A hundred, a thousand, standing on each other's shoulders? Everything in the big city was high, out of reach, even on tippy-toes. It was, the sisters supposed, not so different from living among the mountains. But it wasn't until they rode the train east right through the centre of those very mountains—a magician's trick—that they fully took the measure of their dimensions. In the city, the sisters were mice without tails, looking for tunnels to pass through.

Voices of children came straggling around the bend. "You are my sunshine!" they chirped. A ring of mothers clasping the hands of pale toddlers and cane-wielding elderly was forming around the base of the tower. Aki recognized the families who lived in two old tenement buildings near the fish shop where she now worked. Cramped cold-water flats that decades ago housed returning soldiers from the war and their families. The buildings were separated by a dusty, rusting playground filled with broken see-saws and swings that rattled in the wind. Laundry hung out, but never seemed to dry because there was no sunlight in the shadow of Frankie's high-rises and the Chairman's expressway. Only gloom.

"Please don't take my sunshine away!" Augusta sang out, tuning her voice an octave down from the general chorus; her swollen feet were sluggish but tapped cheerfully on the pavement.

Sad-eyed, furrow-browed mothers stood by their crooked-limbed children, all of them singing. The children were munchkins from *The Wizard of Oz* waiting for the wicked witch to be gone. Augusta had read of the real lives of the Singer Midgets of the movie, paid half for their half-size. It seemed the world shortchanged small people. Strapping American airmen had dropped the bombs on the small people of Hiroshima, after all: small as ants seen from the planes above.

A woman approached, her hair a dark wave cresting around her head, her eyes so wide and fixed they were not to be escaped. "Will you help us help the children?" she asked, then held up a flyer: a child's crayoned orange circle and rays blazing over happy faces beneath.

Augusta dropped some pennies into the donation box. To think her pennies had helped build this tower.

A clipboard with a place to sign her name appeared too.

"We have to stop them from building more high-rises. We could have trees and sunshine here. A park by the lake for children to play." Behind them, photographers were snapping pictures of the mothers and their children.

"Stop who?" Augusta asked, though she feared the answer.

The woman tilted her chin to the top of the tower, way up to its impossibly highest point, teeny-tiny in the sky, to where Frankie might be looking down on them.

========

At last Frankie heard their voices, still girlish and chatty. They burst through the doors.

"Frankie!" Augusta sighed. She took deep breaths. "We were so tired, we had to stop between the fifty-first and fifty-second floors. We had a picnic on the landing!"

And there was Julia. They looked so old to Frankie. Old girls, with long hair streaked with grey. Round shoulders and thick waists in frilled dresses. Aki hung back behind them.

"Julia didn't want to take the elevator," said Augusta. "I told her it was safe, of course. Frankie built it!"

"Two thousand, five hundred and seventy-two steps," Julia announced. "Mama won't approve. You could divide it by four."

Then, shyly, they embraced him, one by one.

"You look distinguished," Augusta said. She gave her curtsy and they all laughed. They were the same after all.

He led them to his office. Augusta stopped in front of the sign that read FRANK HANES and traced it with her finger. "No wonder you didn't get our letters," she tsk-tsked. "They were for Frankie Hanesaka."

They looked him over as he had them: his fine clothes, his fine desk, the view.

"You're King of the Castle," Augusta laughed. Though not everybody liked the king, they'd noticed.

After only a moment, Augusta took a step closer. No use beating around the bush. "We need our money please, Frankie," she said politely.

Frankie was silent. He stiffened and took a step back. It was up to him to look out for and after them. He was first-born and only son. All they knew was to follow one after the other like the months they were named for. They hadn't changed, just gotten older. They provided him the measure of how far he'd come, just how high up he'd pulled himself. High Hope's was no hopes on the edge of No-Jap Land. They needed a moment to flounder without him before they'd understand.

"We're staying with Mama," Julia said quickly. So he'd know they didn't come to freeload. "Down there." She pointed where Frankie's wall lapsed. "With Captain Jim." How happy they'd been climbing aboard; something new and old at the same time.

Frankie shot to the window. "That boat?"

His mother with the old fisherman? Had she tethered herself to that wreck? To spite her own son?

"The money," Julia pleaded before she might be shushed. "Please, Frankie."

Frankie wasn't listening. Instead, he hurried them all onto the elevator. Down through the sky, pulled to Earth. Through the service exit around the back of the tower to avoid the protesters. Down the street, under the belly of the expressway, and out to the lake. He didn't look back to see where they were, but he knew they were following. Then he reached that unsightly strip of land that yawned with its beggarly mouth between the sleek high-rises he had built.

He strode onto the tumbledown dock and found his mother sitting on the boat as if in her chair on Alberni Strait. The old fisherman wasn't in sight.

He hadn't seen or spoken to her in months. But now here she was aboard a wreck with a stranger, not even a Japanese. She could never be without a man, he knew that, even at her age. She'd latch onto any man to survive. Just as she had to Taiji.

He climbed aboard, his sisters after him. Momoye looked him up and down. He stood tall and distant in his fine suit and overcoat.

"Fu-ranki," she snapped at him, as if he'd just spilled her precious sake.

"Yes, Mama?"

"Give the girls their money." She held out her palm and jabbed her finger in it. The girls weren't asking for much—a drop in the sea of his good fortune. They were middle-aged now, thick at their ankles and their middles, though they hadn't borne any children.

"I didn't take money. I made money," he said.

The shame of him hoarding his pennies when the girls were so shabby.

Aki tried to hand him a book—a bookkeeper's ledger—but he wouldn't take it. He planted his hands in the pockets of his fine coat and shook his head. She opened it to show him: more numbers, small amounts tallied up at the bottom of the page and carried over, page to page to page. With dates as far back as when he'd left Tashme. He recognized the hand.

"Papa kept this," Aki said. "We never asked him to, but he said it was important."

Frankie had never taken a penny from the girls that they themselves hadn't given away; nothing he didn't grow for them into something bigger and greater than their theatre of rickety hopes where they'd chosen to stay, stubbornly timid as mice.

Here they'd have been looked after. They knew he would take care of them; it was insulting to be made to even say it! He was, and would forever be, Man of the House.

How could his mother not know this? She used to know everything before he did. There'd been no asking. Now she was putting his sisters before him. The sisters who made him know he was the outsider with strange blood. Who cared and cried for Yas as they never had for him.

Who cared for Frankie? Who was for Frankie?

His mother stared right into his eyes. Her brows arched as fiercely as ever. "Give the money back," she said.

"Mama!" he cried. He took the ledger and threw it down, his face reddening with stopped-up tears. They trickled inside him, scalding his throat as he climbed out of the boat.

CHAPTER 13

The Man Who Couldn't Cry

Frankie knocked at the front door of the Kidney. How strange to be at the front entrance, a visitor, when he'd slipped in the back door all those years. The makeshift see-through roof had been replaced with a shingled roof, and the trees and bushes around the house had grown so thick that even the doorbell was wreathed in green. It was spruced up, yet overgrown.

His calls to Uri and Hannah had not been returned in weeks, not since those pictures of children had begun to appear in the newspapers. If their partnership was to end, no matter, Frankie told himself: he'd learned everything he needed to know. But Hannah: why had she not called? When after weeks of this silence, Frankie was summoned to the Kidney, he was relieved but uneasy.

The door opened. It was Noriko. Hair grey now, but the same.

How frail Hannah looked. How slight she felt in his arms when she embraced him. Purple chiffon still draped her shoulders, but her face was narrowed and angular, her eyes all the larger and darting.

"Frank, there's someone here who would like to see you."
His heart skipped with a memory. Anne? Annie?

She led him into the living room and on the chesterfield
sat an elderly woman, Uri beside her. She looked familiar but
he couldn't place her. He held out his hand but she ignored it.

"Frank, this is Mrs. Mayfield."

The woman stared at him in silence, letting herself be
stared at in return. He should know her. After a moment she
spoke. "You bought our home after the hurricane."

Then he remembered: the couple who'd left with only
their all-you-can-carry. They'd refused his help. He'd had to
cart the things they left behind to the Salvation Army.

"You paid us a pittance. The other families too."
Pittance. The same word Hannah's friend in the caravan
had used. They'd accept a pittance, she'd told him. Out of
desperation.

"It was all I could afford," Frankie told her, "at the time."
It was true. He'd drained his savings to buy the four houses.
But now he felt his insides draining into a burning hole in his
belly.

"But the City paid you more. Much more," Uri suddenly
said. "You knew they would." Uri stood. "You knew because
I told you, in confidence."

Uri gazed down at him. Instantly, Frankie was reduced
back into that kowtower—worse—that servant who'd learned
to sip martinis on this very seat.

He wanted to make excuses. To voice the uncertainty and
fear he'd felt at the time. How he'd convinced himself he was
helping these people, relieving their burden so they could get
on. Explain how it had been his one chance, the only chance
for him to get on.

"Yes," said Frankie. "I knew." He watched Hannah turn
away from him and then enfold the woman's one hand in both
of hers, just as she'd once held his.

Noriko was waiting to let him out. He slipped past quickly, but she gripped his arm and looked into his eyes.

"You were smarter," she whispered, then shut the door.

What would the Chairman have said? What would he have told him to do? Frankie opened his desk drawer and poured himself a glass of Scotch whisky, then another and another. There was no one left to ask.

In his sleeplessness, he'd watched Hannah turn away from him again and again. When he finally dozed off, he was roused by chanting and singing below. *Tear down the wall!* All day and into the night, it seemed: into his dreams.

Light it up! the Chairman would've said. *They'll love you, Frank, my boy!*

So Frankie did. The very next night. He ordered every bulb in every socket inside each built or half-built building turned on: wall to wall, floor to ceiling. He ordered Christmas lights strung up too. His wall afire, blazing in the night, spreading on water. Frankie stood on the observation deck at midnight. It was something to see. Greater than the beehive burner on Alberni Strait. Brighter than the noonday sun.

It blazed across the waterfront atop the wall, above Captain Jim's boat, high in the sky like a sunset, visible in Rosedale, where Uri saw it from the bedroom window as Hannah at last succumbed to sleep.

The night Baby Yuri disappeared, Hannah hadn't waited for the elevator amid the crush of people leaving. Foolishly, she'd rushed down the steps after Frank. At last, into the April night that should not have been snowy and so cold. Her heart still grieved the loss of Frank's boy.

Uri had followed his wife's stocking-footed prints pressed in the snow—her slender toes achingly articulated—and found her calling out to Baby Yuri, then to Frank, her voice growing hoarse. In her desperation, he couldn't help but notice how ravishing she appeared to him: hair streaming and flecked with snowflakes, skin blanched white as snow beneath its veil of violet. She held out her chapped red hands to him. *Uri, find Baby! Find him!* Her hands burned in his. *Help Frank!*

It was not his first time grazed by jealousy. But Uri understood she must do everything for Frank, to keep him safe under her wing. She believed in his suffering as she believed in her own. Everything followed as a consequence or in spite of that. Even this swindling could possibly be forgiven, betrayed though she felt.

At five o'clock, the morning after Frank's show of lights, Uri roused his wife, as he did three times a week. No more languorous night-before martini sipping. They ate toast and sipped tea in the cool stillness, windows blind to the garden beyond it. At six, he bundled her up in black mink over her purple chiffon. They drove through quiet streets to the hospital where for five hours he would sit opposite where she sat, her eyes closed; him not knowing if she slept or not, if she was in pain or not, as a mechanism pumped cleansed blood through her veins. A compact, high-functioning machine stood by her side, sleekly encased, doing the work her body no longer could. Uri had grown into the habit of these early risings, attuned to the machinery of her life. They had grown into it together. They could live on indefinitely, he told himself: he, Hannah and the Machine.

Each morning Uri coaxed his beloved out of their bedroom to walk, to eat—though he had to guide her through a dietary minefield. To once again utter those words he'd joyously given up—*My Hannah, she won't be down today*—that was no longer the worst thing he could imagine. The worst was much worse, as he'd always known.

It was later in the morning, nearing the end of Hannah's treatment, when the sun's rays in the east-facing room pooled with the heated output of the hard-working machine. Uri swam in a flooded yard of half-dreams, with Hannah leaning just out of reach with her fishing line; the suck-and-pump sound of the dialysis machines was his own held breath and heartbeat underwater.

When the machine stopped he woke. He knew the routine: the nurse checking levels on the machine, then disconnecting Hannah from it. But this time, her blood, cleansed and precious, spurted and ran down her arm to the dirty floor. A faint mist rolled off it like fog from a sea. Everyone gasped, instinctively lifting their feet.

The nurse quickly stopped it up at the spout on Hannah's arm, restoring the flow to inside her veins. She gave a terse smile. "Lots more where that came from."

An orderly mopped around Hannah's feet, the red swirling to pink, then muddling into the dull brown of the linoleum. Her chiffon was stained. Uri draped her mink coat around her shoulders and led her out. She leaned heavily on him. "I'm wilted, Uri," she said. He could barely feel her beneath the fur.

He took Hannah home and settled her onto the couch with a blanket to rest by the window to their barren yard.

Hannah turned her back to her husband's charmless fussing. Instead she looked out to the spot where her iris isle had once flourished. A muddy pit was all that remained. She refused to meet Uri's eyes, flooding with worry, imploring her to be well— as if she'd willed the affliction and could will it away.

On the mornings they didn't go to the hospital, he lay awake in the chaise he'd placed beside the bed. Lately he'd pained her with seismic shifts in the night, rolling this way and that. Now he waited anxiously for her to wake and rise. Some days she could and would rise, though every part of her body ached in its own right and way. She held out an elbow to be rubbed, doubled up when her belly burned. *Bring me my mink, will you?* She was perennially cold.

"How's my Hannah today?" Uri asked each morning. She resented the question, the fresh new slate he posed, as if he weren't one to be haunted by what had come before. He, Mr. Knew-It-All.

Time and again over the years, Hannah would hear and read Uri's waxing lament of what might have been, on radio, and in magazines. What had become of Uri Slonemsky's *Modern Architecture*, his alphabetical project barely begun with a "U" and an "I"? The what-might-have-been. He would pause and let the interviewer fill the space. The implication he let settle was that he'd turned his attention to Hannah, his beloved muse. Listening, Hannah could not help remembering those he'd turned away, evicted despite her pleas, so that his gold-paned Towers of Finance might rise.

Through the long lit-up night, calls had come. Complaints, compliments, condemnations. Frankie listened, hung up, then stopped answering. He swilled some Scotch and fell asleep at his desk.

In the morning, another call: it was the police.

They'd found Baby Yuri, what remained of him. A few bones of a small boy nesting on a shore west of the city were discovered, embedded with stray threads of the navy sailor suit Baby Yuri had been wearing the night he'd disappeared.

Frankie sat for minutes, hours. The day passed into night and back again. Sounds of chattering children and mothers drifted in and out of his head. It was a journey, round and round in his rotating tower getting nowhere. It was like being in the Ladies' little home, drifting without leaving, and no one coming for him.

He closed his office door. The phone rang, letters and papers and deliveries piled up outside. He was weak from not eating, unable to open the door, to climb down from his tower.

He settled in his chair as his mother had in their house on the sea. He'd been a monkey climbing over and under her. Not unlike Baby Yuri who'd been something else: fish? eel? A creature apart. There was not even a whole human body left to bathe, to swathe, to put to rest and let pass in peace to the next world. He knew he had to call Reiko, but he couldn't.

For the first time, he ventured into the stairwell and climbed the steps from his office to the observation deck.

The wind snatched at him as he opened the door. He stumbled forward beyond the fenced area to the gate that allowed maintenance crews out. He unlocked it and stepped onto the unprotected ledge. He wanted to see the lake—his sea—unobstructed. The clouds were close enough to touch. He inched out bit by bit. This ledge was smoother than a felled trunk, though levelled and no wider. He followed flecks of light here to there, each dissolving or resolving into bird or cloud or thin air. He spied a small creature darting over the water, then diving down. Frankie leaned out farther; the keys slipped from his hand, slunk into the distance below, sparkled, gone.

Then down, down, down he went. Down between the logs that rolled out from under his feet; down from the peak to the lowest rung his fingers slipped. Down through the deepest crack in the sea.

No one could pull him up. Not Taiji, not his mother. Not even the Priest. Frankie's keys bounced off the pavement. The sparkle and clink of them startled the woman at whose feet they fell.

"It's Mr. Hanes," someone said, and everyone turned toward the figure who'd appeared among them.

The swishing crowd tightened into a ring. Mother and child, mother and child, mother and child.

There were not as many as Frankie expected. Fewer than the newspapers were making it seem. They all stared. They were poor. He knew how that looked and how it felt: their faces lean and pale and stained, small enough to cup, one cheek in each hand as he'd thought to do so many times with Baby Yuri but hadn't. His boy had been pint-sized but strong and nourished—he'd made sure of that. A busy body. A tight bud yet to unfurl. Frankie had felt it in his hands whenever he hauled the boy from wherever he shouldn't be.

Frankie felt a tug at his pant leg. He looked down at the small head there and patted it; so small under his palm, the hair soft: not as thick or coarse as his son's.

An adult hand thrust a sheet of paper in front of him: a lump of yellow and lines wriggling out from it. BRING BACK THE SUN, it read in bold grown-up letters: STOP THE HANES DEVELOPMENT.

The hand stayed there until he took the sheet.

"Frank?" A face he knew was looking back at him.

"My father? Did my father build the wall?"

He touched a hand to her shoulder and she flinched.

She'd changed a little: creases at the eyes, lips thinned, down-turned at the ends; her face wore its cares. That hair, that flying mass darker than her mother's, was tied back. Frankie recognized the blouse as the same or something like the one she wore the night they'd met. Of course he remembered. Annie. Anne.

All in a second he looked back to her eyes, which were spilling over with the question. In her other hand, she clutched a set of keys: his keys.

"No," he said. He held an accusing hand to his chest. "I did this."

CHAPTER 14

Eclipse

Frankie stood on the deck of the early-morning ferry, watching a scrap of wood float past. The wind bit his face; autumn had turned to winter in a day. He retrieved the letter he'd folded neatly and tucked into his breast pocket.

Dear Frank,
I have questions for you, my dear boy. Are you sponta-
neously enthusiastic about everyone having everything
you can have? Secondly, if success or failure of this
planet and of human beings depended on how you are
and what you do, how would you be? what would
you do?

    These are questions I have asked myself.

    I am responding in your hour of need to the best
of my capability. You will find the world responding
to your earnest initiative.

    Yours truly, Bucky

He disembarked on Toronto Island. Striding off the gang-plank, he was jostled from behind only to knock a man pushing a cart filled with dry goods. Cans and boxes that skittered across plank after plank and into the lake. Bags of Five Roses flour and cans of Spam, salmon and tuna slowly sank. The waste! He might have waded in after them if not for the cold.

"So sorry," Frankie muttered, reaching for his wallet.

The man retrieved his upended cart; without a word or glance, he turned it around back onto the ferry.

Frankie stood on the quay and gazed at the city. What he saw was his wall and just above it, Cloud Tower; not much else was visible: the Five Roses plant exhaling its floury smoke. Cranes: their arms crooked over his many buildings still rising. And then, between him and the city were the waves, churning up froth, and that made him shiver: this island sat low in the water. He felt marooned at the moment, that feeling of unsteadiness that lived in his stomach as a boy rowing out to sea to get home.

He drew away from the quay and began to walk following the directions he'd been given. He crossed creeks overhung with bowing willows. He passed the odd person and each time thought to ask about Anne or Annie Slonemsky. Each time, he remembered too late and felt sheepish to double back. He walked until he realized that he was walking where he'd walked before. The lights in the tiny frame houses he'd passed earlier were coming on now. Silhouettes appeared in windows.

It was beautiful along these winding paths, really, once he let go of his worry. All was quiet and quaint: a community of small people in small boxes of different colours—white, green, even pink and purple—low to the ground. Faces or fig-ures adorned walls, doors and mailboxes like hieroglyphs; wind chimes dangled from porches and tree branches; wind-mills were planted in the ground. In one or two windows, he noticed a sign: SAVE OUR HOMES! There were footprints in the soft earth, yet wherever he turned, all was still. Apart from life elsewhere. Each shack resigned to being a home just where it was.

Finally he stopped a passerby—elderly, he realized—on a bicycle. "Anne Slonemsky?" the man repeated. No, but an Annie Slone was one or two streets over.

Had she cut off her tail just as he had?

He stepped onto another bridge—or was it the same one? Across it, he found himself before a hutch transplanted from someone's dining room, studded with nails from which hung dresses on wire hangers, pants, shirts, a sweater still holding the rumpled shape of its wearer. Boots dangling from their laces. Toys sitting on a ledge. Flapping in the wind was a woman's grey blouse. He recognized it, Annie's camouflage. Before he could touch it, a hand reached from behind to whisk it away. Had he really seen the blouse or imagined it? Dishes and cups rattled as the owner of the hand rummaged on the other side. Tacked to the front of the hutch was a handwritten sign:

WALK A MILE IN MY SHOES—
OR DRESS, OR PANTS OR SHIRT
FOR FREE!

Then the figure emerged: a woman. She wore glasses, and her hair was like Annie's, but dulled by greys in the sunlight, its coils unsprung. She looked up.

"Hello, Frank," she said. "Good to see you."

He stepped close, smelling pine and cigarettes, and held out a firm hand to shake.

Annie had a cottage to herself, small as it was. It was surrounded by other cottages on tiny plots of wildflowers, grasses and dirt. There was no concrete or bricks out her window, and no lush isle of irises.

Through Annie's years in Montreal, her mother had sometimes mentioned Frank in letters. But Annie hadn't thought of him much beyond that—only when she contemplated her father, his love of beauty and his refusal to see her as she was. Only then did she recall Frank, who clearly worshipped Uri, and his clumsy attempts to mould himself in her father's image, groomed by Hannah.

But not until she'd encountered him two weeks ago outside the tower, his tower, the children all around, did he settle into her. After that, she thought only of him, and remembered what she'd forgotten: that his son had died in a mysterious accident.

Now she found herself grateful to see him. In spite of the wall he'd built. She remembered his hair boyishly flapping down in his eyes.

He was lost. She knew the look of lost in the eyes, in the slump of shoulders. She'd seen it in workers worn down by the sameness and solitude of the tasks they'd been given, with no end or goal in sight, no value conferred on them. But surely he'd had value heaped on him, and stored in the bank.

"How are my parents?" she asked. He looked up in surprise. No, she explained, they didn't know she was living here. It was the first lie, the first secret kept from Uri and Hannah: she'd closed the door to them while living in the same house. She'd meant to tell them. But days had gone by since she'd been here, then weeks, months, then suddenly a year.

"Hannah isn't well," he said in his taciturn way.

"She never was," Annie said.

In his expensive coat and suit, no doubt chosen by her mother, Frankie slumped on Annie's sagging couch, fast asleep. He was tired, he told her, before asking to sit. She recalled he was a man of few words, and that had been much for him to convey. *So very tired.*

At sunset, she lit candles and thought of Hannah and Uri. She always felt generous and endowed at the wick's first flaming, with light enough to last.

Frankie woke to darkness. The last ferry to the city was long gone.

"It's all right," she told him, and he fell right back to sleep. His hair was still so thick and dark, she noticed, but the moonlight through the window turned it silver. In fact he did have a tuft of grey above his temple, to trick this trick of light. She covered him with a blanket and went to bed.

When he rose at last, it was morning. He wandered outside, found a rake and began cleaning the leaves and weeds from the yard. Through the small open window at the back of the house, he glimpsed Annie sitting cross-legged on her bed, very still with eyes closed. He heard her speak: *Flee and be silent, in a brilliant flame, alone, fearful and trembling.* Then nothing: silence. He got on with his work.

Flee and be silent, he thought as he gathered up stray bricks, pieces of wood and shingle. He ventured out on the path leading to the shore and, from there, gazed at the city. His eyes followed the shore west. Somewhere along there, Baby Yuri had given himself to the water.

Annie appeared on the path behind him. "Do you like it here, Frank?"

He nodded. "Yes, I do."

"They say isolation is helpful to the soul."

"What else do they say?" He gave a weak smile. He'd never felt so isolated before.

"The Kabbalists teach that the mystery of life will unfold to the contemplative mind."

He took a deep breath. It wasn't in his nature to wait. But for now he didn't know what else he could do.

"You can stay for a while if you need to. Though my parents may be expecting you back, with me in tow."

Abruptly Frankie glanced up. He hadn't planned on telling her that Uri had sent him, not yet. Annie smiled.

"Thanks," he said. He had a bit of cash, some cheques in his pocket and the suit on his back. He'd noticed some hand-me-down clothes at the hutch that might fit, and there was her couch.

He wasn't Frank, he told her. "Call me Frankie."

Annie looked at herself in the mirror for the first time in weeks and dragged a comb through the tangled nest of her hair. She dabbed on some lipstick, then wiped it off.

She'd become what they called an old maid, a spinster. Thirty had come and gone; forty had just passed. Her youth was no real loss. Hannah had always been the shining beauty; even with age, she naturally drew attention in any room. Annie knew her parents could never admire their plain daughter as much as they admired each other.

As a girl, Anne had read their story, not in words but pictures: her parents' modest wedding ceremony, rabbi-less, in a friend's apartment, her mother in a chic jacket and skirt of purple silk, a matching veiled headpiece and short, white gloves. In each photograph, Uri's head turned away from the camera, his eyes for only Hannah: worshipful, incredulous, assuring himself, *Yes, she is yours*.

Annie had been left to wonder: *Will a boy ever look at me that way?*

If the two of them could see her now, lumpish and lumpen. Gone to seed as she collected flower bulbs to plant in her unruly garden.

With rusted tools and parts he found abandoned across the island, Frankie fixed the splintered window frames on Annie's cottage and nailed down some loose shingles on the roof. That night, he dabbed the dirt from his good suit as best he could and washed out his shirt, hanging it by the wood-burning stove to dry for tomorrow's work. After Annie had gone to bed, he washed his underwear too. He gazed out the window at the dark shadows of trees and houses huddled along the dirt path. Across the lake, the lights of the tower would be shining above the city.

He half-woke to a bulldozer's growl. As if he were back in the Fujimotos' attic amid the razing of half of Cabbagetown, with all the years ahead to be lived over again.

Outside, Annie was shouting. He ran out, bleary-eyed.

"Stop him!" She turned to Frankie in desperation.

A bulldozer rumbled toward the small house behind. A woman, her children huddled close in blankets, stood outside it, not moving. The driver waved a paper in his hand and shouted, even as he kept rolling closer.

Frankie pulled the woman and her children aside as the bulldozer crushed one side of the house.

"What is wrong with you?" Annie shouted. The wall buckled and crumpled. She strode up to the driver, who thrust the paper at her.

An eviction notice, signed by some city official. She reached down and took all the papers from the cab and threw them to the wind.

"It's no use," the mother called back to Annie. She led her two children, a boy and a girl, off to a neighbour's home.

Frankie spotted more of the signs he'd seen before: SAVE OUR HOMES!

"They've been trying to chase everyone off for years," Annie told him. "Decades." Since the island's heyday when there'd been a hotel, theatre, dance hall. Carnivals with diving horses. All gone now, along with three hundred or more homes. First to make way for an airport.

"Where will they go?" Frankie asked.

"I don't know." Annie threw up her arms and sighed. She looked as if she might cry. "You could do something."

"I don't know what," he said. He shrugged helplessly. "I'm sorry."

"It's the expressway and the high-rises that took away future parkland. That's why they want all this back."

She stared hard at him. "Maybe everyone could move into those fancy apartments," she said bitterly, then walked away.

"They couldn't afford it," Frankie muttered.

Later that day, he found her returning with a swarm of people. The little girl whose house had been mowed down scampered past. On the ground, more eviction notices thrown to the wind.

"City Council called them off," Annie said, "for now, at least." She gave a conciliatory smile and even cheerfully hooked her arm in his as they walked back. "For now the sun is shining."

The rest of the day passed quickly, as days here did with chores to do, broken by lunch and dinner. They glanced up at each other every so often, though they had no words to exchange.

After Annie went to sleep, Frankie walked the path over the bridge, past the weeping willows to the shore. It had begun to snow.

He watched the snow taken by the wind over the water. He glimpsed a small, white swaddled mass suspended over the surface, held there as he held his breath. No one else could see this, he knew. *Yuri, my Yuri.* It rose higher, then unspooled in all directions, shaking off what it must have gathered up.

Until Frankie showed up, Annie had been taking the ferry each morning to stand shoulder to shoulder with the mothers beneath Cloud Tower, giving flyers to passersby, even tourists.

She'd been absent since, so she rose early one November morning to rejoin the other women. Frankie was still sleeping and she scribbled him a note.

A few mothers were already there chatting about their children—something done or said to laugh or shake their heads at. Annie smiled at them and busied herself with assembling the flyers and placards. She'd once sewn children's shirts in a factory and, whenever she finished one, she'd tried to imagine buttoning it on some tiny being. Someone belonging to her.

When school let out, Annie went with some of the mothers to collect their children. They were polite, mostly, and fell into a line behind her just as their picketing mothers did. They were used to not getting what they'd learned not to want. On the march back, Annie rewarded them with candies.

"Miss," one said, tugging on Annie's sleeve. The girl stuck out a bright red tongue. "Miss, look at mine!" another said: a green tongue. Annie laughed. A boy slipped his soft, tiny pillow of a hand into hers, oblivious to his effect on her. Had she once been a delightful little being like this to Uri and Hannah?

Then a mother held out a crumpled candy wrapper. "Miss," she said. "We don't have money for dentists."

Annie hadn't thought of that. She apologized and emptied her candy-filled pockets into the garbage, fingers sticky with shame. She fled around the tower away from the mothers and children, and wept.

All the women she'd tried to help with her picketing and petitions, their heads down at their machines in airless firetraps, some younger than her with children of their own. She hadn't helped them. All they'd wanted and needed was to keep their jobs. She remembered being summoned by the foreman to the office from the factory floor, away from the zum-zum of the machines. Inside, overlooking the workers, the noise was muffled. Below, kerchiefed heads were down, necks bent over, hands moving robotically over and over. He spit at her feet. *Troublemaker, riling everybody up! You can't sew a stitch.* She told him she was leaving. He dusted off his hands, pushed her back into the roaring cavern. *Good riddance, Annie Slone!*

Yes, good riddance. The hypocrisy of Anne Slonemsky, Jew of Rosedale, trading in her name to labour alongside the humble factory worker.

Frankie was sitting on the couch when she got back, looking more lost than ever. His face red and puffed. His good suit fraying at the seams. He was bursting with sorrow. She sat down by his side, let his head drop to her shoulder to absorb his dry sobs. "It's all right," she told him.

She let him rest with her that night, let him hold her until he fell away, asleep. She studied him there, his head on her pillow, hair so black, so thick and resilient. His brows darkly shading his eyes. Who was he to deserve her comfort? A rich man whose riches made others poorer, when he should have known better, having been one of the poor himself. But she would not deny him.

A copper red moon shone through the window. A lunar eclipse on the first day of winter: a wonder.

"Come look, Frankie," she whispered in his ear as she slipped out of bed.

He woke to Annie bundling herself in a blanket. She put his coat around him, led him outside and stood him under the brilliant coppery moon. It was veined and awash with spirits passing through it. In moments, the moon turned raw, casting red everywhere.

He stumbled forward and fell; his heart tripped. The cold clogged his breath and scraped his throat. Now his eyes were clouding as he got up: all he saw was the red, red moon. His head was full, the inside straining against its shell. He eased himself back to the ground. Blood in the snow: his unborn taken, Baby Yuri taken, Yas, Taiji.

Annie knelt beside him. She touched his face. He felt tears coursing down, scorching. The hands that wiped his tears chapped red.

CHAPTER 15

Metaphysical Gravity

For my days vanish like smoke; my bones burn like glowing embers.

He'd read that somewhere. On a gravestone in Tashme or the Necropolis in Cabbagetown. What could Frankie have known of his son? He didn't know himself at that age. Just hunger and whimsy, nothing that made sense, at least to Frankie.

"He suffered," Frankie said, choking. The burning cold, the frost splintering his boy's breath, like a blade into wood. Annie could only press herself close. There was no denying.

Baby Yuri had been a tiny bud of secrets. In fleeting moments before he'd squirm from his father's hold, Frankie had felt his own wilfulness to root them out, his inability to just let the boy be.

At the mortuary, he used chopsticks to place what had been found of Baby Yuri's bones into a small urn, which he brought to the island now.

Frankie read and reread every letter Bucky had ever sent him. He closed his eyes to search Bucky's through the thick of his glasses, to see him in that familiar pose with his eyes shut in contemplation, fingertips tenting the air. His voice was always somewhere in Frankie's head, and now Frankie was waiting for an answer to the very challenge Bucky posed: *So, Mr. Industry. The world awaits your initiative.*

Should he take down the wall? To see the wrecking ball swoop across the sky and into it. Giant clouds of rubble rising up and raining down. Sunlight pouring in over the tenement buildings; children at their windows. The lake open wide to the city. But that was impossible.

No, he could not undo what he had done.

What should he do now? Frankie asked himself, over and over.

The things that you see need to be done, and that no one else seems to see need to be done.

A taxi sped Frankie from the Montreal airport onto a bridge crossing the St. Lawrence River. A forest sprawled across the island below, giving way to a rectangular block of oddly shaped buildings, some resembling the models he'd first seen in the Kidney. At the far edge of it rose a huge latticed dome.

"Come aboard, Frank! It will hold." Frankie squinted twenty feet up at Bucky climbing high as a spider scaling its own web, singing: *Just give me a home in a great circle dome, where the stresses and strains are at ease!*

So Frankie did climb aboard. Each metal rung a nine-inch-diameter tube under his foot, each joint in his hands, stable. The sun glinted off its subdivided triangles upon triangles curving into its spherical form. He glanced back down. They'd built the pavilion over water for the World's Expo. They'd filled in the island site for Bucky to assemble—in days!—a model

Spaceship Earth, a 250-foot-diameter geodesic dome floating over the fairgrounds; a giant glowing, sparkling blossom of a planet. He, Frankie Hanesaka, was aboard, whirling in his own uncertain orbit as he rode the vessel. It was no home on the range. It was a home in a dome!

> *Roam home to a dome*
> *no banker would back with a dime*
> *no mortgage to show*
> *no payments to go*
> *where you dream, dwell and spend your own time,*

Bucky warbled.

Later they sat on the ground inside the dome with a bottle of wine and some bread and cheese. Frankie gazed up through the many triangles framing the sky. It was as if he were seeing the world reshaped, through Bucky's eyes and by his restless ingenuity.

"It's time to step into the twentieth century, Frank," Bucky told him. He frowned. "I have seen your towers. There is no advantage in thermally and aerodynamically inefficient cuboid skyscrapers," he said. "You're using Stone Age logic." Bucky gave him a very gentle pat on his arm.

"The advent of metal alloys has brought us to the advantage of structural lightness. That is at the heart of all ephemeralization. That and this." Not for the first time did he place a small pyramid-shaped stone in Frankie's palm. A tetrahedron, the most stable and flexible form in nature. "You remember that, don't you?"

Yes, of course he remembered. The day they'd sat by the dry garden together. He took the stone, squeezed it and put in inside his pocket.

Just weeks later, Frankie saw pictures of the finished

pavilion in the newspaper. Five million people came, up and down, on foot, on monorail, and on moving staircase to the highest point in the dome, to the Space Observation Deck where sat the *Surveyor*, the spacecraft that had landed on the moon.

The first thing Frankie did when he returned was to halt construction on one of his lots and to build a garden criss-crossed by multiple paths to the lake. He built a maze of hedges that led to a Minotaur's see-saw at the centre.

Annie took the children to visit the new garden. There they scrambled through the maze and clambered onto a geodesic climbing structure that Bucky and his students had erected. Instead of monkey bars, it was an all-surrounding web spun from one continuous rope.

Annie climbed up too, and found herself near the top with one of the older boys.

"Stand up, Miss!" he urged. He tried himself, but tumbled down a rung through the dome's centre. "Stand up!" he shouted from below, tilting up his face to her. "You can do it!"

Frankie noticed her lifting her hands off the rope.

The other children stopped playing and looked up at her, crouched on a rung like a timid monkey. They began to clap and cry, "Up, Miss Annie! Up!"

"No, no," Frankie warned.

The wind ruffled her grey blouse and dark trousers as she squinted into the sun. There was her island across the harbour. She held her arms out and looked down at the tops of things: of trees and flower blooms, the children's heads, their silken, shining crowns.

She felt light, even her pendulous breasts. She gazed down at Frank, who'd begun to wave his arms. *Love is metaphysical gravity*, a Bucky-thought, came to her.

She stood up. The lake was smooth and lucent as her mother's silk chiffon. "Be careful, Miss!" one of the girls called up. The wind rose; she wobbled, reached for the air and slipped down past rung after rung. She thudded to the ground.

Annie woke in a hospital room. Frankie leaned in close. She was fine, the doctor said: a little bruised and scraped, and with a child sprouting in her womb.

Hannah pressed Annie and Frankie to move to the Kidney. Hannah, the grandmother-hen-to-be, fluttered about, exhausted and joyful. Annie wondered if her mother would hang on or simply cede to what was to come. She suspected that Hannah's wishes would exceed, as they always did, what was possible. But a child would come of this, and that was more than enough.

Annie stayed on the island, and little by little, Frankie moved more than a frayed suit there too.

Annie rode the ferry often to visit Hannah and Uri, or to sit in Frankie's flower garden by the water while the children played under the sun. Only her belly grew, thankfully; her breasts were already plumped for the job to come. She didn't mind: her body felt useful, housing and labouring for two.

Overhead, the Chairman's expressway was collapsing bit by bit; a falling chunk of concrete narrowly missed a bus at rush hour.

Annie and Frankie rode the ferry to shore, weathering the blustery wind on deck. She held tight to the rail while her insides sloshed. The wind lifted the tails of her coat; nausea bent her over the railing toward the water. Her feet were just lifting off the deck when Frankie clamped onto her and pulled her back.

She slipped his hand under her blouse and onto her belly: hard and soft, gelatinous, fragile as glass. It was an egg, a planet moving inside her.

More than anything, no matter what other forces intended, Frankie meant for this child to be.

Behind the Kidney, the entire yard had been neglected since Frankie left: overgrown in patches and parched in others. The gravel waves of the dry garden had long been overtaken by dandelions and crabgrass. Where the iris isle once lay, a profusion of wildflowers and ferns had taken root. In the midst of it was planted a delightful lark of a thing: a house of glass. Big enough to sit in (a wooden stool had been placed inside) but small enough to graze your head on its ceiling. A simple cube. You had to look carefully to distinguish between the living things fluttering in and around it, and their reflection.

It struck Annie that she was standing in her own house, her first architectural feat, drawn as a girl with a No. 2 graphite pencil and her father's slide rule. How she had longed to colour it with Laurentian Peacock Blue, Poppy Red, Emerald Green, Deep Yellow and Blush Pink! But Uri had snatched the sheet from her sketch pad before she could. Now he'd built it.

"For my Annie," he said. "Welcome home." He hadn't called her Annie since she was that girl. She hugged him with child-like abandon.

He'd been right: let the sky fill it.

Uri and Annie waltzed belly-to-belly in the living room to Coltrane's bebop "My Favourite Things." One of Bucky's favourites. Annie consented to one martini that sent her spinning. She collapsed on the couch.

Uri was now fat and Hannah thin, with hair dyed a paler shade. She wore beige instead of the purple that now had more life in it than she did, so she said. The two of them spoke and moved slowly and in concert, holding out a hand to the other or lending a word to finish a sentence.

"If only the irises would bloom again," Hannah sighed, "now that Frank is back and my Annie is home."

"If only," echoed Uri, patting her hand.

The next morning Annie sat opposite her mother at the renal clinic in the seat Uri normally occupied. Blood, her mother's, trickled into a tube. Annie felt light-headed and full-bodied. She swooned and fainted to the floor.

The nurse was holding a cool cloth to Annie's forehead when she came to. Hannah was drowsing beside the humming, pumping machine, the tube looping like a red skipping rope in and out of her mother's arm.

Frankie spent hours watching Annie sit in the Glass House cradling her belly. She let her hair grow longer and wilder, like the surrounding bluebells and buttercups and Queen Anne's lace.

He went walking alone at the lake one night. He'd had a stone pathway built in front of the lakeside buildings. More gardens to come, including beds of roses. The water was unriled. Above, a full moon. He sat down on an abandoned couch, a rolled-up carpet by his feet, clothing strewn about. Owners and their belongings cast adrift. He thought of Mr. Fujimoto and his family in the Regent Park tenements, the walk-ups that were too cold in winter, too hot in summer, and sunless all year round.

Farther along, parked in the empty middle of the rubble, sleek in the moonlight, Frankie came across a black Cadillac, rusting, tires flat, front bumper crushed. Inside, a woman slept across the front seat, doors locked. A coat clutched tight around her, calves tucked close. A half-eaten box of chocolates sat on the dashboard. Suitcases piled in the backseat. Nowhere to go.

He passed Captain Jim's land. Smoke billowed from a garbage can. Cardboard boxes sat on their sides and clothing hung from a line strung between two sticks stuck in the ground.

One of the boxes stirred; a man snored. His mother was no doubt asleep in the boat, the Captain too.

She didn't know about the baby. Not yet.

He reached the terminal just in time to see the ferry depart. He sat down for a long wait.

Bucky then appeared just above him, hovering on Cloud Nine in the dim light. His glasses were strapped tight to his head as always.

I was thirty-two years old when I lost my child. I was penniless and unknown: empty and bankrupt. Bucky's broad hands held loosely onto the struts.

"What do you do with nothing?" Frankie asked.

Do more and more with less and less. Then do everything with nothing.

Bucky adjusted the first watch on his wrist twelve hours ahead. Beside him, on a small boat ferrying them across Tokyo Bay, Mr. Minamoto pointed above the grey city blocks to the stark orange and white of Tokyo Tower. They sailed by the future site of Tokyo Sky Tree, the latest project of Minamoto Industries. It would surpass Tokyo Tower as Japan's tallest structure, though it would fall short of the Cloud Tower by eight feet.

His country was small in land mass but surrounded by sea, Mr. Minamoto told Bucky. His people were small in size but were growing taller now with improved nutrition. The population was ever increasing. "Buildings must be bigger and taller," he said. "Doorways higher."

After hearing Bucky lecture at Meiji University a decade earlier, Mr. Minamoto knew the future of his Japanese empire lay not on land but at sea. *Three-quarters of our planet Earth is covered with water which may float organic cities. Floating cities pay no rent to landlords.*

Japanese knew how to construct modest islands. They were now passing a small bunker isle built in the days when Japan guarded its borders from foreign invasion with samurai and cannons.

"A city to house a million people is technologically and economically feasible," Bucky had told Mr. Minamoto. "So light, it can float and withstand an earthquake."

Bucky spoke of floating cities dotting the oceans, enabling flying, sailing and stepping stone travel around the globe. Each tetrahedronal city might start with a thousand occupants and grow symmetrically to hold millions. So much new to do with the old: seemingly obsolete buildings, ships, airplanes, submersibles. *Weaponry converted to livingry!* So much to be gained: efficiencies distributing raw and finished cargo; bottom-of-the-ocean intelligence of marine life and oceanography.

Aqua City was the name Mr. Minamoto already had in mind for the million-person community he would eventually build in Tokyo Harbour. Harbour Town, Water Town, Ocean City. These were more floating cities he and Bucky could build elsewhere. Stepping stones, in Bucky's words, for world-around travel. In the future, almost everyone would have to live on water as land became used up.

A week went by, then another and another. Annie was long, too long, overdue, said the doctors. They'd warned her, of course, of difficulties that might come with pregnancy at her age. She lumbered slowly and stiffly by Frankie's side around the island paths. Walking soon became too difficult, with her weakened joints and swollen ankles.

One morning she woke with a peculiar sensation in her skin. Hour by hour, little by little, it tightened over her joints, then her whole body, compressing the child in her belly. By nightfall, she could barely expel or take in anything. She could hardly swallow because the lining of her esophagus had hardened.

Annie could not eat, drink, pee or move her bowels. Her body was frozen. The baby could not move either. At the hospital, doctors detected its steady heartbeat, though it wasn't as strong or constant as before. By the next morning, Annie could not speak. She was trapped inside herself, her cries unheard, even by Frankie, leaning in as close as he could, desperate to receive. He whispered, shouted, clapped his hands; prodded her lips. He massaged her from head to toe. No matter how awkward, how foolish, how helpless he felt, he did whatever he could think to do.

Annie! My Annie! But she could only gaze back at him, imploring him.

To do what?

The doctors called it *morphea*, a word for hardening, but was it *localized morphea* or *morphea profunda*? *Systemic morphea*? Which was worse? They could not say. For any of these conditions—diseases—there was no cure. The body was simply taking Annie's fate into its own hands.

Her face became a mask, as when he'd glimpsed her in meditation through the window of her island shack. Frankie searched for a window inside that window, for the Annie he knew who'd pulled him from sleep out to a burning moon.

The doctors could do nothing for Annie, much less the unborn child. When Frankie insisted on bringing her home to the island, they prepared him for what would or might come. He spooned water into her mouth, propping her head back and torso upright to receive it. He chanted whatever chant came into his head; whatever prayer, whatever he found in her books.

Uri visited. He patted his daughter's stiffened hand and read to her. First *Alice in Wonderland,* showing her wondrous pictures along the way, then *Sleeping Beauty*, both books he'd read to her when she was a child. She didn't stir.

The Priest, the God named seventy-two times over: all the world was against Frankie. Always had been. It was inescapable, a fact he was born into. He wailed on the outside as he had on the inside, throwing himself on Annie's unmoving body. He wailed as if he were inside the Ladies' stifling bedroom, wailing as he should have, as he hadn't done, to rescue himself. He found Annie's eyes fixed on the door, not moving. There was a knock.

He rose slowly and opened it to find Aki there, with his mother.

They sat with a bowl of warm water, Frankie and his mother, gently bathing Annie's body. Her eyes followed their movements over her motionless limbs and her swollen belly. Slowly his mother began to chant a prayer he'd never heard. She lit a stick of incense and waved her hand to put out the flame. She passed the incense near to Annie's face and gave Aki a piece of paper to read from.

Aki looked to Frankie then to Annie, her one eye weeping.

> In the morning, we may have radiant faces. But by
> evening, we may turn into white ashes.
>   Each of us can take refuge in the Buddha of
> Infinite Life who promises to embrace all beings who
> recite his Holy Name: Namu Amida Buddha.

Momoye returned with Aki to Captain Jim's boat. She sat in her chair on the deck and took out the old photograph of the Priest and some incense which lit easily in the still air. The picture was older than old now, fading into the nothing it had come from. She propped the picture on a table beside her and left incense to burn in front of it.

She'd been struck by how Frankie's face had settled into its bones, its natural contours. He'd come to unmistakably resemble her, for better or worse.

"Who was he, Mama?" Aki asked, looking at the picture.

"Someone who tried to help others," she answered.

Far away in the Sea of Japan, a tidal force was growing, out in dark and light waters, currents tightening into fists in shoals and great depths. High tides were rising higher, low tides ebbing lower. Several ships were drawn aground, a few houses carted to sea.

In the small, dark apartment where the Fujimotos lived, the stems of tea leaves turned in their cups, standing up and then tilting down. The stems in Momoye's tea were swirling, and the waters of Lake Ontario began to rise and rock Captain Jim's boat.

It was nothing like the time of the storm, but ferries were stopped and a general alert was sounded for anyone on the water.

On the island, Annie lay in her bed, pale and rapidly thinning. Frankie remained night and day by her side. The wind grew fierce, and the island began to rock beneath Annie's bed, like a boat. As it did, pent-up sounds and words blew from Annie's mouth. Frankie sprang up. Annie howled and, bit by bit, she unfurled: her pouches and passageways; her fingers, toes, then her legs creaked open. Water gushed from between them, bursting from a dam. The water slowed then with a new gush, a small reddish head poked out, then a shoulder, another shoulder, a tiny hand and then another, then a torso, then legs. Frankie knelt at the foot of the bed to catch the baby in his hands as it crested out on a final wave. He grasped the child and didn't let go.

The boy was tiny and creased. He cried a little to show he was alive and fine, then sucked up the air. Annie's arms reached out. "Is it all right?" she rasped.

"Yes, yes!" Frankie assured her, summoning the memory of what the doctor had instructed. It was simple, really. Then he placed the slick little body into Annie's arms. Annie was drained, her flood subsided, but she was alight with joy. She wept as she held their tiny boy.

As she succumbed to sleep, Frankie lifted the baby in his arms and gently turned him. There was the spot, neither watered down nor blacker than he'd expected. As if a sooty finger had mysteriously reached down to touch.

Frankie covered and swaddled the baby. He ventured outside and held him under the giant moon. By the light of it, Frankie could see everything helpless and wilful in the face of his child.

He was once this: a newborn. Frankie's father might have wanted this moment too; might have wanted everything for his son that Frankie now wanted for his; might have felt this same fathomless swell inside that took his breath.

Since he'd met Bucky, Frankie had lived the experiment of Guinea Pig F: a test. It wasn't until this moment that he understood he'd been daring the world to give back to him all it had taken away.

Frankie called in the new Chairman, who in fact was old, having been in office for some years now.

"Sir," Frankie said. Bucky and Uri stood by his side. "The city is shrinking at the core and bursting at the seams."

"I suppose that's true," said the Chairman.

"Welcome to Torosa," said Bucky, leading the Chairman to the model displayed on Frankie's desk.

It felt good to hear the name *Torosa* on Bucky's lips. A name Frankie had invented for an isle he'd do everything to keep afloat.

Torosa would be a neighbourhood encompassing the shore and harbour of Toronto, the meeting place of waters. A floating module to house one thousand people that could grow symmetrically to accommodate as many as one hundred thousand—maybe more. It would provide each family with two thousand square feet of high-quality living, at a rental cost barely above the poverty rate, yet still enough to sustain the enterprise.

"Mr. Chairman," Frankie said, with a nod at Bucky, "a floating city pays no rent to landlords. It is water-worthy and dollar-worthy."

It was beautiful too. The Floating City was neither ship nor edifice but hive for living, anchored at its shore with schools, supermarkets, light industry; with adjacent flower and vegetable gardens. It could even begin to generate the energy necessary to sustain itself with a floating wind turbine farther out on the lake—the first of its kind. The gateway to Torosa would be a university built by Uri: a glass pyramid echoing the water and sky, and the triangular building blocks of Bucky's Floating City; it would be a Temple of Learning.

We'll soon see, thought Frankie, as he handed the Chairman a glass of Scotch.

TOROSA:
FLOATING CITY

CHAPTER 16

Afloat

Arnon had started out no less a mystery to Frankie than Baby Yuri had been. But the mystery was unfolding to him bit by bit as the boy grew.

Every morning, through three seasons, Arnon swam from the island to the city. He was, true to the Hebrew name his mother had given him, a rushing stream. His eyes were sea green and his long, wild hair streamed like seaweed in the water. His aunt Aki rowed her boat just ahead of him as he swam guided by two beacons: his father's Cloud Tower and his aunt's one eye.

"He's a genius," Bucky proclaimed when he saw Arnon's free-standing, triangulated toothpick and dried pea structures. Bucky made Frankie and Annie promise not to de-genius the boy.

He barely went to school. Teachers told him the sun sets, the moon rises. Yet there were the sun and moon in the sky at the same time, one lit to light the other. Arnon swam each morning as the world slowly turned toward the sun, and swam home each evening as the Earth rolled away from it. His body curved ever so slightly with the shape of the Earth, held in the water by gravity as Spaceship Earth spun its spherical form. The boy's Mongolian spot had faded early on, washed clean away, but his father was ever wary.

Frankie left on the ferry an hour before Arnon, but when he reached the Kidney, his son was already there, on the chesterfield next to his napping grandmother, his wrist clasped within her spindly fingers. Slipping from her grasp, he joined his grandfather at the dining room table.

Uri had built a model of the city—his future wished-for city. Along its familiar streets were unfamiliar buildings, some beautiful, some strangely sculptural. It was his Alphabetical Architecture from *A* to *Z* scattered throughout. Arnon placed tiny figures at the windows. But something was missing.

"Your father would like to tear down Cloud Tower," said Uri, bouncing on his heels. "I wanted to show him the city without it." Uri couldn't bear to lose the anchoring *I* of his alphabetical architecture.

"But you can't," Arnon protested to Frankie. Even though he'd never been allowed inside, never mind climbed its steps. How could he be without his father's beacon?

"We need less tonnage and more light-weight space for people to live in," Frankie said. The tower clouded his head and weighted his heart. He wanted to undo it. But neither Arnon nor Uri would lose their beacon: the highest perch in the land, like the wall, could not be toppled. No one would let him: not the Chairman, not the Fincaps, not the people tuned to their radios and televisions.

He would have to settle for doing what needed doing that he could do.

"Are you ready, my dear boy?" Bucky called out, seconds before that scolding gust of wind swept Frankie off the wharf and plunged him into Lake Ontario. The sky was bright and cloudless, the air calm.

The Priest's doing, of course.

As Bucky plucked Frankie out of Toronto Harbour, tug-boats were pulling hollow blocks of concrete into it. They would form the floating foundation of Torosa's triangular atoll. It would be a honeycomb with cells facing outward on all sides. Each unit's glass doors would open onto a prome-nade winding up and up and up to the rooftop under the sky. As people boarded, they would naturally make their way up there to the air, or down to water level to dip a toe or a fishing line into the harbour. Utilities and supplies would be delivered to an underwater service station by submersibles tethered to land.

Bucky and Mr. Minamoto already had ideas for another floating community connected by bridge to Torosa, and another after that. But one Torosa was enough for Frankie—for now, at least. Waves of people were washing over this New World city or waiting on distant shores to come here. On the water, in the air, there'd be room enough for them all. When Toronto Harbour was full, there'd be space above for Bucky's Cloud Nine, an elevated, domed, climate-controlled, pie-in-the-sky habitat whose science would be perfected in the Crystal Pyramid which first took shape with a single sheet of paper folded by Bucky at Uri's dining room table. A glass tetrahedron, eight hundred feet on each side by four hundred feet high, housing the University of Air and Water. Open to anyone and everyone, Annie liked to say: to people young and old, herself in the middle. Who might be saved from dingy firetrap sweatshops or from dark nights of the soul.

"Are you ready, Frank?" Bucky asked again, smiling. How did the man sustain such buoyancy at his age, this can-do optimism? Bucky had saved him with his old sailor's know-how and inventor's ingenuity, his unwavering belief in realizable reality. A home on Spaceship Earth that could

not be taken away because there was only water under-
neath it.

Uri rubbed Hannah's hands and feet to warm them. Her circu-
lation was never good. He drew back the shutters and opened
the windows. "It's a lovely day, isn't it?"

Isn't it? was appended in good faith to everything he uttered
to her these days. It was the arm circling her shoulder, bringing
her along. Never again would he neglect her, let her fall into the
shadows of his buildings. Like *-msky, isn't it* became essential
to who he was and how he would live out whatever days were
left with his love.

In the chilly early hours, they rose for their tea and toast,
then made their way to the clinic in a taxi, Hannah wrapped
in her balding black mink, which still kept her warm. After
one kidney transplant that had lasted her a few years, it was
back to Hannah and the Machine.

She sat with the machine humming in her heart, thumping
at the walls of her veins as Uri drowsed. She was thinking of
Frankie. Something she had to remind him to do. She pinched
herself as her own reminder. She closed her eyes.

Torosa, the Floating City, was almost complete. The beautiful isle she'd been waiting for, its glass gateway clear and open.
Along the path, flowers—roses, irises—bursting and abounding.
They would cross the bridge together, she and Uri, with Arnon
beside them. The crowd pressing in.

One morning, she summoned Frank to the Kidney. She
had him come up to her bedroom. She was seated, her purple
sleeves folded around her tiny frame. He recognized the smell
that was shadowing Hannah's usual lavender scent; he'd
smelled it on his mother after Taiji died. It was the scent of
life closing in on itself.

She held out her hand, but he offered his arms to embrace

her, then sat down. He looked into the fierce green eyes that the old sum of her had shrunk down to.

"Frank," she said, holding out her hand once again. It was thin and brittle in his, like a bird. But the hand gripped his firmly and shook it with vigour. She pulled their entwined hands close to her sunken breast.

"You remember this, don't you?" The green eyes held his gaze. "The word and the handshake?"

He nodded his head, yes. "I remember."

"Good." Her hand slipped away from his. She made motions of fatigue. Frankie stood.

"You won't forget?" Hannah said.

"No," Frankie replied. "I won't."

The week before Torosa's grand opening, Frankie stood on the Observation Deck of Cloud Tower. From the Crystal Pyramid, paths lined with a thousand roses and hundreds of irises converged at the walkway crossing onto the Floating City. He'd made his dream into a realizable reality.

Yet, his mind still picked at the sore—the snag of land with its wreck of a boat. Beached and grounded, neither afloat nor rooted: the home his mother had chosen over his.

Surely the boat was rotten, Frankie thought. *Unsafe*. He said the word aloud. The fisherman was old, no doubt not right in the head; his mother had been old for some time now. Why not do now what would need doing sooner or later? Frankie's last pulling out from under.

He picked up the phone and called on City Hall, one or two still there whose plots he'd fertilized those years ago.

With his sad, drooping eyes, Mr. Fujimoto surveyed the roses and irises and cast Frankie a fleeting smile. One after another, each of the clan bowed as they passed, clutching boxes and bags of their belongings from the cracked desert of Regent Park. More than the all-you-can-carry brought to the camps. Frankie would soon show Mr. Fujimoto and his son the deep, dark soil heaped at the top of Torosa's Floating City—deeper than he could ever have heaped on his floating garden in Port Alberni's harbour. There they could grow a new chrysanthemum forest.

Of course, there were the children and families of the sunlight Frankie had stolen, older now, some all grown. There were raggedy men who'd been camping out under the crumbling Chairman's expressway.

But his sisters remained back in Hope. They had cashed the cheque he'd finally sent.

Frankie hadn't expected his mother to come, either, and yet he'd hoped. He'd seen Captain Jim's wreck of a boat being tugged across the harbour headed for the scrapyard.

He didn't see her, but she was there, seated on a bench in view of the entrance to the Floating City. She'd grown exhausted somehow, cold and hungry. She was waiting.

Momoye had never truly worried for Frankie. Even when she was pregnant and starving, she'd trusted in her body and the child she was carrying. She and the Priest had left one logging camp for the next across the island and gotten lost. By nightfall, they'd found a rickety shack at the foot of a mountain. He left her there and went in search of kindling for a fire. Snow kept falling through the gaping roof to blanket her belly. Momoye heaved herself up, the door creaking as she opened it. She called and called but the Priest was nowhere.

Through the whirls of snow, she'd glimpsed something, someone. A man with a horse pulling a rickety cart. He approached the shack and found her. It was Taiji who'd come for her, just in time.

Just then, at the edge of the harbour, a familiar face. After all these years? *Nobu?* He wore a hat as she guessed he would, a cowboy's. He was smaller, but she was too—bent. But he didn't look that old after all; his hair was still black, his chest robust—a young man! She raised herself, painfully, and started toward him, his name on her lips for the first time in fifty—more!—years. *Nobu, brother!* But he seemed not to hear, and she was too slow, too tired, and she sat back down.

By day's end, Torosa was almost fully inhabited. It barely bobbed under its new weight. Bucky was there, directing the loosening of reins so that the city might sway on the water instead of fighting the waves and tugging at its moorings.

From the island, Annie watched the honeycomb turn golden in the dusk. Arnon lit a fire in the backyard.

Frankie left Bucky and went ashore to sit alone on a bench among the thousand roses of his garden. These days, the profusion of scents and colours could go to his head. The Queen Elizabeth rose in his lapel had wilted. He imagined how Mr. Fujimoto's chrysanthemums would look above the top deck of the Floating City.

The Earth was tilting into darkness. In that darkness, he made out a slow-moving mass on the water; it was dotted here and there with lights. Frankie stepped up onto the bench.

It was the city unmoored with Bucky at a makeshift helm waving wildly. "I had to try her out, Frank!" he shouted through his megaphone, his silver hair glinting. "We're a sea-stead, Frank. We can go where we want, come hell or high water!"

Frankie waved, speechless, struggling to see as Torosa moved past, picking up speed it seemed, making its way beyond the harbour.

By first light, the city was back in its dock, and Arnon was swimming toward it. The honeycomb of Torosa was pale, its form faint in the mist and morning light—too faint to make out awakenings in any of its cells.

Frankie got up and stretched, stiff from the night spent sitting under the waxing moon that was still in the sky. Slowly he made his way toward the water, stopping here and there to sniff at the roses: sweet, spicy, fusty. One full blossom hung from a limp stem, so he plucked it. There on a bench, he saw his mother staring out at the harbour, waiting, her all-you-can-carry suitcase on the ground beside her.

In 1968, Richard Buckminster Fuller, visionary architect and inventor of the geodesic dome—most notably the American Pavilion at Expo 67—was commissioned to create a plan for the future of the city of Toronto. Fuller, along with his partner, architect Shoji Sadao, presented Project Toronto to City Council. The proposal included a plan for three self-contained floating neighbourhoods in Toronto Harbour. They were never built.

QUOTED SOURCES

Buckminster Fuller developed his own idiosyncratic vocabulary to express his visionary ideas. Throughout *Floating City*, dialogue spoken by the character of Buckminster Fuller is inspired by, or drawn directly from, Fuller's actual lectures or published works. I am grateful to The Estate of R. Buckminster Fuller for allowing me to craft his character in this way. Following are sources for specific quotations appearing as dialogue in the novel:

ix   "LONGING . . . is EXPANSION and INCLUSION."
      Nine Chains to the Moon (Southern Illinois University
      Press, Carbondale, Illinois), 10.

xii   "I sought to . . . on our planet."
      Critical Path (St. Martin's Press: New York), xii.

91   "Fincap"
      Nine Chains to the Moon (Southern Illinois University
      Press: Carbondale, Illinois), 181.

96–7 "houses may be . . . with the wind."
"Designing a New Industry" (Fuller Research
Foundation: Wichita, Kansas), 32.

97 "priest-navigators"
*Tetrascroll: Goldilocks and the Three Bears, A Cosmic
Fairytale* (St. Martin's Press: New York), 88.

100 "What is it . . . and the spiritual."
4D Time Lock (Lama Foundation: Albuquerque,
New Mexico), 33.

109–10 "all the people . . . they may be."
Nine Chains to the Moon (Southern Illinois University
Press: Carbondale, Illinois), vii.

112 "You only succeed when you stop failing."
Buckminster Fuller made this remark while teaching
at the summer institute at Black Mountain College
in 1948. While there, his first geodesic dome was
constructed of venetian blinds, but it collapsed due
to the thinness of the material. He dubbed it the
"Supine Dome."

126 "We could live . . . one world-around network."
Utopia or Oblivion: The Prospects for Humanity,
(Overlook Press: New York), 411.

126 "To survive a . . . sea of tension."
*Inventions: The Patented Works of R. Buckminster
Fuller,* (St. Martin's Press: New York), 180.

162 "Spaceship Earth is . . . miles each day."
Utopia or Oblivion: The Prospects For Humanity
(Overlook Press: New York), 348.

167   "It is feasible . . . expense of another."
      Critical Path, (St. Martin's Press: New York), xxv.

167   "make money or make sense?"
      Grunch of Giants, (St. Martin's Press: New York), xv.

204   "Are you spontaneously . . . everything you have?"
      Critical Path, (St. Martin's Press: New York), xxxvvii.

216   "The things that you see need to be done . . . to be done."
      Critical Path (St. Martin's Press: New York), xxxviii.

216–17 "Just give me . . . your own time."
      *Buckminster Fuller: An Autobiographical Monologue
      Scenario*, documented and edited by Robert Snyder,
      (St. Martin's Press: New York), 153.

217   "The advent of . . . of all ephemeralization."
      *Synergetics 2: Explorations in the Geometry
      of Thinking*, (Macmillan Publishing Company:
      New York), 174–75.

218   "Love is metaphysical gravity."
      Critical Path, (St. Martin's Press: New York), 156.

223   "weaponry . . . to livingry!"
      Critical Path (St. Martin's Press: New York), xxv.

ACKNOWLEDGEMENTS

My family and my friends have kept me afloat all these years of living and writing. I love you and thank you.

To Danito, *querido*, for days and nights of reading, listening and loving that kept me on course.

To Eric, for seaworthy lightness, levity and wit.

To Teo, my brave vanquisher of the seas.

To Edie and Fedor Tisch, Mark Slone, Karen Tisch and lovely Isabella, as well as Laurie Sakamoto for the safe harbour of family. Thank you, Edie, for your loving care of Eriquito and Teito through the years and always being there for us.

A special thanks to my father, Gordon Hideo Sakamoto, for his constant faith in me. His exemplary strength, can-do optimism and lifelong practice of doing more with less are truly in keeping with Buckminster Fuller's philosophies.

To my sisters-in-arms of the Saturday night moms, kids & prosecco collective: Anita, Dalia, Helen, Kathy, Sally, Susan and Van. Thank you for shared guffaws, tears, and sustenance.

Thank you, Janine Lawford, for wisdom and refuge.

For astute comments on drafts early, late and in between, I thank my cherished and talented pals Richard Fung, John Greyson, Mike Hoolboom, Anita Lee, Helen Lee, Ruth Liberman, Karen

Tisch, Kathy Wazana and Lynne Yamamoto. Rebecca Toyne also read an early draft.

Deep gratitude, love and bows to Dalia Kandiyoti and Susan Maggi for narrative epiphanies, the long view and for being there in my desperado hours of revision.

I am grateful to Bruce Kuwabara who, many years ago, told me about Buckminster Fuller's proposed floating neighbourhood for Toronto Harbour. Thanks also to my skyscaper-building father-in-law, Fedor Tisch, for his many insights.

Thank you Ezra's Pound as well as the much-missed Wagamama Cafe and its owner, the late Miwa Yamada, for providing lovely tea and espresso laden havens. Thank you, Lisa and Tim McCaskell, for offering me your cottage as a writing retreat with its inspiring vista of Lake Simcoe.

For funding during the lean years, I am grateful to the Canada Council for the Arts and the Ontario Arts Council, including the Chalmers Arts Fellowship program.

Thank you to my agent, Chris Bucci, for finding a home for my book, and for waiting patiently and faithfully.

I am deeply indebted to my brilliant editor, Craig Pyette, for his belief in my manuscript when it was adrift in choppy waters. Thank you for guiding me toward clarity in my sentences and for helping to bring propulsion and resolution to the narrative. I truly couldn't have done it without you! And thank you for loving Bucky as much as I do.

Finally and apart, I am grateful to my mother, the late Teruko Matsui Sakamoto, for the stories she told me, for the way she looked at the world and helped me find my place in it.

© Daniel Tisch

KERRI SAKAMOTO debuted as a novelist in 1998 with *The Electrical Field*, a finalist for the Governor General's Literary Award for Fiction, the Kiriyama Pacific Rim Book Prize and the IMPAC Dublin Literary Award, and winner of the Commonwealth Writers' Prize for Best First Book and the Canada-Japan Literary Award. Her second novel, *One Hundred Million Hearts*, appeared in 2003 to critical acclaim. She lives with her family in Toronto.

ALSO AVAILABLE

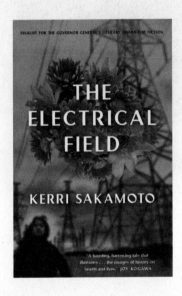

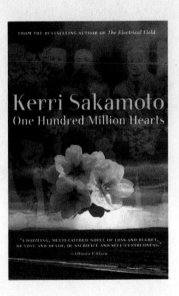